CW01551153

CONTENTS

PART ONE   1

1. Chapter 1   2

2. Chapter 2   16

3. Chapter 3   26

4. Chapter 4   40

5. Chapter 5   44

6. Chapter 6   64

7. Chapter 7   68

8. Chapter 8   81

9. Chapter 9   89

10. Chapter 10   96

11. Chapter 11   107

12. Chapter 12   110

13. Chapter 13   119

14. Chapter 14   123

15. Chapter 15   126

PART TWO   133

16. Chapter 16   134

17. Chapter 17   154

18. Chapter 18   159

19. Chapter 19   168

20. Chapter 20   178

21. Chapter 21   185

22. Chapter 22   187

23. Chapter 23   193

24. Chapter 24   197

25. Chapter 25   201

26. Chapter 26   205

27. Chapter 27   207

28. Chapter 28   210

29. Chapter 29   221

30. Chapter 30   225

31. Chapter 31   229

32. Chapter 32   234

33. Chapter 33   238

PART THREE   245

34. Chapter 34   246

35. Chapter 35   251

36. Chapter 36   252

37. Chapter 37   255

38. Chapter 38   310

39. Chapter 39   319

40. Chapter 40   327

41. EPILOGUE   354

PART ONE
ANDY WISLER

DAY 1

It happens on a perfectly ordinary grey Tuesday afternoon in late March. They're on their way home from school. Andy is pushing his bike and Rebecca is walking next to him on the sidewalk, skipping along to some annoying song playing on her phone.

"We have to make a quick stop at the library," Andy says, stopping by the intersection next to the red brick building. "I need a new book."

"I don't want to," Rebecca says, shaking her head. "I'll just keep walking and you can catch up."

Andy steps in front of her, cutting her off. "No. Mom says we should always go together."

"You're the one who doesn't want to go together. I don't want to go into the stupid library."

"Why not?"

"I just don't feel like it. Books are so boooring!"

"It'll only be a minute. And could you please turn that off?"

Rebecca doesn't pause the song, instead she crosses her arms. She's wearing her thick, purple winter jacket, which makes her look even more stern. "You go ahead into the library," she says, smiling falsely. "But you can't make me go with you."

Andy frowns. "Are you going to wait out here then?"

"Perhaps," Rebecca says, glancing up at the sky.

"Perhaps?" Andy repeats. "What's that supposed to mean?"

"It means: Perhaps I'll wait, perhaps I won't."

Andy feels irritation arise. They've been down this road so many times before, and he knows exactly how it'll end. Whenever Rebecca is like this, there's no way of bending her will. Neither prayers nor threats can make her obey. Still, he points at her and says, putting on his sternest demeanor: "You'll wait here until I get back."

Rebecca doesn't reply; she just stands there, avoiding his eye, humming along to the music.

Andy stares at her menacingly for another moment, attempting to intimidate her into staying put. Then, he crosses the street and parks his bike by the bike rack. As he darts a glance back across his shoulder, he sees Rebecca on the other side of the street, one arm raised to wave sarcastically at him, the way old ladies wave in the movies.

Later, Andy will think back to this moment a thousand times. He'll come to wish he had waved back at Rebecca, even though he knew she only waved to annoy him. But an ironic wave of goodbye would still be a lot better than no goodbye at all.

Then again, if Andy had known what was to come, he would have simply never gone into the library. He would have walked right back to Rebecca, and they would have gone home together and nothing bad would have happened.

But Andy doesn't know the future.

And he's angry with Rebecca at that moment.

So, he scoffs and turns his back to her, then marches into the library.

As soon as the glass doors slide shut behind him, Andy's anger dissipates like fog in the sunny morning air. He's entered the world of books, and he can't be angry here.

Not many people are at the library this afternoon; in fact, he seems to be the only one. It's a small-town library with only a few librarians, and they're only here every other day.

Andy unwraps his scarf and inhales the scent of the books. Ever since he learned to read, Andy has loved books more than anything, and he feels the old excitement bubble up now at the mere thought of the countless universes lurking between the pages. In those universes he can get lost for hours on end. And there is no one bullying or annoying him, no one making demands or yelling at him.

Andy goes down row B and lets his gaze glide across the spines, searching for one that looks intriguing, when, suddenly, the tip of his shoe bumps into something.

He looks down to see a book on the floor. He picks it up. It's an older one with an anonymous, red leather binding. There is no text on the spine, nor on the front cover. Only a title engraved into the leather in scratched gold letters:

THE WENDIGO

Andy has never come across the book before, and he's never heard the title mentioned either; he has no idea what a wendigo is. There's something intriguing about the name, though; it sounds somehow ominous.

He leafs briefly through the pages and skims the text. The story seems promising, so he brings the book to the terminal and beeps it through.

A cold gust of wind leaps at him the moment he steps outside the library again, biting his cheeks and forehead. His gaze immediately seeks the other side of the street, where he last saw Rebecca, but he can't hear her music playing, and she's no longer to be seen.

Of course she's gone. That little brat.

Andy looks in both directions just in time to catch a glimpse of purple, as Rebecca turns down a side street a couple hundred yards away. Andy grabs his bike and takes up pursuit.

Apparently, Rebecca is intent on jerking him around, as she is walking the opposite way from home. Her plan, no doubt, is to give him a good scare by making him believe she's gone home, then, when Andy shows up to find the house empty, he will panic.

But I saw you, you sly devil, Andy thinks, a triumphant smile tugging at his lips. *You're not fooling me.*

Thanks to his bike, Andy is a lot faster than Rebecca, so it takes him only a moment to reach the street where she turned, and once again he's just in time to see her turn down a new side street.

Andy decides to play along.

Rebecca obviously thinks she has the upper hand, since she doesn't know Andy is onto her. So, he rides along at a comfortable speed, following along every time she makes another turn, making sure to stay far enough behind so as to not be seen in case Rebecca decides to look back. She doesn't look back, though, not even once—which proves to Andy just how confident she must be in the fact that she fooled him, and it makes him chuckle to himself.

Then, she suddenly turns into the driveway of a random house, goes to the front door, opens it and disappears inside.

What the heck?

Andy speeds up and reaches the house. He has no idea who lives in there, and the names on the mailbox don't make him any the wiser. He looks up at the house, but can't see anyone in the windows.

Andy just stands by his bike for a moment, brooding.

Could it be a trick? Did Rebecca spot him after all and is now trying to throw him off?

No, he doesn't think it likely she would walk into a strange home just to mess with him. She might be devious, but she's not stupid.

Which means, of course, that Rebecca must know the people who live in the house. Probably someone from Rebecca's class.

So, that was her plan all along. Go to one of her friends' house and let me rush home alone, totally worried about where she might be.

Andy bites off his glove and pulls out his phone. He types a quick text.

You can come out now. I saw you.

He keeps an eye on the front door, but it doesn't open for several minutes. And Rebecca doesn't text him back.

Soon, Andy begins to lose patience. He's also freezing. He puts his bike on the stand, goes up to the front door and knocks on it, loudly.

The door is opened, and a girl from Rebecca's class looks out at him with an expression of mild surprise. Andy can't recall her name—maybe Freya or Faye or something like that.

"Hi," the girl says, as she apparently recognizes Andy. "What do you want?"

"You can tell Rebecca to come out now," Andy says, sniffing. "I'm taking her home."

"Rebecca isn't here," the girl says, her tone innocent.

"Yeah, she is."

The girl shakes her head, causing her bangs to swing. "No, she really isn't."

"Well, I saw her go in."

"When?"

"Just a minute ago."

The girl—her expression still serene—shrugs. "I haven't seen Rebecca since class today. Honestly. It's just me and my mom home."

Andy is growing annoyed with the girl and the way she's covering for Rebecca. Rebecca probably instructed her to play oblivious, and the girl is doing a pretty good job pretending.

He stretches his neck and sees Rebecca's jacket on the rack. "I can see her jacket," he says, pointing. "The purple one."

The girl looks back briefly, then says: "That's *my* jacket."

Andy opens his mouth to answer, but is suddenly struck silent, as something falls into place. He never really saw the girl in the purple jacket up close, did he? No. And come to think of it, he couldn't hear any music playing, either. And the way she walked without glancing back ...

Andy realizes the girl is still looking at him with patient bemusement.

"I, uhm ... I'm sorry," he mutters, backing away. "I think ... eh ... there's been a misunderstanding ..."

He turns around and hurries back out to the sidewalk, finds his phone and calls up Rebecca.

She doesn't answer. After the fourth ring it goes to voice mail.

Right, don't panic now, he tells himself, putting the phone back into his pocket. *She's obviously just gone home, and she knows the way. We've walked it together a million times. Nothing happened to her, she's just—*

Andy is so distraught he goes to cross the street without looking. A yellow van comes out of nowhere, its horn blaring angrily, and Andy leaps back onto the sidewalk, almost tripping over his bike, as the van rushes past. It slows down, and for a moment Andy is sure the driver will jump out and yell at him. But the van only slowed down in order to make a turn at a crossing. It holds and waits for a break in the passing traffic, only one of the brake lights glowing red.

Andy is just about to jump on his bike, when he hears something.

It's a knocking.

He looks towards the van. It could have been the engine. But it could also have been someone knocking from the inside of the van.

Then the brake light goes out, the van revs up, rolls out into the crossing, turns and disappears out of sight.

Andy rides home as fast as he can, panting and sweating under his clothes despite the cold spring air, a nagging sense of dread growing steadily larger in the pit of his stomach all the way.

If Mom finds out Rebecca has walked home by herself, she'll blow a fuse—and Andy will be the one blamed. Mom has instructed him several times that since he's the older one, Rebecca is *his* responsibility whenever there are no grown-ups around.

Never mind the fact that she can be a pain in the butt and fight me every step of the way just because she's in a *foul mood! But oh, no, it's still only **my** fault if something happens to her!*

But there's still hope he can avoid a scolding: if he's lucky, Mom won't be home from work yet, which means she'll never know Rebecca and Andy split up.

Of course, Rebecca might tell on him as soon as Mom gets home—it would be just like her, ratting him out to get him into trouble—but Andy can always deny it, which at least would give him a fifty-fifty chance that Mom will believe his side of the story.

Andy reaches the house, drops his bike in the driveway—which is empty, meaning Mom isn't home yet—and runs to the front door. It's locked. Andy stares at it for a moment, confused. Then he scrambles for the key in his bag and lets himself in.

The first thing he notices in the hall is that the purple jacket is not on the rack. Still, he calls out: "Becca! You here?" then holds his breath and listens. Only silence from the house. Dad always works late, and Cindy is probably out with her college friends.

Andy pulls out the phone and calls up Rebecca once more.

Four rings. Then voice mail.

"Pick it up," Andy hisses and tries again immediately. He knows it won't do any good, but he does it anyway.

This time, there's only a single ring before it goes to voice mail. Which means the call has been declined. Or that the phone was shut off. But why would Rebecca do any of those things? Just to mess with him? It's not completely unlikely, of course—her being somewhere nearby, sniggering at his call—but Andy doesn't think so. Rebecca has never taken a prank this far before.

His heart by now is pounding away in his chest, and the anxious feeling in his stomach has grown into full-fledged fear. He checks the time. It's been more than half an hour since they split up by the library. Would Rebecca really still be mad at him? And if so, where could she be?

Maybe she's still just wandering around town. Or maybe she's lost and can't find her way home. But then why would she turn off her phone? Maybe it ran out of battery.

Andy decides him standing here dialoguing with himself won't do any good. Mom could be home any minute, and when she finds out Andy has come home without Rebecca, she won't just blow a fuse—Andy is afraid her head might simply explode.

So, he goes out to look for Rebecca, locking the front door behind him, as he knows Rebecca has her own key.

Andy rides around town for almost an hour. He checks all the places Rebecca might be: the school, the mall, the park, the playground, even the library. She's nowhere to be found.

Finally, he goes back home. He's really scared now. His last hope is that while he was out looking, Rebecca has come home on her own. That this has all been a mean joke on her part. That she has just been wandering around the streets, biding her time until she was certain Andy was freaking out. He tries to imagine the situation play out. The front door will be unlocked, and he will barge in, call out her name, and she will come striding out casually from the living room to greet him, put her hands to her sides and ask: "What took you so long?"

"What took *me* so long?" Andy will burst out. "How about you? Where have *you* been? I've looked all over town for you!"

And Rebecca will smile her most devilish smile and say: "I took another road." Or: "I met Anna from class, and we talked for a while." Or simply: "That's not any of your business."

Andy has a well-developed imagination, and the conversation is so vivid in his mind, he actually has himself convinced that's how it will play out—he's even smiling to himself as he parks his bike in the driveway the second time. He leaps up the steps and grabs the knob.

His smile withers.

The door is locked.

And when he lets himself in using his key, he finds Rebecca's jacket still not on the rack.

Then suddenly, standing in the empty, silent house, Andy hears something knocking. The sound is coming from his own heart. But it's also coming from the yellow van. It's growing louder and louder inside of him, until it feels like his ribcage is going to break open. That single, red brake light is glaring at him in his mind's eye, burning him with its evil, monstrous stare. His thoughts begin arguing.

She's gone.

No, she can't be.

Someone took her.

No, that's not true.

She's not coming home.

*She **is** coming home!*

Stop being a baby.

Shut up!

Stop pretending.

Shut up!

Andy breathes out heavily and realizes he's seconds away from crying, which makes him even more scared. He clears his throat and swallows hard.

Andy knows there's only one thing left to do now, and he dreads it more than anything. It will wipe out the last hope. It will break the illusion that Rebecca still might show up on her own in a minute or two. It will make it real.

At the age of thirteen, this is the hardest thing Andy has ever had to do—and that includes the time he crashed on his bike and dislocated his shoulder and had to have the doctor pop it back in. The pain, which was already intense, grew to unfathomable dimensions for a few seconds, and the shock of it almost caused him to faint, scaring him out of ever trusting any doctor ever again telling him that "it'll only hurt a bit." But just like then, he has no choice now. The difference is, this time he knows what's coming. Which makes it even worse.

He takes out his phone and makes the call.

Dad answers right away: "*Hey, Andy, what's up?*"

"Dad," Andy says. His mouth is dry. His voice is trembling. "I think ... I think Rebecca is missing."

DAY 50

Andy completely forgets about the book tucked in the back of his schoolbag, until finally one evening, he pulls out his atlas to do his geography homework, and the book incidentally pops out and falls to the floor.

He looks down at it and is instantly reminded of Rebecca. Not that he ever forgot about her, of course, but brief intervals have begun showing up, maybe half a minute or so passing without him thinking of her. Now, at the sight of the book he took out of the library that fateful day, it all comes rushing back for the millionth time, and Andy chokes up.

The first days after Rebecca disappeared were full of questions and police officers and solemn looks and more questions.

"What was the last thing Rebecca said to you?"

"Did you see which way she went?"

"Did you guys fight before you separated?"

"How long were you inside the library?"

"Did you hear her talking with anyone?"

"Did she mention anything about where she might go?"

"Did anyone threaten you or Rebecca earlier that day?"

And so on.

Andy answered to the best of his ability. He also told the police about the yellow van.

"Did you see the van parked outside the library, Andy?" the officer with the deep voice asked him.

"No, but ..."

"Did you see Rebecca through the rear window when the van went past you?"

"There was no rear window. But the knocking ..."

"You said you thought the sound came from the van's engine?"

"That was what I thought at first, yeah, but ... then I got the idea, you know, what if it was Rebecca knocking?"

The officer gave him a long look, then he nodded, and did not ask about the yellow van again.

Andy's not stupid; he can see there's no evidence to support his theory. No one else reported seeing the yellow van near the library that day. Andy didn't see who was driving it. The van could have had absolutely nothing to do with Rebecca's disappearance.

Yet Andy just can't forget about the knocking, or the red brake light staring at him like an evil eye. For every day passing without the police finding Rebecca, Andy has grown more and more certain that the knocking was Rebecca pounding on the inside of the van. If he had only thought to take down the license number, then the police could at least have found the van and checked it out.

He has tried telling both Mom and Dad about it, but neither of them really seem to listen anymore. They've both gone into a strange state Andy has never seen them in before. It's like they aren't themselves anymore.

Mom's eyes are always glazed, and some days she doesn't get out of bed. Other days she walks around the house and tries to do normal things, like vacuuming or doing the laundry. But she keeps stopping, staring out into nothing. As though she forgets for several minutes what she's doing.

Dad mostly keeps to himself and very rarely speaks. Andy sees him cry now and then, when he thinks he's alone. In the beginning, he went for long drives in his car, returning hours later without a word to anyone about where he had been.

One day, when Andy saw Dad take the car keys, he mustered up the courage and asked where he was going.

Dad just looked at him with an empty gaze and said: "Where do you think I'm going, Andy? I'm going out to look for my daughter, of course."

There was no anger in the voice, yet Andy felt the words land on him like bee stings.

No one has ever said it outright, not Mom or Dad, not Cindy or Aunt Clair who had visited a few times, not the police officer with the deep voice or the shrink Andy went to see for a couple of weeks, not the teachers at school or any of his classmates, not even the neighbors or anyone else in town. Yet they all know it. Andy can feel it right under the surface. They all agree on that simple, horrible truth.

If Andy hadn't gone into the library that day …

If he had only kept his promise to not let Rebecca out of sight …

But Andy *did* go into the library.

He *did* leave Rebecca out of sight.

And he's been trying desperately not to think about that day ever since.

But now, as he is standing in his room, staring at the book he took out only a few minutes after he saw Rebecca for the last time, the feelings of dread and guilt and regret come rushing back, and Andy tears up, his bottom lip begins bobbing.

He hasn't picked up a book since Rebecca disappeared, hasn't read a single page; he just hasn't felt like it, although he used to read at least a book a week, usually two or three. But the mere thought of going near the library now makes him almost physically ill.

Andy chokes back the sobs, wipes his eyes and picks up the book. With a sigh, he sits down on his bed and studies the secretive, dark-red cover. It must have gone way past its due date, and he probably owes a library fine on it now.

He opens the book and finds the author name on the title page: Algernon Blackwood. Andy has never heard of that author before, but the book looks to be at least a hundred years old, so the guy is probably long dead.

He absentmindedly leafs through the first few pages, reads a couple of paragraphs, and then he disappears.

The language is fluent and colorful, the descriptions so vivid that Andy has no problem getting immersed in the plot.

The evening grows dimmer outside the window, the church bells chime somewhere in the distance, marking the hours passing by, and Andy turns the pages.

The story plays out way up in Canada more than a century ago. It follows a group of men on a moose hunt, venturing deep into the huge Canadian forests, reaching territory where no man has ever set foot. In there, they encounter something strange. A demonic creature dwells in the forest, luring in people who have gone astray by imitating voices. Wendigo, the monster is called. If it catches you, it'll break down your psyche and suck the life force from within you, until you're nothing but an empty shell. But first, it'll light your feet on fire and poke out your eyes.

Why?

Because eyes and feet are the only two things that can save a person lost in the woods.

Andy feels the fear come creeping like ants on his skin, his heart pounding away in his chest. At one point, he has to close the book and look around, making sure he's still safe in his room and not trapped in an endless forest. A part of him wants to put away the book and never pick it up again. It's late, and he has to get up tomorrow morning to go to school. But another part of him wants to keep reading, *demands* it. That part needs to know how the story ends.

It's just a story. Wendigos aren't real. Get a grip, you big wuss.

Andy takes a deep breath, peels open the book once more and dives back in.

Andy has already read quite a few horror stories in his life. He has even taken on some of the heavier monsters, like Dracula, or Cthulhu, or Pennywise the Clown. But the wendigo scares him in a way none of the others ever managed to do. There is something absolutely terrifying about that invisible thing lurking in the woods, just waiting patiently for someone to come close enough ...

The plot flows along easily enough to begin with, the mood getting slowly darker despite nothing really happening. Until about a third of the way in, that is; then something happens which almost makes Andy scream out loud.

The men have set up camp for the night, when suddenly, one of them is dragged to his feet and flung out of the tent, like some invisible force pulling him away. And as he disappears into the darkness of the woods, his voice can be heard by the other men:

»Oh! oh! My feet of fire! My burning feet of fire! Oh! oh! This height and fiery speed!«

Andy reads the line again and again, and every time he does so, his palms grow sweatier. He understands what has happened to the poor guy, and yet he doesn't. Something—the wendigo—has taken him. And the part about his feet burning—is it meant to be taken literally, that they simply burst into flames, or did the man lose his mind on the spot, like a house of cards collapsing? What exactly does the invisible demon do to him? The text simply isn't clear enough and leaves it up to the reader's imagination—which somehow only makes it worse.

Andy reads on with bated breath. More than once he tries again closing the book. The problem is, his fingers don't obey him anymore; they just eagerly keep turning pages.

When he finally reaches the conclusion of the story, he feels dizzy. He looks to the clock on his nightstand. It's past 2:00 AM. His parents have long since gone to bed. Andy doesn't recall ever having been awake at this hour, not even on New Year's Eve.

He's about to put the book away, when he notices something. On the very last page, a piece of paper is pinned. It's a library receipt, one of those automatically printed out by the terminal when you borrow a book. Someone apparently used it as a bookmark. The text is faded but still readable.

Lisa Labowski, the name on the receipt reads. The date is August 16, eighteen years ago.

Amazing to think the paper has been in the book for eighteen years without someone removing it. Perhaps the book simply hasn't been read by anyone for that long.

Andy reads the name again.

Lisa Labowski ... I think I heard that name before ...

He tries to remember, but he's too exhausted to think straight, so he closes the book and falls asleep the second his head hits the pillow.

In his dreams, Andy travels to the Canadian woods to hunt for moose. It's winter, and it's very cold and dark.

Suddenly, he sees Rebecca between the dead trees. She has her back to him. Andy feels his heart leap and he runs towards her. But it's difficult to move his legs right, so he only very slowly gets closer. Instead, he calls out for her.

"Becca! Becca, it's me! I'm coming!"

Rebecca turns her head sideways, as though she hears him. But something is wrong with her eyes. Is she crying? No, Andy realizes to his horror, it's not tears streaming down Rebecca's cheeks—it's blood.

Then, the wendigo steps out from behind the tree. The demon is even more terrifying than he imagined. It looks kind of like a human, but at the same time not at all. It's much taller and sickly skinny, the skin is ashy gray and paper-thin, clinging to the bones and revealing the dark veins underneath. The eyes are small and dark and deep-seated, the lips are cracked and bloody.

Andy can only look in horror as the creature goes to take Rebecca's hand and leads her away, his sister following along willingly, like a sleepwalker or a zombie, completely unaware of what's going on. Andy tries to scream to her, but no sound comes out of his mouth. Rebecca turns her head to look back one last time just before she disappears into the darkness with the wendigo, and Andy sees her lips mouthing the words: "Help me."

Andy sits up in bed with a choked cry. He stares around his room, his heart in his throat.

"The wendigo took Becca," he whispers hoarsely. "It was the wendigo ..."

DAY 51

The next morning, as Andy is awakened by the alarm, the images from the nightmare have mercifully faded to nothing but vague shadows at the back of his memory.

On his way to school, Andy rides past the town church as usual. The old, white building surrounded by the graveyard is located right up against the park, so Andy takes the shortcut through the park, when he suddenly sees three girls a hundred yards away, blocking the path. Andy recognizes them immediately. It's Sheila from Andy's class and two eighth graders, Kimmie and Stacey. They're posing for a group selfie. When they look at the result, they laugh out loud.

Oh, crap, Andy thinks to himself, realizing he won't be able to get past them unnoticed. *That's just my luck ...*

Ever since Rebecca disappeared, everyone in his class has acted differently whenever Andy is around.

They fall silent. As though not sure what to say. Even the teachers become awkward.

Andy is used to being the quiet boy in class—the one who's always reading a book at recess and only seldom gets any attention or is spoken to. And that hasn't changed, but now he can sense everyone staring at him.

Only Sheila is acting like she used to. She's still bullying Andy like she has always done. In a strange way, Andy finds it somewhat comforting that at least this one thing hasn't changed.

But that doesn't mean he's in the mood for Sheila today. He sees the gate leading into the churchyard and makes a quick decision to cut across instead of going through the park.

Just as he gets off his bike and starts for the gate, he hears one of the girls exclaim: "Hey, isn't that Wisler from your class, Sheila?"

Andy turns his head to see the girls looking in his direction.

"Yeah, it is," Sheila says. "Hey, Andy! Why are you going into the churchyard?"

Andy doesn't answer, but opens the gate and pulls his bike through. He restrains himself from running, just walks briskly along the gravel path winding through the many graves.

"Andy! Hey, Andy! You got gravy in your ears, man?"

Sheila's voice is followed by shrill laughter. Andy is unsure what, but something makes him stop. It's obviously a mistake; he should just keep moving. But he turns to look back.

The girls are at the gate. Sheila is wearing a tight black top, way too cold for this time of year, which reveals her boney shoulders and flat chest. Kimmie is sucking noisily from a McDonald's cup.

Sheila glares at Andy with a stupid smile. "Come on over here, Andy. I need to talk with you real quick."

Andy feels the heat rise to his face. It's part embarrassment, part frustration with himself for stopping. Now that they're staring right at each other, he can't just turn and leave.

Of course you can. Why should you stay and listen to her bullcrap? She's only going to humiliate you. Go. Just go!

But he stays rooted.

"You can have the rest of Kimmie's milkshake if you come," Sheila says alluringly.

Kimmie almost chokes with laughter, spraying out pink milkshake on the gravel. She holds up the cup and dangles it in the air. "Come on, piggy! Come get a treat!" She tries to say something more, but is interrupted when Stacey breaks into hysterical laughter.

Sheila is the only one not laughing. She just holds Andy's gaze, her smile widening ever so slightly. "Seriously, Andy," she says in an almost friendly tone, stepping into the churchyard. "I just have one little question for you."

Andy turns and starts walking.

"Hey, Andy!" Sheila calls out, a clear note of insult in her voice now. "I'm talking to you! Don't just walk away—that's rude!"

Andy keeps walking. Now that he finally got moving, he walks fast enough for his backpack to jump up and down.

"Let him go, he probably got hungry!" Kimmie shouts, sending Stacey into another manic case of high-pitched laughter.

"Fat idiot," is the last, scornful words Andy hears from Sheila, before the girls' voices dissipate behind him.

Andy looks back to see them no longer at the gate. His pulse is beating fast, as though he was just running, and he waits a moment for his heart rate to slow down.

What the heck got into her? I know she's always picking on me, but she's definitely gotten worse lately. It's like she—

Andy's gaze falls on the tombstone by the grave right in front of him, and his thoughts immediately stop as he reads the engravement:

Lisa Labowski

Here lies our beloved daughter

Andy just stares at the name for several seconds. Then he reads the date at the bottom. July 17, eighteen years ago. At first, he doesn't really get it. Not consciously, anyway, but something inside him begins to feel very funny at the sight of the date, until suddenly, it dawns on him.

No ... that can't be. I must remember it wrong.

He needs to know for sure, so he takes off his backpack and finds the book, opens it and takes out the receipt. His fingers are shaking as he holds it up.

He stares at the date on the paper.

Then back at the tombstone.

Then back at the paper once more.

He didn't remember it wrong. Which means there has to be some other logical explanation for the impossible discrepancy in the dates. And there are plenty of possible answers, all clambering in his mind, like eager students wanting to be heard by the teacher.

It has to be a flaw in the library system, one thought suggests. *The machine simply printed the wrong date.*

It's not Lisa Labowski herself who borrowed the book, another one argues. *Someone just took it out in her name.*

It's not even the same Lisa Labowski, a third thought interjects. *There are two of them: the one who borrowed the book and the other one who's buried right here.*

All of the answers are reasonable. All of them make sense. All of them could be true.

And yet, none of them *feel* true to Andy. None of them can fight back the goose bumps making their way up his spine. And if none of the answers are true, then he's left with one simple fact.

Lisa Labowski borrowed the book from the library a month after she died.

Andy can't really shake the thought of Lisa Labowski. All day in school he has to strain to concentrate on anything else, since his thoughts keep going in circles about the dead girl.

Luckily, Sheila has apparently forgotten their little rendezvous by the church; she's busy talking with her friends and doesn't bother Andy. This gives him time to brood.

Did Lisa Labowski really borrow the book after her death? Despite Andy's vivid imagination, he doesn't really believe in ghosts or other fantasy creatures. Part of him wants to think they really do exist somewhere in the world, and that you can encounter them like people do in books and movies, but that's mostly the child in him. The rational, soon-to-be-a-grown-up part of him knows it's all just made up.

And yet he keeps thinking about Lisa Labowski as a ghost girl. So, he decides to investigate—if nothing else, at least to give himself peace of mind.

So as soon as school ends for the day, Andy heads straight for the bike shed, grabs his bike and rides through town.

For the first time since Rebecca disappears, Andy stops by the library. He looks up at the red building. It looks completely the same: friendly and inviting. He has been riding past it almost every day, but hasn't had the nerve to really look at it, much less go in. Even now the thought scares him a little.

But he needs an answer to the Lisa Labowski paradox, so he puts the bike in the rack and strides towards the glass doors. They greet him with their old, familiar hiss as they glide open.

Andy steps inside the entrance and stops to close his eyes for a moment, inhaling through his nose. The atmosphere is exactly as he remembers it, and it brings the same feeling of security and peacefulness it always has. Andy can't help but smile.

I've been so silly. Why was I afraid of going in here? It wasn't like the library caused Rebecca to disappear.

He proceeds to go inside and sees Regan—or Libraregan, as she calls herself on social media—by the desk, busy sorting out returned books. A couple of girls Rebecca's age are sitting by the computers and an elderly man is reading a newspaper in the armchair in the farthest corner.

Andy goes to the desk and says: "Hey, Regan."

Regan turns around with a look of surprise. "Andy? Heey!" she beams at him. "Great to see you! It's been so long—got to be a new record."

"I know." Andy smiles shyly.

He notices Regan is about to ask him something, but then seems to think better of it. Something unsaid passes between them, and her smile fades a bit. Of course Regan heard about Rebecca, but did she also hear how it happened? Does she know it was Andy's fault? If she does, then she doesn't say it. Instead, she asks: "How are you holding up?"

"Okay, I guess," Andy says with a shrug.

Regan is pretty young for a librarian—no more than twenty or twenty-one, if Andy had to guess. She's not much taller than Andy and wears glasses too. But unlike Andy, Regan is very thin. She has a tiny pigment spot on her right cheek bone where the skin is noticeably brighter than the rest of her face. It reminds Andy of a teardrop and gives Regan a look of eternal sadness—although she smiles most of the time. Yet Andy has always sensed a loneliness from her, very much akin to his own, and he's pretty sure she doesn't have a boyfriend; she's in love with books, just like Andy.

"So, what did you read this time?" she says, her smile returning, as she goes on sorting books.

Andy finds the book from his bag and shows it to her. "It's called *The Wendigo*. It's really cool."

"*The Wendigo*? Don't think I've heard about it ... who wrote it?" She takes the book from Andy and opens it. "Algernon Blackwood ... huh, what an old-school name."

"I know," Andy says. "I never read anything else by him—did you?"

"I think I'd remember a name like that, so no, I probably haven't." She hands him back the book. "Is it a horror story?"

"Yeah, and it's freaking scary. Definitely too scary for you, Regan."

Regan puts her hands to her sides. "I'll have you know I've read several horror books in my time, thank you very much. In fact, I recently finished *Pet Sematary* ... and now I have to sleep with the lights on for the rest of my life."

Andy sniggers. Then he remembers why he came. "I need to ask you something, Regan."

"Sure."

Suddenly, Andy doesn't know how to put the question. Somehow, "Are dead people allowed to borrow books?" doesn't really seem like the right way to go about it.

"It's just because ... uhm ... I found this note ... here, let me show you." He leafs through the book till he gets to the last page. The receipt isn't there. Then he remembers he put it in his pocket. Or was it the bag? "Eh ... give me a second," he mutters and begins rummaging for the note.

"Do you mind me helping the gentleman behind you, Andy?" Regan asks, and Andy looks back to see the old newspaper guy standing in line with an impatient look on his face.

"Yeah, sure," Andy says, scurrying aside. He keeps digging for the library receipt, but he can't find it anywhere. "Damnit," he murmurs, scratching the back of his head. How can he put the question to Regan if he doesn't at least have the note proving Lisa Labowski was dead at the time the book was lent out?

He glances towards the desk, where Regan is still talking with the old man. Andy looks down at *The Wendigo*, flipping through the pages absentmindedly, just to double-check if he by chance put the receipt in somewhere else, when a certain paragraph catches his eye. It's the one where the man is pulled from the tent. Andy immediately feels his skin begin to prickle, and he can't help but read the passage one more time.

What happens next is the most curious and inexplicable thing Andy has ever experienced.

The line is changed.

Of course that's not possible.

Words printed in a book can't change; they're ink on paper.

But the line has changed nonetheless.

And it's no subtle change, either. Had the wording been only slightly different, Andy could have explained it by him simply not remembering the line correctly. But the words he reads now are nothing at all like the ones he read last night.

The line, as Andy recalls it, went:

»Oh! Oh! My feet of fire! My burning feet of fire! Oh! oh! This height and fiery speed!«

But now it's only one word:

»hello«

Andy is dumbfounded. He reads the word twice over, then a third time, spelling it out, scrutinizing every letter.

He's not reading it wrong. And there's nothing wrong with his eyes, either. The new word is really there. It shouldn't be, but it is.

I must be at another place in the story ...

He reads the paragraphs leading up to the line, but he's not in another place. The man is awakened in his tent, and just as he shoots out through the opening and disappears into the night, he screams out in distress, that disturbing line which ...

Which now is completely wrong.

"Andy?"

He jerks and spins around, almost dropping the book.

Regan—who is no longer talking to the old guy—is looking at him with an uncertain smile. "Are you okay? I heard you muttering to yourself."

"There's ... there's something wrong," he croaks. "With the book."

She looks at *The Wendigo* in his hand. "The one you just read? What's wrong with it? I thought you said you liked it?"

"Yes, well, it's ... I'm just ..."

Regan eyes him patiently.

For a crazy moment, Andy considers the possibility that she is the one playing a trick on him. She was holding the book in her hands a moment ago—could she have switched it for another one?

Of course she couldn't. This is the same book.

"There's an error in the text," Andy says. "Look."

He shows Regan the page and lets his finger run down the text until it reaches the line. They both read it.

Andy gapes.

Regan frowns. "Well, it does sound a bit odd, I'll give you that. Burning feet of fire, what's that mean? I don't think it's an error, per se, but I agree it's a weird way to phrase it."

Andy attempts to moisten his lips with a dried-up tongue. "Yeah, very weird," he manages.

"That book really did a number on you, didn't it?" Regan asks, squeezing his shoulder. "You look like you saw a ghost!"

Andy murmurs something about him being very tired due to the fact that he was up all night reading. Regan laughs heartedly and says she knows exactly what he means; she usually refers to the phenomenon as a "book hangover." Then she goes back to sorting books.

Andy is just standing there for a minute, discretely holding the book at arm's length, as though it is something poisonous. He goes to row B to put it back on the shelf, when he suddenly gets the urge to look one more time.

Why would you do that? a voice in his mind immediately objects. *What could you possibly have to gain? If the text is normal, there was no need to check in the first place. If it's changed again, then there must be something wrong with your head. Do you really want to know if you're going crazy?*

The voice makes a good point, but Andy looks anyway. His curiosity gets the better of him. He opens the book once more and finds the page.

The line is changed again. But to something new this time.

»afraid?«

Andy slams the book shut, shoves it in a random place on the shelf and leaves the library in a hurry, not even bothering to answer Regan, who says his name from somewhere. As soon as Andy is outside, he grabs the bike, jumps on it and rides home as fast as he can.

DAY 54

Andy naturally concludes the library must be haunted, and he swears to never go near it again, ever. Instead, he begins to spend his free time at home in his room.

Ever since Rebecca disappeared, Andy has avoided being in the rest of the house as much as possible, only leaving his room to eat or go to the bathroom. He just can't take The Silence—that's how he thinks of the word, with a capital S.

Before Rebecca, his parents would no doubt have noticed how Andy isolated himself.

Mom would have asked him if he was feeling okay, would have checked his forehead with her cool palm.

Dad would have come into his room, sat down on the bed next to him and asked him if everything was okay.

But those kinds of things are in the past now, and his parents are simply drifting through the days, hardly noticing anything. Andy will sometimes imagine them going on like this, growing more and more distant, talking less and less, until they completely lose the ability to speak or recognize anyone around them. Or maybe they will even begin to grow transparent, simply fade away like ghosts, until one day, there will be nothing left but the occasional creak of a floorboard from Dad's office or the faint smell of Mom's perfume. No one would be able to explain exactly what had happened, only Andy would know that The Silence had finally swallowed up both his parents.

Still, there is one other thing besides food and bathroom visits which can make Andy venture out of him room, and that's Tweety. When Rebecca went missing, Andy took it upon himself to feed and look after her parakeet. Whenever he enters Rebecca's room, he's greeted by a squawking voice: "Hello, ugly!"

"Hello, Tweety."

Tweety reminds him in many ways of Rebecca, and Andy suspects that parakeets adopt the personality of their owners just like dogs will. As Andy steps inside and closes the door behind him, the bird gives a whistle and flies up on its perch. He hesitates for a moment, like he always does, looking around the room. Everything is neat and tidy. The bed is made, the floor is clean, not a trace of dust or laundry. It's almost like Rebecca moved out and the room is now waiting for a new occupant.

Andy dislikes the thought, and besides, it's not true; Rebecca will come home, of course she will. No one else will move into this room.

"Most children who run away from home get found within twenty-four hours," Andy recalls one of the officers telling his parents. "In rare cases, it takes up to a week."

The word, which the officer discretely avoided, and which no one has said aloud yet—at least not when Andy was listening—is of course, "kidnapped." Although Andy hasn't heard the word uttered, he can sense it lurking in the air all around him, immersed within The Silence. And behind it, buried even deeper, lies another word—a much, much worse one.

For some reason, Andy is reminded of the nightmare he had recently about Rebecca being taken by the wendigo, and his stomach tightens. What if it wasn't merely a dream, but some sort a warning? He once saw a documentary about twins who were able to sense each other's pain and distress even over great distances. Perhaps he and Rebecca have a similar connection?

"Hey, you!" Tweety calls out, pulling Andy from his train of thoughts. "Whaddaya looking at?"

Andy goes to the cage and pours seed into the bowl.

"Bon Appetit! Bon Appetit!" the bird squawks and begins eating.

Andy stands for a moment and studies it, the shiny green feathers and the gleaming orange eyes. "What do you think, Tweety? Will Rebecca come home?"

"Becca!" the bird answers and stops eating for a moment, as though it genuinely remembers.

Andy feels his heart speed up. It's silly, he knows that; of course the bird doesn't know who the word refers to, it simply repeats what it's heard.

"Becca!" it says again.

"Is that a yes? Do you think she will come home?"

The bird eyes him intently for a moment, then it says: "Hello, ugly!" and resumes eating.

Andy bites his lip, his gaze growing distant. "Up to a week," he mutters, not even aware he's speaking aloud. "Seven days."

It's almost two months since Rebecca disappeared.

DAY 57

Of course Andy can't avoid the library for the rest of his life; he needs something new to read. And after only a couple of days, The Silence is getting on his nerves.

Besides, it isn't really the library that scares him, it's the book. Or rather, the strange, changing line.

The notion which he has been trying to ignore is that the line wasn't just a random thing, but a meaningful message addressed to him. Not any reader, but him, Andy Wisler.

Andy has been going over the scene in his head several times. It really was exactly as though the book was talking to him.

No, not the book. The message came from someone else.

The name trying to force its way into Andy's mind is of course Lisa Labowski. But that wasn't only not possible, it was also insane.

Andy often reads books where the main character encounters something inexplicable, and usually the reader is given a rational explanation later on in the story, but sometimes ... sometimes it turns out there aren't any.

That's just stories. I'm not a character in a book. This is the real, boring world. And there is no such thing as books with changing lines.

So, Andy makes up his mind to be brave and go back to the library. He decides to wait until Friday at five o'clock. At that time the library will probably be empty.

He lets himself in with his password and begins by walking casually around the rows, making sure he's alone. Then he takes his time checking out Regan's newest display of popular books. Nothing really catches his attention, though, so he goes on to the rows.

He keeps glancing nervously over at row B, but as the minutes pass by and nothing happens, the calming atmosphere of the many books makes him feel at ease. He even begins to smile to himself.

God, I've been so stupid. I got scared by a brief moment of imagination. That's all it was. I'll bet I can go to the book right now and read the line and it'll be exactly as it has always been.

And he decides to do it. Just to put this silly thing to rest once and for all. He goes to row B and finds *The Wendigo*. He takes it out, leafs through the pages and finds the scene with the tent.

The line goes:

»Oh! oh! My feet of fire! My burning feet of fire! Oh! oh! This height and fiery speed!«

Andy lets out a long breath he wasn't even aware he was holding, and his shoulders drop down an inch. Apparently, he wasn't quite as confident as he acted, but he's still glad he looked, because now it's confirmed.

"It was just my imagination," he mutters. "Nothing more than that."

He puts back *The Wendigo* and finds another book which looks promising: *Solaris* by Stanislaw Lem. He sits down in the armchair by the far corner, kicks off his shoes and makes himself comfortable.

Andy reads the first chapter. He sits quietly and turns the pages, completely undisturbed and utterly absorbed by the story.

Solaris is about a young astronaut visiting a space station on a foreign planet called Solaris. But as soon as he arrives on the station, it becomes clear that something is wrong. What remains of his colleagues still on the station are frightened and scattered and acting extremely weird. When the main character talks to one of them, the dialogue quickly turns odd as the colleague warns the protagonist of great undefinable dangers aboard the station.

»Who could I see?« I flared up. »A ghost?«

»You think I'm mad, of course. No, no, I'm not mad. I can't say anything more for the moment. Perhaps ... who knows? ... Nothing will happen. But don't forget I warned you.«

»Don't be so mysterious. What's all this about?«

»Keep a hold on yourself. Be prepared to meet ... anything. It sounds impossible I know, but try. It's the only advice I can give you. I can't think of anything better.«

»But what could I possibly meet?« I shouted.

»lisa«

Seeing him sitting there, looking sideways at me, his sunburnt face drooping with fatigue, I found it difficult to contain myself. I wanted to grab him by the shoulders and ...

Andy is so caught up in the story that he reads on another few lines before it finally dawns on him. He stares at the last line of dialogue. The way it's written; no capital letters. No punctuation. And the name ...

Everything inside of him stiffens up, as though his body temperature has dropped way below zero. He stares at the name, feeling his skin turn to ice all over.

It's her again! his mind screams at him from someplace far away. *She's in this book, too! Get out of here! Run!*

He manages to get up on shaky legs while squeezing the book hard enough to crinkle the pages, afraid that it might jump on him if he lets go. Then, he drops it all at once, while simultaneously spinning on his heel and bolting for the exit. His elbow graces one of the shelves and knocks down a couple of books, but Andy pays no mind, he just runs as though his life depends on it, only slowing down as he approaches the glass doors.

"Come on, open!" he cries out, as the automated doors take their sweet time gliding aside. They're no more than a few inches apart when Andy leaps forward to squeeze through—but then, completely unexpectedly, the doors close again, almost pinning Andy's nose. He stumbles backwards, taken aback, staring at the doors. "What? No, no, open! Open up!"

He flails his arms, stepping back and forth, trying desperately to activate the doors again.

They finally react, gliding apart once more—but this time, they only open one inch before slamming shut again.

"What's wrong?" Andy demands shrilly, almost with tears in his eyes now. "Why won't you open?"

He grabbles at the doors, trying to force his fingers in between them to pry them apart, but to no avail.

He steps back, panting, staring at the doors as they attempt to open a third time, then a fourth and a fifth, but every time they're slammed shut, as though some invisible force is outmuscling the electrical system.

As soon as Andy thinks the thought, he realizes this is exactly what's happening, and he backs away, his heart pounding in his throat.

It's her ... she won't allow me to leave ...

He wheels around, expecting to see a ghost girl standing there, but he's still alone.

The building is completely silent—except for the strained opening and shutting of the doors behind him.

Andy steps forward tentatively as he looks in all directions, scanning the library for any windows. They're all way up high, too high for him to reach. For a moment, he considers running to the bathroom and locking himself in there, but it's small and has no windows, and the thought of him being stuck in there is claustrophobic.

There is only one way out of the library, and that way is being blocked; which means he's trapped.

A new flood of fear rushes through his body, sending out icy darts of adrenaline all the way to his fingertips.

"Who are you?" he whispers to the empty air, his voice shaky. "Why are you keeping me here?"

Andy holds his breath and listens. There's no answer, except for the roaring of his own pulse.

"What do you want from me?" he demands a little louder.

Still, no reply.

The doors behind him have given up the fight and stopped trying to open. Andy moistens his lips with a clammy tongue and swallows dryly.

Why doesn't she answer me? Or show herself?

Maybe she can't. Maybe the only way she can communicate is ...

He goes back towards the armchair, walking slowly, all his senses poised. He's ready to turn and run at the slightest indication of something ghostly showing itself. But nothing ghostly does, and he finds the book exactly where he left it.

Andy sits back down, his back and buttocks drenched with sweat underneath his clothes, his fingers cold as icicles as he picks up *Solaris*. The text on the page is yet again normal, and the dialogue between the two characters plays out exactly as you would expect it to, no mention of the name Lisa.

Andy clears his throat, then whispers. "Can you ... can you hear me?"

He expects the text to change right in front of his eyes, the letters morphing into some other message.

But the text stays the same.

Andy frowns. To his surprise, he's both relieved but also a little disappointed that he didn't get an answer.

Maybe she can't do it while I'm looking.

The sudden impulse makes Andy shut the book then open it again. And there, on the middle of the page, one single line, completely out of context, screams up at him like a drop of blood on a clean bedsheet.

»yes«

Invisible ants appear on Andy's lower back, crawling up along his spine and spreading out over his shoulders. He glances around, looks behind the armchair, but finds no one.

He's completely alone.

And yet he's not. Someone is here. Talking to him.

"What ... what do you want?" he croaks, the words barely audible.

He closes the book and opens it again.

»talk«

Andy blinks at the word. He had expected something a little more dramatic than that.

"You just ... you just want to talk? Okay. I guess we can talk a little."

He clears his throat, wondering how to small-talk with a ghost.

"So, uhm ... did you talk with anyone else than me?"

He closes and opens the book.

»no«

For someone wanting to talk, Lisa Labowski comes off as awfully curt. Perhaps, Andy wonders, it's not easy for her to talk through the book. Afterall, it must take some effort to change the words on the page. He decides that he should probably be the one doing most of the talking.

"So, have you always been here?" he asks. "Ever since you died, I mean."

»yes«

Andy ponders that reply and exactly what it entails.

How many times has he visited the library? How many hours has he spent here? Every time he has been carelessly strolling around the shelves or sitting here reading a book, an invisible ghost girl has been very close by. Watching him. Maybe she has even touched him. It's a crazy thought.

Another question pops into his mind. "Haven't you been awfully lonesome? I mean, all those years since you died, with no one to talk to."

For the first time, Lisa offers Andy more than a single word reply.

»no time«

He's pretty sure what the answer means, that time stands still when you're dead, or at least moves very differently. Maybe those eighteen years Lisa Labowski has been here in the library haven't felt like eighteen years at all.

But that answer begs still another question. "Where are you exactly? I don't get it … If you're dead, how can you be here in the library and in the books?"

He shuts the book and opens it again. Lisa's reply makes no sense at first.

»church bells«

Then he hears it. The bells from the church across the street are ringing out.

Andy checks his phone, but the battery is dead. He looks instead up at the clock on the wall. "Oh no, it's six already! I've got to go. It's my mom, she'll worry if I'm out too long. But … I'll be back again tomorrow. Maybe, you know, I mean, if you feel like it—we could talk some more then?"

Andy's hands are shaking a little as he closes and opens the book—but this time, it's not so much from fear.

»yes«

"Cool," Andy says. "I'll come right over from school."

He brings the book with him as he leaves the library.

Andy notices nothing of the world around him all the way home. More than once, a car honks at him, as he's about to make a turn or cross the street without looking. His thoughts keep going back to the conversation he had with Lisa Labowski.

It's difficult to grasp there was a real girl behind the short lines. At least real in a sense. Not living, but still somehow able to communicate with him from somewhere ... from where, exactly? That last question didn't get any answer.

Andy imagines how Lisa must be able to enter the books in order to change the text. Maybe she sees the universe of the book exactly like he sees the real world. Like a space traveler who can jump from one dimension to another.

This image in his mind spawns a host of other questions. Like, is it only the books at the library, or can Lisa visit any book in the world? Could she be in his backpack right now? Andy doesn't think so. He believes Lisa is somehow tied to the library.

There are also more far-reaching questions to be answered. If Lisa Labowski is really living some sort of afterlife, is she the only one? Could there be others? Do all people get to live on in books when they die? Or could it perhaps be only people who love books and read a lot, like Andy himself? And are there other people out there who have encountered a dead person living in a book?

The more he thinks about it, the crazier everything seems. Like something a child made up in his imagination. Still, his belly feels bubbly with anticipation at the thought of going back to the library tomorrow. He is almost—

Andy's thoughts are abruptly disrupted as he turns into the driveway of the house. The front door is yanked open and his mom comes rushing out. She runs to him and pulls him into a crushing embrace, almost tipping him over, her breath coming in rapid gasps.

"What ... what's the matter, Mom?" Andy asks. "What's wrong?"

Mom's hands are fondling his back, squeezing his sides, checking his arms, and Andy realizes this isn't a hug.

"Are you okay?" she breathes in his ear. "Are you hurt? Did anything happen to you?"

"I'm fine," Andy says, trying to pull back. But Mom grips him firmer, strokes his hair and checks his skull as though looking for bumps or bruises. Andy shoves her back. "Relax, Mom. I told you, I'm not hurt."

She grabs him by the shoulders, and as their eyes finally meet, Andy sees that his mom is not simply worried; her face is contorted in an awful grimace, causing her to look almost like a stranger to him. "Where have you been? Where have you *been*, Andy? We were worried sick! I spoke with all the neighbors, and your father is out looking for you, and I was just about to call the police ... Where have you *been*?"

Andy gapes at her. "But ... but I've just been at the library, like I alwa—"

"Don't you dare lie to me!" Mom exclaims, tightening her grip around his upper arms, her voice growing half an octave higher. "We've been at the library and you weren't there. So where were you, Andy? Did you go home with anybody you don't know? Did you talk to any strangers? Did anyone give you a ride in their car? I've told you over and over again never to say yes to anybody who—"

"Mom, please!" Andy almost yells to outshout her. "I was only at the library. I promise! You must have been there right after I left."

"Then why don't you answer your phone?" Mom's voice is close to a pitch of hysteria, and her grip is hurting him. "I called you like ten times—why didn't you pick up?"

"My battery is dead," he says.

"Your battery is always dead! Or your phone is in your bag, so you didn't hear it, or it's on silent, or you forgot it at home, or ..." She sighs, shaking her head violently. "Sometimes I think you do it on purpose."

"I'm sorry, Mom."

"Sorry doesn't cut it. You're not—"

"Helen? Oh, I see you found him."

Andy turns his head to see Paul Herbert come trudging across the street. The old widower lifts his dingy old cap, exposing the bald head for a second. "Where was he?"

"He came home on his own," Mom says, straightening herself, but only lets go of one of Andy's arms—like she's afraid he might take off. "He says he was at the library. We must have just missed him when we were there."

Paul Herbert raises his thick, white eyebrows in a look of relief. "I see. Well, I'm glad he's fine."

Mom nods, absentmindedly brushing her bangs aside. "I'm sorry we got you worried too, Paul."

"Don't worry about that," Paul Herbert says, sending Andy a brief smile. "And don't be too harsh on him now, Helen. Boys his age so easily forgets time, and—"

"Thank you for your concern, Paul," Mom says, turning to go back inside, hauling Andy along.

The Silence is extra oppressive that evening as the family sits down to eat dinner. Andy feels Mom glancing at him every few seconds, almost like she expects him to disappear into thin air if she takes her eyes off him for too long.

Cindy is home and has joined the family for dinner—both of which happen still less often. Andy still hasn't gotten used to her new haircut: Cindy's hair is long on one side, buzzcut on the other. She also wears a lot more makeup around her eyes than she used to, and her clothes are mostly black and worn-looking. She pokes at her food with her fork for five minutes, then excuses herself and takes her plate to the kitchen. A moment later, Andy hears her running up the stairs. Sometimes, Andy wonders if Cindy has even noticed Rebecca is gone. In a way he envies his older sister for her ability to simply not care. Since Rebecca disappeared, Cindy has seemingly been more concerned with her looks than mourning their little sister. Andy hasn't seen her cry even once.

Suddenly, Mom puts down her knife and fork and says: "Well, let's talk about it."

Dad looks up from his plate. "About what, hon?"

"What do you think, Henry? About your son's behavior."

"Oh, right." Dad looks at Andy. "It wasn't very smart, Andy. You had us all very worried. From now on, we need you to keep better track of time, okay?"

"Okay, Dad."

Dad nods, then resumes eating.

Mom glares at Dad. "Is that all you're going to do about it?"

Dad looks up once more, shrugging. "What do you want me to do, Helen? The boy knows he messed up. He promised not to—"

"Yeah, well, apparently we can't count on his promise, can we? He promised to follow Rebecca home from school, and look what happened."

Andy feels like Mom just punched him in the gut. A moment of thick Silence slugs its way through the dining room, until Dad finally says something.

"Helen," he sighs. "Please think about what you're saying ..."

"I'm not the one who needs to think!" Mom exclaims. "How can we ever feel at ease if we can't know whether our son will come home again or not? Or don't you even care? Don't you care if Andy also disa ... disa ..." Mom can't get the word out. Her lips start to quiver.

"Calm down, hon," Dad tries and reaches across the table.

Mom moves her hand away and breathes sternly a few times. Then she looks at Andy. And there it is again, that strange expression on her face, and suddenly, Andy can see it very clearly, that it's no longer his Mom. Not really. The eyes are all wrong.

"If your father won't be strict with you, I'll have to," she says coldly. "You're grounded for the entire weekend."

Andy shrinks at the thought of two whole days as a hostage in the looming Silence. And what's worse: He won't be able to keep his promise to Lisa.

"It's about time you learned to think about other people, Andy," Mom goes on, her voice lower and less angry, but somehow that's even worse. She looks him straight in the eye, a look of anguish on her face. "Your actions have consequences. Can't you see how terrified you make us when you don't come home on time and we can't reach you? After what happened to your sister ... don't you ever think about that?"

Andy looks down at his plate, his chin begins to jump up and down. He fights back the tears with all his might, but they squeeze out anyway. He feels like jumping up and running upstairs.

But he doesn't.

He just sits there, his head lowered as he starts to sob. He doesn't run to his room, for in a way he understands the punishment is just.

What he has sensed ever since that terrible day, what has been hovering over his head like a heavy cloud, what he has been reading off of the faces of everybody in his life, has finally been stated outright by his mom.

I promised to follow Rebecca home from school, and look what happened.

The words echo in his mind, causing his face to burn and the tears to flow faster.

It's my fault Rebecca disappeared. It's all my fault.

Later that evening there's a knocking at Andy's door. He's on his bed, reading *Solaris*—though he can hardly concentrate on the story, as his thoughts keep going back to Rebecca.

The door opens and Dad looks at him. "Can I come in?"

"Sure." Andy sit up and discretely wipes his cheeks, but the tears from earlier have dried up.

Dad closes the door after himself and goes to sit down at Andy's desk. "Your mom didn't really mean what she said—you know that, right, Andy? She's just afraid, that's all. Afraid of losing you and afraid that Rebecca won't come home."

Andy nods, digesting the words. He believes the second part to be true, the part about his mom being scared. He's not convinced about the first part though.

Quietly, he asks: "Do you believe Rebecca will come home, Dad?"

"Of course I do," Dad says promptly. But to Andy, he doesn't sound very sincere.

He broods for another moment, as he feels the words bubbling up from deep inside, and then he finally says it outright: "I know it's my fault. I shouldn't have gone into the library that day."

The confession hangs heavily in the air. Dad doesn't reply right away, just stares into empty space.

Andy badly wants him to say something, anything. He can even agree with what Andy said—as long as he doesn't just keep quiet. Anything is better than silence.

But Dad doesn't say anything.

"Dad?"

Dad blinks. "Yeah?"

"What if Rebecca doesn't come back?"

"Don't think about that, Andy. She'll turn up."

"Yes, but ... what if? What will happen then?"

Dad looks to the window and the dim evening sky outside. He sighs deeply and says: "Then I guess we'll just have to live on without Rebecca."

Then, as though the conversation is over, he simply gets up and leaves the room with no more words, not even looking at Andy before closing the door again.

For several long minutes, Andy just sits there on his bed, feeling his heart beat heavily in his chest.

How could Dad say it like that? How could he even pretend like everything will eventually return to normal if Rebecca never comes home? Of course it won't. Nothing will ever be normal again without Rebecca.

The thoughts keep going around and around, and Andy feels fresh tears building up in his eyes. He's just about to give in and begin to cry, when something changes.

Something inside of him.

It's like a shift, subtle but significant.

A feeling he hasn't felt before arises and fills him up, strong enough to drown out the impending sobs and force back the tears; it even pushes aside the guilt. Andy is not quite sure what the feeling is, but he's suddenly reminded of Lisa Labowski.

And then he finally recognizes what's going on inside him.

He has a strong impulse to act instead of just feeling sorry for himself. If he can talk with a dead girl in a book, then anything is possible. And since it's his fault Rebecca disappeared, it's also his responsibility to find her again.

Andy gets out of bed and begins planning.

DAY 58

He is awakened by his alarm at exactly 0:00. The ring-tone is dialed all the way down; that way, he doesn't risk waking anyone else in the house.

Andy gets up and gets dressed. His clothes are laid out and ready. So is his backpack, which he puts under the blanket and arranges it just like he practiced earlier. With a little effort he manages to make it look exactly like he's still in bed. He goes to the door and looks back at the bed, making sure it looks right from over here—which is where Mom or Dad will be looking from, in case either of them gets up to take a pee and decides to check on him.

As the final touch, Andy takes his phone and starts the recording he made. It's a three-minute-long audio file of him snoring discretely. He sets it on loop and hides the phone next to the pillow. Then he steps back to get the full impression.

It looks totally realistic—in fact, with the added sound effect, Andy gets an eerie feeling of really looking at someone sleeping in his bed.

"Perfect," he whispers to himself, realizing he is smiling. He can't recall the last time he smiled. He can't recall the last time he felt this good, either. He's not exactly happy, but he feels motivated, which is a big step up from sadness.

Now for the second part of the plan, he thinks to himself as he turns to the door. *Getting out of the house unnoticed.*

He leaves his room and slips downstairs. He knows which steps give off screeching sounds, so he deftly avoids them. In his jacket pocket is his own key to the house, and he uses it to lock the front door after he steps outside.

The night air is cool and crisp and quiet. Andy goes to the garage, unlocks his bike and takes it outside. He rides down the street, stops at the nearest light post and finds the map he printed out.

The town is not that big; he doesn't know the exact population figure, but besides the church there is a mall, a drugstore, a nursing home, and of course the school and the library.

He pulls out his marker, locates his own house on the map and puts a tiny X. He does the same with Paul Herbert's house.

"Two down," he whispers. "Only the rest of town to go."

He puts away the map and marker, turns his bike lights on and heads down the street.

Andy spends two hours riding around town.

Surprisingly, he's not sleepy at all. On the contrary, his senses seem somehow heightened, and his lungs welcome the chill air. He only meets a couple of late drivers; besides that the streets are quiet and empty.

He checks every driveway. Every single house gets an X on the map. Where there are closed-off garages, he peeks in through windows or opens the doors slightly—if they aren't locked, of course. If they are locked—or if he is for some other reason unable to get a visual of the car—that particular house gets a dot on the map; which means "scheduled for a later checkup."

A few places he's surprised by automated lights turning on, almost causing him to trip over his own bike in a frantic attempt to get out of sight.

And at one house, a large dog chained up in the carport starts barking at him furiously, probably waking up half the street. By the time the owners could get out to see what the dog was barking at, however, Andy was long gone, riding his bike like a desperate fugitive.

He can't skip even a single house; he needs to cross them all off the map. If he misses one, he might miss the one where the yellow van resides.

Half past three Andy rides back home. He's dead tired and a little disappointed. He honestly didn't expect to find the yellow van on this first night of searching, though; that would be too much luck to ask for, as he has only cleared a very modest portion of the town. He's still determined to spend as many nights as it will take.

When he comes home, he puts the bike in the garage, lets himself inside, sneaks upstairs, throws himself on the bed and immediately falls asleep.

DAY 60

Andy spends all Saturday and Sunday in his room. They are the longest days of his life.

He has finished *Solaris* and reread another book, though he had a hard time concentrating on the reading, since his thoughts were constantly darting back and forth between Rebecca and Lisa Labowski. The thought of her waiting for him at the library is plaguing him. He keeps imagining her standing behind the glass doors, gazing out, a frail ghost girl with a look of sadness in her eyes. Or maybe not sadness—maybe something else. Disappointment? Frustration? Anger, even? How will she react to him standing her up like this, when he promised to be back the next day?

At the same time, Andy is fighting a constant battle with his thoughts which keep telling him Lisa Labowski isn't waiting for him, that she was never really there, that it was all just a trick of his imagination.

Andy finds that idea even worse. For some reason, the prospect of talking with a ghost fills him with great excitement—even though he knows absolutely nothing about her or her intentions.

Which is why he decides to Google her.

It's a pretty rare name, not exactly the kind of name you hear every day. And he's in luck: He finds an article from a local newspaper about a thirteen-year-old girl by the name of Lisa Labowski who died in a car accident right by the intersection of Low Banks and Glenmore Ground—which is the one next to the library building.

So Lisa was hit and killed by a car right outside the library. Perhaps that's why her spirit ended up in the books? Maybe, on its way to heaven after leaving her dead body, it got entangled somehow in the world of the books, which enabled her to live on even though she should be dead.

The only other thing helping Andy to keep his spirit up is his nightly excursions.

In three nights he has crossed off more than two hundred houses—and yet there are still so many left. Being awake half the night is also starting to take a toll on him during the day.

Finally, Monday arrives and Andy is back in school. He fights his way through the lessons, struggling to keep his eyes open.

As soon as he hears the bell, his energy shifts completely, and he bolts out the classroom and makes for the bike shed.

Just as he rounds the corner, Sheila steps out right in front of him. Andy has no time to react, so he bumps into her, nearly knocking her over.

"Watch where you're going, Fatty!" she yells at him, shoving him hard in the chest. Andy is so surprised he loses his balance and trips, falling to the asphalt. He breaks the fall with his left hand, scraping it pretty badly and even drawing blood.

Sheila just scoffs and walks away.

It all happened so fast and unexpectedly, Andy is still befuddled as he gets back up, carefully dusting dirt off his bleeding palm.

Sheila has never done something like this before. Usually, she just taunts him.

He looks in the direction she left and sees her standing not far away, joined by Kimmie and Stacey. Sheila smiles and points to him, making the older girls laugh out loud.

Andy frowns. *She did it on purpose. She was waiting for me.*

Now that he thinks about it, Sheila actually darted him menacing looks more than once during the day, when their eyes incidentally met. He was too tired to read anything into it, but now it's clear to him that Sheila was just waiting for the right time to strike.

I don't get it, Andy thinks, as the mean trio turns and walks away, still sniggering. *What did I do to piss her off?*

He can't think of an answer, so he unlocks his bike and hurries on towards the library.

Regan isn't at work that afternoon; instead Andy is greeted by Stanley, an older librarian with a meticulous grey beard always dressed in shirt and tie. Stanley is chatting with a younger man by the autobiography section as Andy slips by them and heads for row B.

He pulls out *The Wendigo* and brings it to the armchair, which luckily is unoccupied. He makes sure no one is within earshot, before he whispers to the book. "Lisa? It's me, Andy."

He opens to a random page and reads the lines, but they all seem normal.

Maybe she didn't hear me.

He clears his throat and says a little louder: "Lisa Labowski? Can you hear me? It's Andy Wisler."

He scans the page—still nothing.

Perhaps she's in a different book right now?

He gets up and picks another book at random. He whispers to it, opens it and checks—but finds no reply from Lisa.

A sinking feeling settles in Andy's stomach. Is Lisa Labowski not real after all? Was it all just make-believe?

Then something occurs to him.

He gazes at the book, biting his lip, before speaking softly. "I'm sorry I didn't show up when I said I would. I didn't mean to stand you up like that. My mom grounded me because I came home late."

He holds his breath and with shaky hands he opens the book once more. This time, one of the lines pops out at him.

»hello«

Andy feels a jolt of excitement. But it's quickly dampened by a feeling of guilt. Somehow, he senses a lot of different feelings in that single word on the page; sadness, hesitation, anger. The thought of Lisa being trapped in the world of the undead all alone with no one to talk with for eighteen years—and the first time she reaches out, she's almost rejected. He realizes he needs to say something more.

"I ... I thought of you all day. I was really looking forward to speaking with you again."

There's no answer this time. But Andy feels that Lisa heard him, and he gives her a minute before he opens the book again. This time, there's a question:

»hand?«

Andy looks to his left hand and remembers the scrape. It's not bleeding anymore, but it still throbs a little. He discretely closes it. "It's nothing," he mutters, aptly changing the subject. "There's something I've been thinking about: How can you see me? I mean, are you, like, looking out from the book? Like it's a window or something?"

Lisa's reply is both cryptical and very fascinating.

»worlds behind worlds«

Andy imagines being inside the world of the book, to be able to hear all the sounds of the story, smell all the odors, being able to touch the characters and perhaps even talk with them. He imagines it must feel completely real. And still, there's another reality—*his* reality, the reality of the living—right under the surface. Like two photographs blended together.

The thought almost makes him dizzy. "So, does that mean you're actually in both worlds at once?"

This time, he gets no answer. He tries again, but still Lisa is silent.

"Lisa?" he asks tentatively. "Is something wrong?"

The lines remain unchanged. For a moment, Andy fears he might have said something insulting, something to make her upset. But he can't imagine what that would be, and he—

"Andy?"

The voice is right next to him, and Andy jumps in the chair.

Stanley is standing there, a pile of books under his arm, looking from Andy to the book in Andy's lap. "Are you ... talking to the book?"

"I ... uhm ... yeah, well ... it's just ..." Andy stutters, searching frantically for a plausible excuse. "I guess I got a little carried away ... by the story, you know." He tries for a smile, which feels more like a grimace.

Stanley stares at him for a long moment. He's far more old fashioned and rigid than Regan, always talking slowly and deliberately. Andy halfway expects him to wrinkle his nose and walk on, but to his surprise, a faint smile tugs at Stanley's mouth. "It's amazing when a book can make you forget everything else around you. Sorry to disturb you, Andy."

Stanley gives him a nod, then walks to the nearest shelf and begins putting books in their places. He whistles low as he makes his way around the shelves, disappearing out of sight.

Andy's pulse takes a minute to calm down. When it finally does, he asks the book: "Lisa? You there?"

And when he opens the book, Lisa says:

»yes«

Andy thinks for a moment. Lisa got quiet when Stanley was here. But why? Didn't she want him to see what she was saying? Perhaps she wants only Andy to know about her. That at least seems like a logical explanation—and it makes Andy feel special.

On the other hand, it also somewhat fans the flame of the creeping doubt at the back of his mind, the doubt about whether the ghost of Lisa Labowski is real or not.

If she's simply a figment of his imagination, it would make perfect sense that Andy imagines her not wanting anyone else to come in contact with her—just like she avoided Regan the first time Andy saw the strange lines in the book—as that would cause the illusion to break down.

In order to know if she's real or not, Andy decides he needs to know more about her.

"There are so many things I'd like to ask you," he tells her. "Like, did you live here in town? When you were alive, I mean."

He shuts the book and opens it again.

»yes«

"Right. And who were your family? Do they still live here?"

Andy closes and opens the book again, and this time, Lisa's reply takes him by surprise.

»my turn«

"Oh! Sure. I mean ... you want to ask me something? Go ahead."

Closes and opens.

»siblings?«

"Uhm, yes, I've got two sisters. One older sister called Cindy, but she's hardly ever home. I don't even feel like I know her anymore, and I can't remember the last time we talked. My other sister's name is Rebecca. She's younger than me. She's ..." Andy stops himself short. "Right, my turn to ask. I want to know about your family. Are they still in town?"

Lisa doesn't answer his question; instead, she poses another one of her own:

»rebecca?«

Andy frowns. "I thought we were supposed to take turns? You already asked a question."

He closes and opens the book a few times, but the line doesn't change and doesn't go away. It's obvious Lisa wants to hear about Rebecca.

Andy sighs. He doesn't want to argue with a ghost. "All right. Rebecca is ten. She can be a real pain in the butt, but also very sweet. If, for instance, she already ate all her candy and I still have some left, then she's *really* sweet. Let me see, what else? Oh, she's good at drawing. She likes to draw birds. We used to go looking at birds together back before she—"

Andy realizes at the last moment what he's about to say and closes his mouth. He closes the book, too, then opens it again, looking for a reply from Lisa.

But there isn't one.

Andy can sense her waiting; can sense the question still hanging in the air.

He breathes deeply, then begins talking in a low voice. "Rebecca is missing. It happened two months ago ..."

He tells Lisa everything. For the first time since Rebecca disappeared, he allows himself to go through everything that happened that day. It makes him sad to talk about Rebecca like this, but it also somehow makes him feel lighter once he's done.

He closes the book and opens it again. This time, Lisa speaks.

»sorry«

Andy smiles sadly. "Thank you. I guess it's even harder on my parents. They almost never speak anymore. But once I find Rebecca, it'll all be all right again. I'm looking for her, you see, at night. Or rather, I'm looking for the yellow van I told you about. As soon as I find that, I'll find Rebecca."

»police?«

Andy shakes his head. "I already told them about the van, but they don't believe it's got anything to do with Rebecca. But I know it was her knocking. I just know it."

This time, Lisa doesn't reply.

Andy waits for a minute, then tries again.

Still nothing.

He says her name a few times, but still Lisa remains silent. He looks around to see if anyone could be within earshot, but he's all alone with the book.

Then, finally, Lisa speaks.

»saw it«

Andy feels a tug in his intestines. "What did you see? The yellow van?"

»outside«

Andy's heart speeds up. "Did you see the yellow van go by right outside the library? When was it, Lisa? Do you remember? And did you get the license plate?"

His hands shake as he shuts the book and opens it again.

»no«

Andy feels his heart sink, but only a little. Now he knows the yellow van drove by the library at least once, which means it probably belongs to someone here in town or nearby. It makes him more optimistic about finding it.

He sits for a few minutes, brooding. Then he decides to turn the conversation back to Lisa by saying: "I read an article about you. I know how you died. What's the last thing you remember from being alive? What's your last memory?"

Half a minute passes, before Lisa says:

»blinding sunlight«

An image comes to Andy immediately of Lisa sitting on a porch in the afternoon sunlight, enjoying the warmth on her face. The thought makes him smile. "That's a beautiful memory. You want to ask me something now?"

»tired«

"Oh, okay," Andy says, feeling embarrassed. "Well, I was about to head home anyway. I guess … I guess I'll see you around?"

Lisa doesn't reply.

Andy feels his cheeks burning without really knowing why. Is Lisa tired of talking with him? Does he bore her? Or is she really exhausted? Maybe it takes great effort for her to talk.

He gets up and goes to put the book back in place. Just before he does, he checks it one last time. There's a line from Lisa.

»took rebecca«

Andy's insides turn to ice. He whispers: "Do you know, Lisa? Do you know who took her?"

He almost doesn't dare to close the book and open it again, but he forces himself. The new line screams up at him:

»wendigo«

Andy suddenly finds it hard to breathe. He never mentioned the wendigo to Lisa when he told her about Rebecca. Now he's reminded of the ominous dream he had where the demonic creature abducted his sister.

"The wendigo ... isn't real," Andy croaks. "It's just made up ... like vampires and werewolves."

Lisa replies right away, repeating herself:

»met it«

Andy almost can't squeeze out the next question, and it comes as barely more than a breath: "Where?"

The reply from Lisa, on the other hand, comes promptly:

»library«

DAY 61

The next morning, Andy rides his bike to school as usual. And although it seems like a day like any other, to Andy it feels like everything has undergone a shift of sorts.

He's more hopeful than he's been for months.

He's also scared and dead-tired—the latter due to the fact that he was out again last night for three hours straight looking for the yellow van—and the fear comes from what Lisa told him yesterday.

That the wendigo took Rebecca. That she has even seen it, because it visited the library once.

Andy never seriously considered the thought that something other than a human could have taken Rebecca. But now it all makes sense. How he chose that exact book, the story about the wendigo, on the day Rebecca disappeared. What his nightmare meant. And why the police can't find out who took Rebecca. How would they ever do that if they're only looking for a person?

Andy has always seen a clear distinction between what could exist in real life and what could only exist in books. But then again, ghosts have firmly belonged in the latter category, and that conviction has certainly been put to the test.

Somehow, the more he talks with Lisa, the more he becomes convinced that she's real. That he has met her for a reason. In books, nothing ever happens by accident—there is always a deeper meaning—and Andy is getting a growing sense that the real world has somehow been mixed up with the world of books.

He is riding through the park, so wrapped up in his thoughts, that he doesn't notice the strange sound until the third or fourth time he hears it, even though it's quite loud in the cool quiet morning air. It's a brief, sharp rapping.

dakka-dakka-dakka!

Andy stops his bike and looks in the direction of the sound. Apparently, it came from the trees at the bottom of the park. A few seconds pass by until the sound repeats.

He recalls Rebecca often talking about the wood-peckers residing in the park. She always hoped to see them, but as far as Andy knows, she never succeeded.

dakka-dakka-dakka!

There it is again. It's almost like the noise is calling for him. He puts his bike on the stand and steps out onto the wet grass. The sound keeps repeating with short intervals, guiding him, leading him to the trees. As he crosses the tree line, large, cold drops of dew fall from the branches, hitting his hair and his jacket. Andy hardly notices; he's too focused on the sound. He's getting closer. He's almost—

And then, right beside him: *DAKKA-DAKKA-DAK-KA!*

Andy spins around, staring at the tree he just passed. There are no leaves on the branches, since the tree is dead. He can tell from the white bark the tree is a birch. But he can't see the woodpecker anywhere.

Slowly, he walks around the tree. He scans the thick trunk up and down, scrutinizing every branch, but sees no birds.

And then he sees it.

The hole.

It's right in the middle of the trunk about ten feet up. Perfectly round, no larger than a ping-pong ball. The rapid tapping sound comes again. It comes from inside the hole.

Andy has an idea. He purses his lips and whistles.

Almost immediately, a small head peaks out from the hole. It's black-and-white and has a pointy beak. The woodpecker looks down at Andy, turning his head slightly to do so.

For a couple of seconds they just stare at each other.

Then the bird loses interest. It pulls its head back in. And a moment later the rapping continues.

Andy's heart is racing. Rebecca loved birds. He needs to show her the woodpecker's home right away. She will be ecstatic when she—

Then he remembers that Rebecca is gone, and his excitement dissipates. He's struck by a deep sadness—until he recalls he has someone new he can share his discovery with.

"It's building a home for itself," he tells Lisa that same afternoon. "I think it wants to put its eggs in there. Maybe it will even hatch them out and have babies! I really wish you could see it. Wait a minute—you can! I could just bring the book to the park."

He closes and opens the book, and the reply from Lisa shouts at him:

»NO«

"Okay, okay," Andy mutters, his cheeks reddening. "It was only a suggestion." He broods for a moment, then asks tentatively: "What happens if you leave the library?"

»death«

Andy stares at the single, ominous word, feeling a cold shiver run down his spine. What does "death" mean? Lisa is already that—but then again, not really. Part of her is still alive in the books.

If she leaves the library, she will die for real.

The thought of Lisa really dying fills Andy with an unexpected sense of dread. He wouldn't want to risk losing his opportunity to talk with her. Already he feels a strange bond with the dead girl, having exchanged but a few words with her and still knowing next to nothing about her.

Andy senses Lisa saying something, and he opens the book.

»rebecca?«

"I'm still searching for her every night," he says, yawning at the mere thought of being up half the night. "I haven't found her yet, but I will. I just need to find that yellow van."

»brave«

Andy feels heat go to his cheeks. "Me? Oh, I think anyone would do the same if someone in their family disappeared."

»not me«

The line befuddles Andy at first. Then it starts to make sense. He frowns. "Lisa, did you … also disappear?"

»I«

The line seems cut short, as though Lisa interrupted herself.

Andy closes and opens again. This time, there's nothing.

"What is it, Lisa?" he whispers. "What is it you're trying to tell me?"

A couple of minutes pass by. Andy keeps closing and opening the book. Finally, a new line appears.

»gone«

Andy sinks back in the chair. It's obvious to him that Lisa almost remembered something important, but then lost it again. He bites his lip, then says: "You told me the wendigo once visited this library. Do you remember what it came for?"

This time, Lisa replies right away.

»book«

"You remember which one?"

This time, no answer.

"Lisa?"

Still nothing.

Andy waits patiently. Several minutes pass. He checks for an answer now and then, but Lisa thinks for a long time.

At last, she speaks again. What appears on the page is the longest line Lisa has ever spoken to him.

»anatomy of the human eye«

Andy feels a rush of adrenaline. "Okay!" he bursts out. "Okay, hold on a minute. I'll try to find it."

He puts down the book and eagerly goes to search for the book Lisa just named. Judging by the title, he assumes it's a nonfiction, so he goes to that section.

He finds plenty of books on the subject of the human body and different parts of it, including one or two about the eye and the vision, but he finds none with that specific title.

Andy goes to the terminal and makes a search for the book, but gets no hits.

He returns to the armchair and asks Lisa: "There seems to be no book by that title—are you sure you remember it correctly?"

Andy closes then opens the book, but receives no reply from Lisa. He waits half a minute then tries again. Still no answer. He waits again several minutes this time, but still Lisa doesn't say anything.

Finally, Andy concludes that Lisa is tired. She probably spent the last of her strength giving him the name of the book, and she has no more energy to speak today.

Andy is left with a mixture of excitement and disappointment. He was really hoping to find the book the wendigo has read. He's not sure why, but something tells him that book would provide him with a vital clue; perhaps even lead him to the wendigo—and by that, to Rebecca.

DAY 78

The days begin to look alike. Andy's life falls into a certain routine.

In the morning, on his way to school, he checks in on the woodpecker. The bird is working away tirelessly building its home, the rapping sound growing more and more hollow with each day, as the hole inside the tree apparently grows steadily larger.

After school he goes by the library to visit Lisa. Some days he's not alone and they can't really talk. Other days Lisa is more talkative than others.

Andy tries a few times to get her to remember something more about the wendigo—anything that might help him find it. But whenever he brings up the subject, Lisa becomes oddly quiet, as though talking about it to her is either strenuous or uncomfortable. So mostly, they talk about ordinary stuff.

In truth, Andy is doing most of the talking, telling Lisa about his life, sharing his fondest memories and also his ideas for stories he wants to write someday, when he hopefully becomes an author.

When at home, Andy keeps to himself in his room, avoiding The Silence as best he can.

He goes to bed right after dinner and is awakened by the alarm around midnight, enabling him to sneak out of the house to go look for the yellow van. He has several hundred houses crossed off his list by now, but there are still even more to go, and progress slows down with each night as he needs to go still farther away from home in order to find new houses to check off.

Mom has become even more strict about the time that Andy must be home from school—five o'clock sharp—so Andy does his best to maximize the time he can spend at the library. He packs his bag two minutes before the bell sounds. He keeps his jacket ready by his side. And he bolts out the door the minute class ends. It takes him only four minutes riding his bike from school to the library, and only six from the library and home; this gives him a total of fifty minutes in which he can speak to Lisa.

This routine gives Andy a certain amount of comfort. He feels safe knowing what the day will bring, he enjoys the excitement of talking with Lisa, and he's satisfied with the progress—however slow it may be—he is doing at night. There is also a touch of pride in his work; at least he's doing *something* to find Rebecca, unlike everyone else.

Then suddenly one day, something happens which breaks the routine.

One morning, on his way to school, Andy stops by the woodpecker's tree as always. He stands still and listens. And then he hears it. Tiny chirping voices calling from within the tree. Andy breaks into a smile. The sound can only mean one thing.

At that moment, something comes whooshing over his head. The woodpecker lands by the opening in the tree, holding something in its beak. Before Andy can make out what it is, the bird disappears inside the tree. The chirping noises grow more eager. A moment later the woodpecker pops back out and flies off to find more food for its babies.

Andy just stands there, awestruck.

"The babies have hatched," he whispers to the book as soon he sits down in the armchair at the library that same afternoon, still panting from riding his bike as fast as he could all the way from school. "The woodpecker, I mean. I heard them—it was so amazing, Lisa."

He opens the book, but finds no reply from Lisa.

He checks to see if anybody could be within earshot; no one is. In fact, he's the only one here right now. Maybe Lisa simply waits for him to go on—so, he does.

"I saw the parents fly off and come back with food. And I made a recording of the sounds so you could hear them. Here, hold on a minute."

He takes out his phone and finds the recording. He's just about to hit play, when he suddenly feels a cold shiver run down his back for no discernable reason.

Andy looks at the book. "Lisa? Is something wrong?"

He closes and opens the book. The line from Lisa make the tiny hairs at the back of Andy's neck all stand on end.

»it's coming«

He knows immediately who—or rather, what—Lisa is referring to. He darts a look at the window, but can't really see anything from where he's sitting.

"Is it coming in here?" he whispers, his ears stiff, listening for the sound of the automated doors.

He closes and opens the book a few times, but Lisa has gone silent again.

Andy gets up, his legs shaky, and goes to the window. The parking lot in front of the library is empty. So is the sidewalk as far as Andy can see.

Then, it comes into view. Andy's heart feels like it explodes in his chest.

The yellow van drives right past the building.

Before he can even think, Andy is running for the exit. He almost clashes with the glass doors, squeezing out as soon as they're far enough apart. He stares down the street, but the van is already out of sight.

"Damnit!"

Andy runs to his bike, jumps on it and heads off, pedaling harder than he ever did. He spends twenty minutes searching the nearby streets, checking every possible turn the van could have taken. But he doesn't find it.

Andy rides back to the library, trudges back inside, his thigh muscles aching from the effort, and slouches back down into the armchair. "I didn't catch it," he sighs, wiping sweat from his brow. "It was so close. If I had just come a little bit closer, I could have glimpsed the license plate ..."

Lisa doesn't say anything, so Andy just sits there in silence for a while, feeling the sour sting of disappointment.

"My plan isn't working," he mutters. "It could be months before I find that stupid van if I have to keep searching like this. I'm still only halfway. If only there was a quicker way ..."

He senses Lisa saying something, and he opens the book.

»memory«

Andy sits up a little straighter. He can feel the hesitation of the word, feel how Lisa is concentrating not to lose the memory again. He says nothing, gives her time. Then, he closes and opens the book again.

»kidnapped«

Andy stares at the word. His tongue is like sandpaper. He can't talk, so he just closes the book, then opens it once more.

»yellow van«

Andy's heart is knocking against his ribcage. He closes and opens the book several times, but Lisa says no more.

"Who did it, Lisa?" he finally asks. "Who kidnapped you?"

No answer.

"Was it the wendigo? Was it the same one who's taken Rebecca?"

No answer.

"Please, Lisa. Say something. Do you remember anything else?"

This time, Lisa answers him.

»blinding sunlight«

Andy reads the line a couple of times, trying to figure out what it means. Lisa mentioned the memory of the sunlight blinding her before, but he must have misinterpreted it since she brings it up again.

What does it mean? Why is Lisa's last memory of blinding sunlight?

Andy feels like he's very close to a breakthrough. For some reason, he knows whatever happened to Lisa has something to do with Rebecca. He just needs the last few pieces of the puzzle.

"You got to give me something more, Lisa," he tries. "I can't figure it out."

He holds his breath as he closes and opens the book.

»tired«

That's the last word Lisa speaks to him that day.

DAY 79

The following morning, Andy wakes up exhausted.

He was out again last night, spending three hours riding around looking for the yellow van. Part of him knew he wasn't going to find it, but another part of him felt optimistic since seeing it yesterday.

He plans on going straight to the library after school as he always does. He can't wait to find out if Lisa remembered anything else which might help him.

On his way to school, he rides through the park as usual, wanting to check in on the woodpeckers, and maybe snap a picture of one of the parents to show Lisa.

As soon as he enters the park, though, he becomes aware of a sound quite unfamiliar. It's a loud rumbling, almost like a car engine revving away, except angrier.

Andy stops and stares at the sight which meets him. Many of the trees are tipped over. Two men in bright-orange vests and chainsaws are busy cutting more of them down.

Andy feels his stomach tighten up into a painful knot of fear. He can't see the woodpecker's tree anywhere.

He drops his bike and runs over to the place it used to be. Sawdust is everywhere, the smell of freshly cut wood thick in the morning air, mixed with petrol from the chainsaws.

Andy stops dead in front of the old birch.

It's lying flat on its side. The woodpecker's hole is pointing up into the sky.

Andy's heart turns to stone. He feels nauseous and dizzy as he slumps down on the trunk, burying his face in his palms, fighting the tears.

He can't believe it. They cut down the tree and killed all the baby woodpeckers. The thought makes him want to scream.

At that moment, the chainsaws stop. Silence falls over the park. Andy can hear the men talk with each other; their voices lighthearted. One of them even laughs.

How could they? How could they cut it down and kill those poor babies like that?

Then, suddenly, Andy hears a chirping. He stares at the hole next to him, his eyes widening.

One of the babies is still alive in there! Then, another one chimes in. And a third.

Andy jumps to his feet. He can't believe it: the woodpecker babies have survived the crash!

A loud chirp makes him spin around. In one of the trees still standing, high up on a thin branch, sits one of the parent woodpeckers. It has brought food.

Andy backs away. He's no more than a few yards distance from the birch, when the woodpecker swoops down, lands on the tree and dives down into the hole. The babies tweet eagerly inside.

Andy looks in stunned amazement as the woodpecker reappears and flies off. A few minutes later, the other parent comes, bringing more food.

Andy hardly believes what he's witnessing. The woodpeckers seem to pay little heed to the fact that the tree has been cut down. Apparently, they're still firmly determined to feed their babies.

"Hey, kid!"

Andy turns around.

One of the men is waving at him. "Better not play around here right now. It's not safe. We're cutting up the trees."

Andy points at the birch. "You cut down a tree with a family of woodpeckers inside!"

The man frowns and comes to him. He's younger than Andy took him for, maybe only twenty years old. He lifts his helmet, revealing a pimply forehead.

"Jesus," he mutters. "Looks like you're right, kid. And they're all still alive in there, judging from the sound."

"Yes, and the parents are still bringing them food," Andy says.

As though to prove him right, one of the woodpeckers lands on the birch at that exact moment and slips into the hole.

"Jesus," the guy says again, smiling broadly. "I'll be damned. Hey, Tommy! Come over here a second."

The other guy joins them. He's very overweight and sports a thick moustache. He heaves as though he just ran half a marathon. "What's up, Cliff?"

"Check it out," the young guy says, pointing to the hole. "That's a woodpecker's hole. There's a whole bunch of younglings in there—just listen!"

Tommy looks at the hole, breathing through his mouth. "You're right. Shoot, what a shame we didn't see it before we cut it down. We could have left it standing. Now they're probably not going to make it."

"They will!" Andy exclaims. "The parents are still feeding them."

Tommy looks at him, raising his bushy brow. "You sure about that?"

"It's true," Cliff says. "I saw one of them just a minute ago."

Tommy scratches his neck thoughtfully. "Well, whaddaya know."

"You think we can do something?" Cliff says. "If we just leave it here, the guys will come tomorrow and chop it to chips like the rest."

Andy lets out a gasp of horror at the thought of the woodpecker babies suffering such a terrible death.

"I don't know," Tommy says. "We could move it out of the way, I guess, except it's way too heavy."

"What if we cut out the middle part?" Cliff suggests, snapping his fingers. "We only need to move the part where the hole is, right?"

Tommy shrugs. "I guess it's worth a shot."

Andy feels his hopes rising. He takes a few steps back as the men puts their helmets and earmuffs on.

"Better cover your ears," Cliff tells Andy, then he pulls the string, and the chainsaw roars to life.

The men go to work cutting out about three feet of the birch trunk. The chainsaw bites into the tree eagerly, causing the sawdust to spurt into the air. Meanwhile, Andy notices both woodpeckers waiting and watching in a nearby tree.

The men turn off their chainsaws again. By working together, they raise the piece of the trunk upright. The babies are chirping away inside.

"At least the noise didn't kill 'em," Tommy remarks, looking around. "Right, if we drag it over there ..."

The men pull the tree stump across the soft ground and prop it up between two younger trees which have been spared.

"I hope we didn't scare off the parents," Cliff says, looking around. Andy can't see the woodpeckers anywhere.

The three of them step back a little and wait. The minutes go by. No sign of the parents.

"Hmmm," Tommy growls. "Don't look too good. Maybe we shouldn't have moved it."

Cliff doesn't answer; he glances at Andy.

"Well, there's really nothing more we can do," Tommy says. "We'd better get back to it, Cliff."

"I hope they'll be back," Cliff says, darting Andy a smile. "At least the babies have a fighting chance now. Good thing you spotted the hole, kid."

Andy stays behind as the men go back and resume their work.

He looks at his phone. It's half past eight. He should have been at school more than half an hour ago. He doesn't care, though. He needs to make sure the woodpeckers will keep bringing the babies food.

At that moment, something comes whooshing over Andy's head. The woodpecker flies to the piece of the birch tree and lands on the ground in front of it. It looks around, as though checking out the new surroundings.

"Go on," Andy whispers. "It's okay. Go on!"

The babies chirp from inside the hole.

The woodpecker looks around one last time. Then, it flies up and slips through the opening.

"Yes!" Andy shouts, throwing his fist to the sky. "Yes, yes, yes! They're going to make it!" Without really thinking, he shouts out: "Cliff! Hey, Cliff!"

Cliff is wearing his earmuffs, but still he hears Andy call to him, stops and looks over at him. Andy points to the birch and holds up a thumb.

Cliff smiles broadly and returns the gesture.

Andy feels very relieved as he hurries back to his bike.

He's almost an hour late for school.

He runs down the hallway and reaches his classroom. He's just about to knock, when the door is opened.

Their math teacher Otto looks at him in surprise. "Oh, hi, Andy! Didn't think you'd come today."

"I'm sorry," Andy mutters. "I was just a little late."

"That's okay," Otto says, smiling. "I'm glad you're here now. I just called your mom."

Andy freezes. "What? Why?"

Otto shrugs. "I was worried about you. You need to call in sick if you can't make it to school, remember? And since I hadn't heard from you, I decided to call and check. Your mom sounded pretty worried, so I think I'll call her back and tell her you're here now."

Otto goes to his pocket when a voice cries out: "Andy! Oh, thank God!"

Andy's stomach curls up. He turns around as though in slow motion to see Mom come running towards him, her hair fluttering. She grabs him and hugs him tight.

"Oh, dear God," she breathes. "There you are ... there you are ... oh, God, I was so scared ..."

"Mom, calm down," Andy says, trying to pull free. "I'm fine. I was just a little late."

Mom pulls back, and as Andy looks into her eyes, he can tell right away it's New Mom. "A little late?" she repeats shrilly. "Otto calls me because it's been almost an hour and no one knows where you are! You call that 'a little late'? Where were you, Andy? Where *were* you?"

"I ... I was at the park," Andy says, glancing through the open classroom door. Several of his classmates have come to look at the scene. Andy feels the heat rise to his cheeks.

New Mom doesn't seem to care one bit how many are looking. She just stares right at Andy, her pupils contracted. "The park? What on earth were you doing in the park?"

"I had to save the woodpeckers, Mom," he murmurs. "They had cut down the tree, and ..."

"Woodpeckers?" New Mom exclaims. "You're on your way to school, and you go looking for birds? My God, what's wrong with you, boy? Don't you ever think anymore?"

Otto clears his throat. "Well, Andy is here now. I'm sure he'll be more careful about the time in the future."

Mom looks at Otto briefly, as though only now noticing his presence. "Thank you for calling me, Otto. I'm terribly sorry about this."

"Don't be," Otto says, looking at Andy. "Come with me now, Andy."

Andy is very thankful to Otto. The teacher obviously senses how embarrassing the situation is for Andy. And if Otto hadn't interfered, New Mom could easily have worked herself up into hysteria. Andy tries to walk away, but New Mom grips him by the arm.

"Hold on," she says. "Since you can't be trusted to go alone anymore, I'll drive you to school from now on, and I'll pick you up afterwards."

"No, Mom," Andy says, shaking his head in horror. "I'll go straight to school from now on, I promise. You don't need to—"

"I don't care about your promises," New Mom interrupts harshly, pointing to his face. "This is the way it'll be. Got that?"

Andy stares at her, and he can tell there's nothing to do. The frustration bubbles up inside of him. He's painfully aware that both Otto and his classmates are watching him, awaiting a reaction. Andy feels like screaming. His face is burning.

"Okay, Mom," he mutters.

New Mom's expression softens a bit. She releases him and sends Otto a smile which is really more of a grin. "Please don't hesitate to call me again if anything else like this happens."

"I will," Otto says, forcing a smile.

Andy hurries into the classroom, cutting through the masses blocking the doorway and heads for his desk. Somewhere in the crowd he can hear Sheila laughing scornfully.

And from the doorway, he hears Mom's voice: "See you at two o'clock, Andy. I'll be parked by the bike shed."

Andy doesn't answer.

The humiliation is complete.

DAY 80

"It's the most embarrassing thing I've ever experienced," Andy tells Lisa. "And I can only come here with her as my warden now." He nods at the window. "She's parked right outside, waiting. Once my ten minutes is up, she'll come and get me."

Lisa doesn't answer him.

Andy sighs heavily. "And now Sheila will have something new to bully me with—it's just great."

This time, there's a reply from Lisa.

»sheila?«

Andy realizes he has never told Lisa about Sheila. "It's just a girl in my class. She's a real pain in the butt. She's always badgering me. I don't know why, though, but it got a lot worse after Rebecca disappeared. She's even started hurting me. Remember that day I had a scratch in my palm? That was her. She shoved me so I—"

Andy shuts up as he suddenly becomes aware of what he's saying. He sounds like a complete wuss, complaining about a girl bullying him.

Lisa says something.

Andy opens the book.

»fight back«

Andy is very surprised by Lisa's answer. "What do you mean? Should I … shove her back? No, I can't. She's a girl."

»bring her here«

Andy bursts into laughter at how unexpected the line is, then he looks around guiltily. Luckily, no one is around to hear him.

"Why?" he asks, smiling at the book. "Why would I bring her here? What would you do to her if I did? Beat her up? You're only a ghost, remember?"

As soon as the words leave his lips, Andy hears how mean they sound. He didn't mean for them to come out like that, not at all, he's just in a bad mood.

"I'm sorry, Lisa," he sighs. "It's just—"

Andy stops as the chair begins shaking. At first, he thinks it's his own legs, but then the shaking grows more intense, and the chair almost tips over.

"Holy crap!" Andy exclaims, jumping to his feet. He stares at the trembling chair. "What the …? Lisa, is that you?"

Suddenly, it's not only the chair shaking, but all the shelves around him. Books begin raining down, thudding to the floor, the noise growing deafening. It's like an earthquake going through the building, two of the shelves even tipping over with a couple of loud crashes, books spilling out everywhere.

Then, it stops.

It's over just as suddenly as it began. A few more books slide to the floor, then complete silence falls over the library.

"Oh my God," Andy whispers, looking around at the devastation. "Why did you do that?"

He opens the book still clutched in his hand. Lisa doesn't answer him.

Andy realizes that while the room is no longer trembling, his entire body is shaking. He's terrified. Suddenly, he doesn't want to be here anymore. He feels like someone is standing very close, staring at him with eyes full of rage.

"I ... I have to go," he says to the empty air. "The ten minutes are up. I'll ... I'll see you around."

He turns and leaves the library in a hurry.

DAY 81

The next day, Mom drives him to school as promised.

As they pass by the park, Andy almost crawls out of his seat to look for the birch tree.

"What are you doing?" Mom says. "Sit down, Andy."

He sits back down with a sigh. "I can't see them from the street anyway."

"See who?"

"The woodpeckers."

He can feel Mom eyeing him. "We can stop by the park on the way home," she says.

Andy looks at her, but now she's looking straight ahead.

"As long as you keep our agreement and come straight out to the car as soon as class ends," she adds, still not looking at him.

"Fine," he mutters.

They reach the school and Mom drops him off. Andy looks around the parking lot as soon as Mom drives off, hoping that no one was around to see him. But of course, someone was.

Sheila is coming towards him, flanked by her two faithful cronies, Kimmy and Stacey.

Oh, crap ...

"Well, look! The baby just got dropped off at the daycare," Sheila taunts right out the gate.

Andy sighs heavily. Normally, he would avoid looking her in the eye and head in another direction in a hurry. But something keeps him from moving. Lisa's line from yesterday suddenly appears in his mind's eye.

»*fight back*«

Andy stays where he is. He feels the old, familiar fear come rushing up from within; but instead of reacting to it, as he's so used to doing, he brushes it aside.

"I'm not in the mood today, Sheila," he hears himself saying—his voice surprisingly firm.

Sheila stops in front of him, widening her eyes dramatically. "Uh, whaddaya know? The baby talks!"

"Don't call me that."

"You don't tell us what to say," Kimmie brays.

Andy doesn't even look at her; he holds Sheila's gaze. "I mean it, Shelia. I'm done with this."

Andy's heart is pounding away like a jackhammer, trying to make its way into his throat. But to Andy's great surprise, he finds himself not caring anymore. He doesn't care about the fear, and he doesn't care about Sheila. He's not the old Andy any longer, the nervous, submissive Andy who would let Sheila walk all over him because he was afraid. He's still afraid, mind you, but he's even more angry. And those words are still flashing in his brain, like a silent fire alarm.

»fight back« ... »fight back« ... »fight back«

The cronies are both cackling now, yet Andy doesn't hear a word of it; he's still just staring at Sheila, who's staring back at him, a devilish smile on her lips.

"I wonder," she says, her voice playfully soft and sinister. "What will happen if we keep you here until class begins? You think the teacher will call your home again? You think Mommy might come running again? You'd like that, wouldn't you, you big baby?"

Cries of shrill laughter come from Kimmie and Stacey.

"I'll only tell you this once," Andy says, his voice still firm. "I'm going to go to class now. And don't you try and stop me."

Sheila's eyes grow narrow. "You don't talk to me like that. You don't have the right to—"

Andy simply walks right by her, cutting between her and Stacey.

Sheila is so surprised, she doesn't even have time to react.

"Hey!" she shouts after him. "I'm talking to you!"

Andy walks towards the entrance. He wants to run, but he forces himself to walk. He doesn't want it to look like he's fleeing.

He can hear Sheila come running after him.

"You stop right there!" she hisses, grabbing his arm. "I'm not done talking with you!"

Andy doesn't turn around, but he jerks his arm free with such force, he almost sends Sheila flying. She struggles to keep her balance, then she just glares at him in stunned disbelief. Her cronies come running to the rescue, shouting angrily at Andy. He just walks on towards the entrance.

Sheila doesn't try to catch up with him again.

Andy heads down the hallway, his pulse still beating like a heavy metal band, his armpits are drenched from sweat. But a tentative smile is lurking at the corner of his mouth.

I did it ... I really did it!

He can't believe it. He stood up against Sheila, and he won! It's almost too good to be true.

In fact, it *is* too good to be true.

As he steps into class, most of the students are there. A few of them look at him, and Andy feels like he can tell a difference on their faces. He feels like a whole new person, and he's pretty sure his classmates can tell. He straightens his back and goes to his desk.

Just as he puts down his backpack, Sheila comes into the classroom. She's no longer accompanied by her cronies, but her expression makes it clear immediately that the matter isn't settled yet. Her eyes seek out Andy and fire lightning at him.

"There you are, you fat piece of shit," she snarls. "You just think you can walk away from me like that? Who the hell do you think you are?"

Heavy silence falls on the room. Everyone freezes up and looks from Sheila to Andy.

Andy doesn't answer. He ought to sit down, but his body doesn't obey; it just stands there, next to his desk, firm like a soldier in line.

Sheila breaks eye contact to look around for something. She goes to the whiteboard and grabs the pointer stick out of the holder. It's a three-feet-long, thin aluminum spear, and in Sheila's hand it looks like a nasty weapon.

She turns to Andy, and now she's once again smiling. She waves the pointer stick back and forth like a windshield wiper as she walks towards him.

"What are you going to do with that?" Andy asks in a low voice.

The bell sounds right at that moment, and Andy feels a jolt of hope. He might be saved by the bell, quite literally. The trouble is, sometimes it takes five minutes before the teacher shows up. And Sheila doesn't even react to the bell.

"I just want to ask you a question," Sheila says, stopping a few paces away from him. "That's all. Just one simple question."

As they stand in front of each other, Andy is both taller and broader than Sheila by a significant margin, yet Sheila's voice clearly betrays that she feels like the one in control—and that she enjoys that feeling.

"Fair enough," Andy says. "Ask it then."

"Why are you so fat?"

A couple of the other students snigger nervously.

Sheila breaks into fake laughter. "That was just a trick question! I already know why you're so fat: you eat too much."

"Stop calling me that."

"Why should I? It's true. You *are* fat, Andy."

Andy glances towards the door. Students are coming in at a steady pace, yet no sign of the teacher. The classroom has turned into an arena, everyone looking at Sheila and Andy, the newcomers quickly realizing what's about to go down and joining the circle.

"All right, here's my real question," Sheila says. "But I warn you ..." She taps him on the shoulder with the pointer stick. "If you don't answer correctly, I'll have to punish you."

"If you hit me with that," Andy says through gritted teeth, biting back the rest of the sentence.

"Then *what*?" Sheila hisses, stepping close to him and staring up into his face. Andy can smell her perfume. "Then what, you fat moron? Are you going to run home to your Mommy crying?"

Andy can't reply. He can't get any more words out. His blood is boiling. Every muscle is seething. He manages to shake his head once.

Sheila smiles. "Good. Here's my question, then. It's about your sister."

A rush goes through the room, then everyone falls even more quiet. Sheila just mentioned Rebecca, whom no one talks about.

Andy feels something brewing in his chest. It feels like thunder.

"Now, I know the police say she's disappeared," Sheila begins in a lighthearted tone. "But isn't it the truth, simply, that you ate her?"

No one laughs this time. The silence is as thick as sand.

Sheila stares at Andy, smiling and holding the pointer stick ready to strike. "What do you say, Andy? Did you eat her? Is that what really happened to poor little Rebecca?"

Andy forces his jaw to unclench, enabling him to whisper: "Fuck you!"

Sheila's smile vanishes. "Wrong answer." She swings the stick. It hits Andy on the thigh, hard enough to produce a loud smacking noise. Andy doesn't feel anything, though. He doesn't even flinch.

Instead, he draws back his right arm and hurls it at Sheila, connecting his open palm to her cheek with brutal force. The slap is much harder than he anticipated. Sheila's head is flung sideways, she stumbles and halfway falls over a desk. The pointer stick lands on the floor with a metallic sound.

Then, a few long seconds of silence.

No one moves.

Sheila straightens up, wobbles briefly, then lifts her hand to her cheek, which is already a fiery red. She stares from her hand to Andy, her face a mask of shock and confusion. Then the mask crumbles and she breaks into tears, right before she whirls around and runs out of the classroom.

In the doorway she almost collides with Otto, who enters at that exact moment.

"Wow, Sheila, where are you going? Class is about to begin ..."

Sheila just squeezes past him and disappears out of sight.

Otto looks to the rest of the class. "Was she crying? What happened in here?"

No one seems to want to answer. The students just exchange hesitant glances. A few of them look at Andy.

Andy is suddenly able to move again. He sits down in his chair. The rest of the class follows his example and finds their seats.

"Well," Otto murmurs, shrugging. "I guess I'll find out if it concerns me, won't I? Right, let's get to work ..."

DAY 84

Andy is certain punishment awaits him. He's sure the principal will show up, telling him they need a talk. Maybe he'll even get expelled. And of course, once Mom hears about it, he'll be grounded for life.

Or maybe Sheila won't even tell on him. Maybe she'll simply take matters in her own hands and show up with a gun at recess to shoot him. Andy almost prefers that outcome; at least it'll be over quick.

But to Andy's utter amazement, none of the scenarios come true. In fact, nothing further happens.

The rest of the day proceeds in a surprisingly normal fashion. Sheila doesn't turn back up. Apparently, she left school when she ran out of class.

The only difference is how his classmates are looking at him. To begin with, their eyes are anxious, almost scared. But then, little by little, as they find out Andy hasn't turned into a raging monster, they become softer, warmer even—and by the end of the day, a few of them have even smiled at him. That hasn't happened since Rebecca disappeared. In fact, being completely honest, Andy can't remember any of his classmates having *ever* smiled at him.

Mom shows up after school. They go by the park as she promised, and Andy checks on the woodpeckers. He can still hear them in there, chirping away.

Afterwards, they go by the library. Andy had actually decided to tell Mom they could skip the library today—after what happened last time, he was afraid to show himself, much less talk with Lisa. But now he's not remotely scared anymore.

Regan greets him with a smile when he steps inside. "Hello, Andy! Gosh, did you hear what happened? Apparently, an earthquake hit the library yesterday."

Andy stops dead in his tracks. "An ... earthquake?"

"Yeah, I know, it's insane! Come look at this."

She shows him into her office and finds a videoclip on the computer. "Now, I'm really not supposed to show you this—it's from the surveillance cameras."

Andy feels his skin on his scalp tighten all over.

"But since no one is on the recording, I think it's fine," Regan goes on. "The angle is a little off; the camera moved slightly just as the shaking began, but we fixed it. Well, here it is, are you ready?"

She runs the clip, and Andy sees a black-and-white overview of the library exactly where he sat yesterday—except the angle is just far enough to the side that the armchair isn't in the shot. He sees how the shelves start to shake and books fall out.

"Holy crap," he whispers.

"I know," Regan says. "Luckily, no one was here—I checked in the system. They're sending someone from a local news station later this afternoon to talk with me about it. Isn't that crazy? I mean, there's never been an earthquake within five hundred miles of here!"

"That *is* crazy," Andy admits, swallowing dryly, trying to think. It isn't true that no one was here yesterday—*he* was. He let himself in using his card. But why doesn't that show in the system?

And who moved the camera so that I wasn't in the shot?

Andy feels goose bumps pop out all over his back.

Regan talks some more, and Andy tries to nod at the right places. Then a woman comes to ask for Regan's help finding a book, and Andy is released.

He goes to the armchair. The shelves have been fixed and all the books are back in place—it must have taken Regan hours to sort it out.

Andy takes a random book and sits down. For a moment, he just sits there, the book on his lap. He doesn't really know what to say. He can sense Lisa is there, waiting.

Then, finally, he says: "I fought back."

He waits a moment longer, then opens the book. A single word from Lisa.

»good«

***

That evening, Andy waits for someone to call Mom; either from school or maybe Sheila's parents. But part of him knows it won't happen.

And that part is right; Mom's phone never rings.

DAY 87

Sheila doesn't come to school the next day. Or the day after that.

Andy begins to think she'll never show up; that she maybe moved to another school. But on the third morning, right after Mom drops him off, he sees her standing in the schoolyard, waiting, alone.

Andy hesitates for a moment. He can tell Sheila has already seen him, but she just stands there, her expression blank.

Okay, this might be it, Andy tells himself, breathing deeply. *Round two is about to begin. Be tough. Don't let her get away with whatever she's going to try.*

He walks towards her, stopping a few yards away. His fists are buried in his pockets, clenched firmly. For a moment, they just stare at each other, like two cowboys in a western.

Then Sheila says: "Hey." No anger in her voice.

"Hey yourself," Andy retorts, a bit uncertain.

Sheila rubs her arm and looks away. Then she takes a few steps closer. Andy stands his ground, thinking it's a trick. He darts a quick look around, suspecting Kimmie and Stacey to be sneaking up on him; but no one else is around.

Sheila looks at Andy's feet as she says: "Look, I'm sorry for what I said about Rebecca."

She sounds so sincere, Andy is taken completely off guard. "That's ... that's okay."

"No, it really wasn't. It was very mean."

Andy has no idea how to react or what to say. The situation is so unexpected, almost surreal. Part of him is still suspicious, expecting this to be some sort of devious ploy to get him to lower his defenses so that Sheila can really hurt him when he's most vulnerable. But something tells him she's being honest.

"I guess I'm sorry I slapped you," he says.

Sheila scrapes the ground with her shoe. "I probably deserved it; I hit you first."

"It didn't really hurt."

"So ... we're friends, then?"

"Uhm, yeah, sure."

Sheila looks up at him briefly, before she turns to walk away, but then seems to think better of it and turns back around. "You know, my older sister died."

"Oh," Andy says stupidly. He had no idea Sheila even had a sister.

"She was about Rebecca's age when it happened," she goes on, her voice very low, almost a whisper, and Andy must strain to hear her.

"I'm ... very sorry," Andy manages. "How did it happen?"

"She drowned. One day, she just vanished. The police never found her, but they found her clothes and her bag in the stream down in the park. They think her body ..." Sheila breaks off as her lower lip begins to quiver. She bites it to make it stop, but Andy can see tears in her eyes now. "Her body must have been taken by the stream out to the ocean and eaten by fish. I was only six back then, but I still remember how we used to play." A single tear runs down Sheila's cheek, and she quickly wipes it away, then looks him straight in the eye. "I hope Rebecca comes home."

Sheila turns around and leaves.

DAY 95

Following the episode with Sheila, the days go back to normal and begin to look very much alike again.

Andy is still looking for the yellow van at night; he feels his efforts might be in vain, but he doesn't know what else to do, and at least doing *something* is better than nothing.

The trips have grown longer, since he needs to go farther away from home to find streets he hasn't crossed off the map yet. There are only a few hundred homes left by now, and with each night, Andy's hope of finding the yellow van dwindles.

One night, as Andy returns home at about 3:30 AM, he puts his bike in the garage and lets himself in through the front door, making as little noise as possible.

By now, he's done it so many times—slipping in and out of the house like a burglar—that he hardly thinks about it. That's why the surprise is so much bigger when the lights in the hall suddenly flick on.

Andy spins around.

In the door to the kitchen he sees Mom. She's dressed in her robe. Her hair messy and her eyes puffy. Behind her, on the counter, is a glass of water.

For several long seconds, the two of them simply stare at each other.

Andy has no idea what to say or do; his mind is blank with shock. On Mom's face, however, a terrifying transformation begins, as she turns into New Mom in front of Andy.

"Where ... have you ... been?" she breathes, barely moving her lips.

Andy tries to answer, but he can't.

New Mom steps closer. "I asked you a question, boy." Her voice rising ever so slightly. "Where have you been?"

"I ... I was just ..." Andy gropes for the words. Perhaps he can still get out of it. An idea pops into his head. "I just remembered I forgot to turn off the lights on my bike. I went out to check, just in case I—"

New Mom is at him in three longs strides, grabbing both his ears before he can even react.

"Don't you dare lie to me!" she screams. "I saw you from the kitchen window! I saw you come riding on your bike! Where have you been?"

Andy tries to get loose, tries to pull away, but his back meets the wall. "Auv, Mom!" he howls. "Let go!"

"What is this?" New Mom lets go of one of his ears to snag the map out of Andy's hand. She stares at the crumbled paper. "It's a ... a map," she says, breathless with horror. "Have you been all over town? In the middle of the night?"

"I was just—"

New Mom drops the map and twists Andy's ear all the way around. The pain is intense. Andy can feel the spit hitting his face as New Mom screams at the top of her lungs: "*Have you gone insane, boy!? Have you gone completely insane!? Do you want to disappear like your sister!? Do you!? Is that what you're trying to do!?*"

"No, Mom!" Andy cries. He's on his toes, grabbing her wrist with both hands, trying desperately to relieve the pain from the twisted-up ear.

She grabs him by the hair with the other hand and shakes his head back and forth, still screaming into his face: "*Do you want to disappear!? Do you!? Do you!? Answer me! Do you want to disappear!?*"

Andy no longer understands the words; the world is an inferno of pain and fear. He hears himself crying and shouting over and over: "I'm sorry! I'm sorry!"

Then, a new voice cuts through: "**Helen!**"

Andy is able to turn his head just enough to see Dad's legs coming down the stairs.

"What are you doing?" he shouts in disbelief. "Let him go!"

New Mom doesn't let go. She just turns on him like a hawk, spitting: "Your son has been out riding around all over town! He's been making fools of us, Henry! He's gone insane! He's—"

"Let go of him, Helen! He's crying!"

Only when Dad rushes to grab Mom does she finally release Andy, and the pain lessens somewhat. He stumbles sideways, his hand going to his ear, feeling warm blood.

"What the fuck is going on?"

A new voice from the staircase. Cindy is standing there in her nightclothes, glaring around at the scene with eyes big from shock.

New Mom is still standing in the middle of the hall. The halogen spots in the ceiling cause her to look more like an animal than anything else. She's breathing heavily, her lips wet from spit, her eyes wild. Her right hand is red from Andy's blood. "He ... he lied to us," she hisses between ragged breaths. "He's been making fools of us all ... he's going to disappear ... just like Rebecca ... he's going to disappear ... he's going to disappear ..."

Dad comes to Andy; his eyes are worried and alive—*really* alive. Like they used to be before Rebecca disappeared. "Are you all right, Andy? God, you're really bleeding."

Andy can't answer, he's still crying too much.

"Disappear ... disappear ..." New Mom keeps saying. "He's going to disappear ..."

"Helen, damnit," Dad says, turning around. "You've almost—" His voice changes abruptly. "Helen?"

Andy looks past Dad just in time to see New Mom turn her eyes up, then collapse to the floor.

Cindy screams.

"It looks a lot better already," Dad says, squeezing the Band-Aid back in place on Andy's earlobe. "It's no longer bleeding."

They are in Andy's room. Andy is sitting on his bed; Dad is standing in front of him.

"What about Mom?" Andy says. "What happened to her?"

"She just got a little too riled up," Dad says. "She's sleeping now."

"Did the ambulance come by? I thought I heard someone talking downstairs."

"I called them just to be sure. But they said everything will be all right. Mom just needs to rest for a few days. She's under a lot of pressure right now. You understand that, don't you?"

Andy nods. There's a dull throbbing in his earlobe.

Dad sits down next to him. "You need to tell me what you were doing riding around town, Andy."

Andy takes a deep breath. "I was looking for Rebecca."

Dad squeezes his shoulder. "That's thoughtful of you, Andy. But you don't need to go looking for her. The police are doing that. They'll find her."

Andy throws out his arms. "But they have no idea where to look. I saw the van, Dad. The yellow van. That's the one I'm looking for. If I find it, I'll find Rebecca."

Dad sighs. He sounds exhausted. "You can't go on like this, Andy."

"But you went looking for her in the beginning. You told me so yourself."

"That's different. I'm a grown-up."

"But I—"

"Listen to me, Andy. You can't be riding around town in the middle of the night looking for some van just because you think it's got something to do with Rebecca. We need to trust the police and wait."

And there it was. The magical word.

"I don't want to wait, Dad! Waiting isn't doing anything for Rebecca. I want to *find* her! It's my fault she disappeared, so it's my responsibility to find her again."

"We went over this already, Andy. It's not your fault that—"

"But it is! It *is* my fault! And you know it—I can tell by your face."

Dad is quiet for a while. He looks down on the floor. Andy's heart is pounding away in his chest.

When Dad looks up at him, his eyes are once more dull and blank. The aliveness has gone away again. "No more excursions, all right? Please give me the map."

Andy realizes it's over. Dad is no longer on his side. He hands Dad the paper.

Dad gets up and trudges to the door. He looks back to say: "I'll be locking the door to your room at night from now on, Andy. Just until this is over."

PART TWO
REBECCA WISLER

DAY 1

Rebecca glares at Andy as he crosses the street.

Does he really think she's going to wait out here in the freezing cold while he goes looking for a stupid book? Well, if so, he'd better think again. Rebecca decides to give Andy a good scare.

He parks his bike by the stand and looks back over at her one last time, his expression hilariously forbidding, like he's trying to browbeat her from across the street. Rebecca sends him her sweetest smile and a little wave.

He huffs, turns around and marches into the library.

As soon as he's out of sight, Rebecca runs down the sidewalk, her bag jumping up and down. By the entrance to the park are two large elm trees, and Rebecca hides behind the nearest.

She peeks out and holds her breath in excitement. From here, she has a good view of the entrance to the library, yet Andy won't be able to spot *her*. Once he comes out, he'll think she went on homewards, and then he'll hurry to catch up with her.

Rebecca smiles at the thought of tricking Andy like this.

This is what you get for being a jerk.

A minute passes, but Andy doesn't come out.

Rebecca needs to pee really bad. Typical Andy, taking his sweet time.

"Come on," she whispers, shifting her weight from one foot to the other. "Come on, stupid Andy!"

Still, the glass doors don't open.

Then, she hears it.

dakka-dakka-dakka!

Rebecca spins around, staring into the park, her eyes scanning the trees. She immediately knows what made the sound. It's the woodpecker. She's heard it a few times before, and every time she and Andy walk through the park, she keeps an eye out for it, yet she never managed to actually see it.

dakka-dakka-dakka!

There it was again!

Rebecca can even tell which direction the sound came from. This might be her greatest chance to get to finally have a look at the woodpecker.

She forgets completely about teasing Andy and heads into the park, running with excitement. The sound came from the far end of the park, where there's a large area of younger trees. She can't see the bird in the first trees, so she ventures farther in. It's still early spring and only a few of the trees have leaves, so the woodpecker will be easy to spot on the naked branches—provided it hasn't flown off yet. Rebecca scans every treetop meticulously as she goes on.

dakka-dakka-dakka!

She lets out a gasp. The sound was closer and a little to the right. She changes direction and speeds up.

The trees are bigger and stand closer together now, making everything a little dimmer, but Rebecca hardly notices. She reaches some bushes and pushes her way through, then she almost trips over an old, rusty bike someone left here several years ago.

Rebecca looks up as she walks on, listening intently, but now the woodpecker has fallen silent.

She's amazed at how far the trees go on; come to think of it, she's not quite sure what's on the other side of the park. But she needs to see the woodpecker, so she presses on. If only she could—

"Help me!"

Rebecca stops abruptly. She holds her breath and listens.

Was that a voice? Someone calling for help?

Now there's only the slight breeze, pushing at the treetops and causing the old leaves on the ground to stir and rustle. She picks up something on the wind, a foul smell; probably a dog turd, except it's even worse than that.

She turns to look back but suddenly she can't tell exactly which way she came from; the forest has grown too thick to see very far, and it looks the same in every direction. She can't even hear the sound of traffic anymore.

Am I even still in the park?

She feels a faint trace of budding panic.

Of course she is still in the park; where else would she be?

Rebecca isn't normally very easily scared. She's not afraid of the dark, not afraid of spiders, and she can even watch scary movies without having nightmares afterwards.

But this is different. She can't put her finger on it, but something is wrong here. She wants to get out of the forest as fast as possible. She doesn't even care about seeing the woodpecker anymore. In fact, she wishes she had never left Andy. She considers for a moment taking out her phone and calling him for help, but Andy will no doubt tease her for getting lost.

Besides, she's not *that* scared. Not yet.

She pulls herself together. She just needs to pick a direction, that's all. Whichever way she chooses will eventually lead her out of the trees. She knows the town pretty well and can easily find her way home from wherever she might end up.

That awful smell again, stronger this time. It smells like something rotting.

Rebecca is just about to move on, when the voice comes again.

"I'm hurt. Please help me."

This time, she can tell it really is someone calling and not just the wind. A girl, probably around her own age. She sounds like she's about to cry.

Rebecca turns towards the sound but can't see anything between the trees. Or can she? She squints.

Rebecca's eyesight is perfectly fine—not like Andy, who needs glasses—and she glimpses something far off. Something yellow. She walks closer.

Rebecca reaches an almost overgrown dirt road obviously no longer in use. An old, mustard yellow and rusty van is parked right in the tire tracks. Rebecca can see through the dark windshield that no one is behind the wheel. She goes around to the back. The back doors are open. She hesitates. The stench has grown stronger still.

"Ugh, what *is* that?" she whispers, wrinkling her nose.

"*It really hurts*," the voice whimpers—coming from inside the car. "*Won't you please help me?*"

"Sure, I'm coming," Rebecca says, instinctively responding to the pleading tone of the voice, as she steps over to the van, grabs the handle and opens the door.

There is no girl in the car.

There's not even a human being.

The creature staring out at her might *look* like one, but Rebecca can tell right away the face belongs to something very different.

Something monstrous.

Everything happens very fast, too fast for Rebecca to react.

The creature lunges at her. She's pretty sure she fights to get free; she might also be screaming. The only thing she knows for certain, though, is the feeling of the creature's cold, strong fingers.

Then she's lying in the dark, dazed and terrified, as the engine roars to life and the car begins moving. Branches are scratching along the outside of the van, screaming against the metal. Besides the terrible, rotting stench, she can also smell oil and dog in the stuffy air.

She tries to get up, but loses her balance and falls down again right away. She feels something, a car wheel. She recalls briefly having seen it before the light went out and left her in complete darkness.

Except it's not complete darkness.

Rebecca stares at a thin, vertical line of daylight. She crawls towards it. The car makes a turn, causing her to roll sideways, bumping hard into the wall. It hurts badly enough to make her scream out in pain, but there's no time to sulk, she knows that. She needs to get out, while the car is still in the forest. If they make it onto the real streets, it will be too dangerous to jump out.

Her thoughts are going a million miles an hour, flickering around her head like a murder of scared crows, each one trying to out-shout the next.

I'm being kidnapped! What does it want with me? Maybe it wants to kill me! I've got to get out!

Rebecca reaches the strip of light separating the two back doors. She fumbles for a handle but finds nothing.

The car makes another turn, but this time she's more ready for it, and manages to keep upright. She feels the ground smoothing out underneath the car as they speed up.

Oh, no! We're driving on asphalt now!

But they must still be in town. Which means they can't go very fast. Rebecca just still might be able to jump out without hurting herself too badly. Even if she should break an arm or bruise herself bloody, it would still be a thousand times better than being taken by the creature.

The problem is, though, the doors can't be opened from within. She pushes and struggles, but nothing helps.

I can't get out!

Rebecca begins to scream. The sound is ear-piercing inside the confined room of the car, yet she's not sure it can be heard from outside, due to the rumble of the engine. She places her mouth to the strip of light and screams at the top of her lungs: "*Help! Help me! I'm being kidnapped! Heeelp!*"

Suddenly, the car stops, sending Rebecca sprawling backwards, landing hard on her back. She sits back up and listens. The engine is still going, but the car isn't moving.

Then, the sound of the front door opening. The car tilts slightly as the driver gets out. She counts four quick footsteps. Then the light strip is blocked out by a shadow on the other side, and next the doors are yanked open.

Rebecca isn't prepared for the daylight, and it blinds her. She only just has time to glimpse the tall, skinny figure, as it reaches in to grab her. Rebecca fights back, but the creature pulls her in, and again she feels the hard, cold hands as they turn her around so that she faces away from the open doors.

It's going to kill me!

She screams again, but something soft is jammed into her mouth, followed by a sharp, unpleasant taste. Rebecca chokes and tries to spit out the thing in her mouth, but the creature swiftly wraps something thin and hard around her head and tightens it. A shove in her back and Rebecca falls to her hands and knees. Before she can get up, the doors are already shut, and she's once again left in the dark.

Rebecca tries to scream, but no sound comes out this time. She fumbles over her face and feels the cloth in her mouth. A strip of what feels like plastic is tied around her head and keeps the cloth tightly in place. Her fingers find what feels like a knot at the back of her head, but she can't loosen it.

The car moves again.

Rebecca crawls to the light strip and puts her eye close to it. She sees a residential street unfamiliar to her. But at least they're still in town. She screams with hardly any sound and begins banging on the doors.

The car just rolls leisurely through town. The creature is obviously not in a hurry; it knows Rebecca can't get out and now she can't scream for help, either.

As they ride through town, Rebecca peers out at a world which feels miles away. She sees pedestrians, cyclists and people in other cars, and every time she screams for help and hammers away on the doors until her fists ache—but none of them hear her.

Then, suddenly, she remembers her phone. Instantly, her hand goes to her pocket, but she finds it empty. A sinking feeling in her stomach as she recalls how the creature's fingers dug into the pocket. Her bag is also gone.

The car jerks sideways, almost throwing Rebecca to the floor again, and the horn blares angrily. Rebecca looks out of the thin strip and sees—

Andy!

She can hardly believe it. Andy is standing on the sidewalk with his bike, a stunned look on his face as he stares after the van which apparently almost ran him over.

Rebecca screams as loudly as she can into the cloth which is soaked with saliva, and hammers away on the doors with both hands.

To her surprise, the car slows down and comes to a full stop. Rebecca stops banging. For a moment, she is sure the creature will jump out and run to grab Andy, too, but she can't hear the front door open.

She stares at her brother. He looks right back at her. His expression one of confusion and—suspicion?

He's listening! He heard me!

Rebecca starts banging again, just as the car revs up and gets moving again, turning left. The view changes and Andy disappears from sight.

*But he heard me! He **heard** me!*

But what good does it do her? Even if Andy did hear her, he can't catch up with the van now, not on his bike. And if he calls the police, the van will be long gone by the time they show up. It doesn't work like in the movies, where police cars always seem to be parked right around the corner whenever someone dials 9-1-1. It could be several minutes. And by that time, the creature will have taken her far away, maybe all the way out of town, and it could have stopped at a rest stop, and it could have killed Rebecca in the most horrible way imaginable.

Rebecca keeps banging on the doors, but now her effort is weak. She begins to cry. The car drives on. Within a few minutes, it reaches the town limit and speeds up. It heads out onto the highway as Rebecca sees the last houses grow distant.

Still, she keeps banging until her legs give in and she sinks to the floor, sobbing.

She has no idea how long they drive for. Time feels odd in the darkness. Sometimes it seems to move very fast, others it stands almost still.

To begin with, she noticed every time they made a turn, trying to print the route into her memory. But by now they've turned so many times she's lost count.

Every time the van slows down, Rebecca is certain the creature will pull over, come around the back and kill her. But every time she draws a sigh of relief, as the van only slowed down in order to make a turn.

Then, suddenly, the ground turns to gravel. Rebecca can hear it rumble beneath the tires. A few more minutes pass. Then, they finally come to a full stop. The engine is still going. The front door opens and the creature gets out.

This is it! It's going to kill me now!

Her heart feels as though it explodes in her chest. She jumps to her feet and steps away from the doors, as far back as she can. She tries to ready herself for the doors to open, tells herself to not become blinded this time, to get ready to fight for her life.

But surprisingly, the doors don't open. The footsteps don't come around the back, but head away from the van in the opposite direction. She listens intently.

Someplace not far from the van she picks up the sound of metal rattling. Then, the footsteps come back towards the car. It rocks gently as the creature gets back in behind the wheel, then they are moving again.

Rebecca goes to the doors to peek out. They have just passed through an open and very tall wrought-iron gate, and now they enter a large gravel courtyard. Old buildings appear on each side.

The van stops again. This time, the engine dies with a few, dry coughs. Rebecca can hear her heart pound away in the silence that follows.

The creature once more gets out of the car. Steady footsteps through the gravel. Rebecca backs up and readies herself again, staring at the strip of light. But the doors are still not opened. Instead, she hears the metal rattle once more.

It went to close the gate.

Rebecca listens as the footsteps move farther away from the van. There's a sound of a door opening. Then, silence.

Rebecca breathes quickly through her nose. Her jaw is aching, and her cheeks are burning from where the plastic strip is gnawing at the skin. She can hardly fathom she's still alive. But it might only be a matter of minutes. The creature probably went inside the building to find something to kill her with.

I need to get out of here before it comes back! This could be my last chance ...

She kneels down and feels her way across the floor, searching for something, anything she can use to pry open the doors. All she finds is the tire, a roll of rope, an empty cardboard box and a crooked metal pipe of some sort. None of it can be used as a door opener.

Suddenly, she hears the footsteps return—two pairs of them, now. One pair of long, steady steps, and one much smaller, much faster.

Rebecca picks up the pipe and backs away from the doors. She's not sure how hard she'll be able to swing the pipe, as it's very heavy in her hands, but she's determined to do her best.

The strip of light disappears.

The lock turns.

The doors open.

Rebecca squints at the bright daylight and holds up the pipe, ready to swing at anything which might come at her.

But nothing does.

She blinks as her eyes adjust to the light. She sees a slice of the courtyard, but the creature is nowhere to be seen. In the gravel, however, a few yards away, sits a small dog that looks up at her with a look of curiosity, its tail wagging gently.

Rebecca holds her breath to listen. *Is it a trick? It has to be ...*

She swallows hard and fights to hold back the tears. It's hard; she's never been this scared before, has never been in a situation like this. She shifts her weight from foot to foot, the pipe growing slippery with sweat from her palms.

The dog gives off an impatient whimper and moves its head a little. A tiny bell hanging from the collar rings briefly as the dog looks at her like it's trying to say: "Why are you just standing there? Come on out here. It's okay."

Rebecca can't take it anymore. She drops the pipe and makes a run for it, jumping out of the open doors. The dog pulls back in surprise as Rebecca comes flying out. But she never lands on the gravel. A long, slender arm shoots out and catches her midair.

Rebecca squirms, kicks and punches. The creature wraps its arms around her, pinning her against its boney body in a crushing embrace, preventing her from moving. It's way too strong; way stronger than a human. It can easily break every bone in Rebecca's body. The stench from it fills her nose as she is carried towards the building. She screams into the cloth until she almost can't breathe.

The creature brings her inside what looks like a quite ordinary, yet very messy, home. The air is stale and stuffy, smelling heavily of dust and cigars.

The creature carries her upstairs, down a hallway and into a tiny room with old, nicotine-brown wallpaper. Then, it throws her facedown onto a bed without any sheets.

Before Rebecca can get up, a hand is placed right between her shoulder blades, pushing her down into the mattress, squeezing the air out of her lungs.

As Rebecca struggles in panic to breathe through her nose, she vaguely notices her shoes and socks being pulled off. The pressure on her back eases off just enough for her to lift and turn her head sideways, heaving in long, whining breaths through her nostrils. Then a cold, strong hand locks around her ankle, and she hears a strange whistling noise which reminds her of the sound a hot stove gives off when you spray water droplets onto it.

Then comes the pain.

It's sudden and sharp and shoots up through the ball of her foot.

Rebecca screams and tries to kick, but the grip around her ankle is like iron, and the creature presses her back down as she tries to wriggle sideways.

The pain in her foot eases slightly as the seething noise stops. Still keeping her pinned to the mattress, causing Rebecca to once again feel like she's suffocating, the creature shifts its grip to the other foot, and then the noise and the pain come again, just as bad as before.

Rebecca screams, cries, coughs and retches all at once, fighting to get air in through her nose and trying not to throw up into the cloth, which would definitely cause her to choke.

Then she's abruptly turned onto her back.

Rebecca flails her arms aimlessly, trying to tear at the creature, sensing only a blurry outline of it through teary eyes.

It grabs both her wrists, seemingly with little effort, and pins them both atop her head. Rebecca squints her eyes, anticipating pain and tries to turn her face away, but the creature's cold fingers clamp down on her chin and turns her head back to neutral. She tries again to scream, but manages only a muffled sigh, as the creature's fingers go to her left eye and force it open. Through tears, Rebecca gets a glimpse of its greyish face soaring above her with the brown ceiling as a backdrop. Then she feels a drop of cold, thick liquid in her eye, blurring her vision even more. A second later, it begins to burn and sting. The creature moves to the other eye and repeats the procedure.

During the whole operation, the creature is completely silent. Rebecca can't even hear it breathing—only her own, panicked noises.

Finally, it rolls her over on her side and lets go of her wrists. Rebecca's hands immediately go to her stinging eyes, rubbing them, but that only makes it worse. She feels the creature fumble at the back of her neck. There's a snap. The pressure around her head disappears, as Rebecca is able to spit out the soaked-through cloth and heave in deep, freeing breaths.

She tries to open her eyes, but they burn too badly, so she simply scrambles to the far end of the bed, pushing up against the wall. Her feet are burning, and her eyes sting like mad. She forces herself to breathe quietly, allowing her to listen.

The room is quiet. It sounds like the creature left.

But no. Rebecca can smell it. The rotten stench and the sour odor of cigar. Only now, it's mixed with the scent of something burned.

She manages to pry open one eye a few millimeters, and she gets a glimpse of the ragged figure standing there, next to the bed, staring down at her, what looks like a lit cigar dangling from its lips.

Rebecca knows the creature only just got started. She knows it's only taking a short break from torturing her. Any second, it will resume.

"Lea ... leave me be," she whimpers, her mouth still wooly from the cloth. "Please just ... leave me be ..."

The creature doesn't answer. Rebecca doesn't know if it understands her; if it even talks. Then she recalls the small, whimpering voice of the girl from the car, and she trembles even more. She blinks and tries to look at the creature, but it's painful having her eyes open.

Then, it suddenly speaks. The voice is nothing like the one it used to lure Rebecca to the van. It's low and rusty, like it's very rarely used.

"Welcome home, Alice," it says.

Rebecca sobs. "I ... I want to go home ... if ... if you take me home ... I promise not to tell anyone ... I promise!"

She halfway sees, halfway hears the creature turn around and walk out of the room, closing the door gently behind it.

Rebecca doesn't move for a while. The stench of burnt skin, smoke and fear is heavy in the air.

She tells herself to get up and try to get out. But her eyes are still stinging, and the pain from under her feet has grown worse. She carefully feels the ball of her feet with her fingers and finds two small wounds on the soft skin. They're no bigger than a penny, but they're bleeding.

While it happened, Rebecca thought the creature cut her with a knife, but now she can piece it together: the circular shape of the wounds, the smell of burnt skin, the cigar.

It burned me.

Rebecca begins to cry again, her thoughts going back to Andy. Did he really hear her knocking from inside the car? Yes, he must have. He turned his head to look straight at her.

Even if Andy didn't hear her, by now he must have realized Rebecca is missing. He probably already told Mom and Dad. They must be out looking for her. Did they call the police yet? If Andy heard her knocking inside the van, he will tell the police—maybe he even had time to see the license plate.

Rebecca feels a faint hope at the thought.

They'll come for me. Andy heard me. They'll come for me.

She keeps repeating it in her head. It keeps all the scary thoughts somewhat at bay. She's very exhausted from being terrified for so long. Now, as the immediate danger seems to be over, the fear drains away slowly, leaving Rebecca to drift off into something close to sleep.

DAY 2

Rebecca awakens abruptly and sits up with a jerk.

What comes back to her first is the pain in her feet. It has turned into more of a hot, pulsating sensation, but it's still painful. Her eyes, however, are a little better; they don't burn or sting as much as they did before she drifted off. But her eyesight is still somewhat blurry, even after she has blinked several times and rubbed at her eyes.

The dusty taste of the cloth is still in her mouth, and she can feel dried-up saliva on her cheeks. She's terribly thirsty.

She looks around the room. It seems to be a child's room, most likely belonging to a girl, judging from the old-fashioned dolls on the shelf on the wall. Aside from the bed, which is placed under a slanted wall, the only pieces of furniture are a bookcase, a desk with a wooden chair, an old chest and a tall, built-in closet.

The floor has a worn-down rug and the ceiling hangs very low, like it's about to fall.

Rebecca has no idea how long she was out for. The room is dimmer now, outside the single window the sky is dark grey. She slept very deep with no dreams; in fact, it felt more like she was unconscious. For all she knows, she could have been gone for hours, perhaps even a whole day.

She swings her legs over the edge of the bed and carefully puts her feet to the floor, immediately sparking darts of pain from the burn wounds.

She manages to get up and wobbles to the window. The view is blurry, almost like the glass was wet from rain, but she can make out a large garden encircled by a tall, thick hedge, and on the other side are open, naked fields. No other houses are visible for as far as Rebecca can see. Out by the horizon lies a brownish belt, most likely a forest. For a hopeful moment, Rebecca thinks it might be the forest next to the park, but then she remembers how long they drove to get here; it must be another forest.

She turns and staggers across the room to the door, her feet throbbing worse with every tentative step. She tries her best to only put weight on her heels, but it's difficult walking like that. She reaches the door and tries the knob, expecting it to be locked, but it turns willingly.

Rebecca peers down a long, dark and narrow hallway with no windows and three doors, all closed. At the end is the staircase leading down.

She can neither see nor hear the creature; it could be lurking right behind any of the doors, or maybe at the bottom of the stairs. She breathes through her nose, sensing faintly the rotten smell in the air.

Rebecca's heart is beating in her chest. The hallway reminds her of a river in Africa, and she's a gazelle who needs to cross it, not sure if a crocodile is waiting just below the surface, ready to strike.

Rebecca bites her lip. *Do I make a run for it? What if it catches me? What will it do to me?*

She decides not to risk it, not like this. She can't run on her aching feet, which means she'll have a very poor chance of outrunning the creature if it comes after her.

So, she closes the door again and limps back over to the window. She's on the second floor, and there's a long way down to the lawn. Below the window is a tiled terrace. Rebecca is okay with heights, but jumping from this high up will undoubtedly result in something fracturing—if that happens, she'll have zero chance of escaping.

She moans and sits back down onto the bed, relieved to take the pressure off her feet which are really hurting now.

Perhaps she needs to wait, just a little while. Only until her feet are better. Hopefully, her eyesight will get better, too.

Besides, she's sure help is on its way. The police will come. Andy heard her—she knows he did. He told them about the van. They're probably working hard to trace it right now. Maybe they're even on their way out here. She imagines three police cars racing down the highway, sirens blaring. It's a very comforting image. She hopes they'll shoot the creature dead once they get here.

Rebecca's gaze falls on the basket sitting on the desk. It's about the size of a shoebox. She frowns.

Was that here before? Or has the creature been in here while I slept?

The thought gives her the shivers.

She goes to look in the basket. There's a packet of Band-Aids. A roll of gauze. A tube of cream and a tiny, brown bottle.

Rebecca strains her eyes to read the inscriptions on the labels. There are some difficult words, and she needs to spell her way through them.

Burn gel, it says on the tube.

And *Chlorhexidine – for disinfection*, on the bottle.

The basket is a first-aid kit, Rebecca realizes with surprise. The creature put it here, so she could tend to her wounds.

Next to the basket is a big glass of water. Rebecca sniffs it, not really sure she can trust to drink it. Maybe the creature put poison in it.

But why would it do that? If it wanted to kill her, it could just as easily come in here and do it itself. She would be powerless to stop it.

So, she drinks the glass of water, gulping down every last drop. It washes away the dry taste in her mouth and feels wonderful in her throat.

She brings the basket to the bed and uses first the chlorhexidine, then the burn gel on the wounds. The first one stings badly, but the second one soothes the pain again. She uses the gauze to bandage her feet.

Afterwards, she lies back down, feeling a little better, staring up into the blurry ceiling. She recalls the image of the police cars and feels even better still.

They'll come for me soon. Andy heard me, and he told the police about the van. I just need to wait. They'll be here any minute ...

Rebecca dozes off again.

DAY 3

The next time Rebecca awakens, the room is dimly lit by a faint daylight. She notices right away the pain in her feet is less intense, and as she blinks her eyes open, her sight is almost back to normal, only a small fuzziness around the edges.

She lies still for a moment, listening. She had a dream that policemen were storming the house, shouting and shooting downstairs. The sound of the firing guns and the men's voices were so real, she believes for a second it might not have been a dream at all. But the house is completely quiet, which probably means the police haven't come yet.

That's okay, she tells herself. *They will soon.*

She sits up and feels the bandages. One of them has come a little loose, and she spends a minute fixing it. As she works on the bandage, she becomes aware of a pleasant smell. She looks around the room, noticing she's able to perceive a lot more details now, and she sees a plate on the desk. Which means the creature was in here again.

Her stomach rumbles from hunger. It's amazing, actually, that she can be hungry in a situation like this, but she is. So, she stands up carefully. It's still painful, but with the help of the bandages she's almost able to walk normally.

She goes to the desk and sits down. Sniffs the plate. It's mashed potatoes with small brown lumps, which look like bacon.

She considers again if the creature might want to poison her, or maybe give her something which puts her back to sleep so it can do things to her. But again: why would it make the effort, when it can do what it wants to her already? Besides, there was that thing it said.

"Welcome home."

And then some name, Rebecca can't recall what it was. But apparently, the creature thinks Rebecca lives here now.

"Well, it's wrong," Rebecca whispers to herself. "I'm going back very soon to my real home. The police will be here any minute now."

Meanwhile, she might as well eat something. She lifts the fork and takes a tiny bite. There is nothing alarming about the taste. She takes another bite, then another, and soon she's shoveling down the meal.

Once the plate is empty, she wipes her mouth with her sleeve, then gets up and goes to the door. Again she finds it unlocked.

Rebecca feels a lot braver now, with her stomach full and her head well rested. Still, her heart rate immediately speeds up as she slips out into the hallway. She steps as carefully as she can, but the ancient, worm-eaten floorboards give off tired moans nonetheless. She flinches every time there's a new stab of pain from the wounds. The hallway seems like it's a mile long.

Finally, she reaches the staircase, her mouth dry and her armpits clammy, and she halts for a moment, holding her breath and listening.

Is that someone talking?

It is. And it's not the voice of the creature. It's a man's voice, deep and calm. Someone else is downstairs—maybe the police really have come after all!

Rebecca feels her hope go up. She begins to descend the stairs one step at a time while grasping the greasy banister for support.

She stops four steps from the bottom and crouches down. From here she can see a tiny kitchen bathed in a grey daylight. The stove is really old and greasy, and there seems to be no fridge. The counter is stuffed with plates, newspapers and garbage. But other than that, the kitchen is empty. Yet the voice of the man is still audible.

Who's talking?

Rebecca spots the radio on the windowsill, and immediately, her spirits sink. No one has come for her. She's still alone in the house with the creature. And what's worse: she has no idea where it currently is.

Only one door leads out from the kitchen, and it's open. Rebecca can make out another dim hallway out there.

She gets moving again. Her feet are hurting now, but she ignores the pain and pushes on, hoping to reach the front door and get out of the house before the creature shows up.

Halfway through the kitchen, a subtle ringing makes Rebecca stop in her tracks. She turns to look. In the corner is an old wicker basket. The dog is looking up at her with a curious expression. She completely forgot about the dog. It's a brown dachshund.

"It's okay," Rebecca whispers, afraid the dog might bark to alarm the creature. "I just want to get out of here."

As though the dog understands her, it sighs, then rests its chin on the edge of the basket.

Rebecca presses on. The hallway leads to several other rooms. One of them is a living room. Another is the scullery. At the sight of the front door, Rebecca's heart jumps.

She moves quickly, hardly sensing the painful jabs from the soles of her feet. She is just about to grab the knob, when something tells her not to. Instead, she looks down and sees a dog hatch at the bottom of the door. It's too narrow for her to squeeze through, but she crouches down to have a look. With her hand, she flips up the hatch and peers outside, the cool, early evening air seeping in.

She sees a section of the courtyard and one half of the garage, in which the yellow van is parked.

Then the creature comes into view, and Rebecca almost screams.

The figure trudges across the gravel on its long, thin legs, dressed in blue overalls. It has something which might be a pair of large hedge shears in one hand. It's only a brief glimpse, then the creature is gone from view again. Rebecca can hear the crunching footsteps disappear out of earshot. She carefully closes the hatch again and goes into the living room.

Just like the rest of the house, everything in here is as old as Rebecca's grandma. The furniture looks worn and forgotten. There's a heavy couch, a rocking chair, a piano and a tall grandfather clock. There's also an open fireplace completely black from soot, and through a row of dirty windows Rebecca can see the terrace.

She limps to the garden door and turns the handle. This one opens with a squeak. Rebecca looks back across her shoulder as she hears the bell chime. The dachshund has followed her into the living room and is now standing there, eyeing her expectantly.

"I'm leaving now," she tells it. "You want to come with me?"

The dog tilts its head, but doesn't move.

"All right," Rebecca says. "Bye, then."

She steps outside and closes the garden door. The terrace is obviously never used: the garden table is green from moss and weeds are growing tall between the tiles.

Rebecca staggers out on the lawn and continues toward the hedge. She squeezes through the branches and comes out the other side. From here, she has a clear view over the open fields and forest in the distance. She stands for a moment, hesitant, not sure which direction to go in.

Does it matter? As long as I get far away from here …

She begins walking, and—

And steps directly into something.

"Ouch," she moans, steps back and rubs her nose and forehead. She stares at the chain-link fence right in front of her. She didn't see it before, because the thin, grey metal bands blend in perfectly with the overcast sky.

The fence is ten feet tall, and at the very top sits a row of barbed-wire, making it impossible to climb over. Rebecca begins walking sideways, following the fence all around the outside of the hedge, her hope of finding a way out dwindling with every yard.

Finally, she reaches the front of the house, where the hedge ends and the open courtyard begins. She stops and peers out from the corner of the hedge. The fence runs all the way around the courtyard, too; the only place it's interrupted is by the gate where they came in with the van. Even from here, Rebecca can see the chain holding the gate shut and the metal spikes pointing to the sky on top of the gate.

She turns to go back to look for another way out, and there, between the hedge and the fence, is the creature.

It has snuck up on her completely silent, the cigar between its thin lips, the garden shears in its hand.

Rebecca screams. She ought to flee, but the shock has locked her in place. Instead, she holds up her arms in an effort to protect herself, as the creature comes towards her.

But it doesn't grab her.

It simply walks right by her.

Rebecca blinks and turns to look, as it trudges out onto the courtyard and into the garage.

Why didn't it hurt me? Why didn't it pull me back inside the house?

Slowly, things begin to fall into place for Rebecca. There really is only one logical conclusion as to why the creature didn't mind her being out here: it knows she can't get away.

Rebecca panics. She runs back along the fence, ignoring the pain from her feet, searching desperately for an opening or even a tiny hole to squeeze through. But she finds nothing. And less than two minutes later, she's back by the courtyard, only on the other side of the house.

Rebecca grabs the fence and tries to climb it. She's pretty good at climbing trees, and she manages to reach the top. But as soon as she tries to grab hold of the barbed-wire, she cuts her hand, screams and falls to the ground.

She jumps back up and begins shaking the fence. "*Help!*" she screams. "*Help me! I've been kidnapped! Hello! Can anybody hear me? I need he—*"

She is cut short as something grabs her from behind. The creature drags Rebecca into the house, upstairs and into the room with the brown wallpaper. It throws her down on the bed and then repeats the procedure of burning her feet and dripping the thick liquid into her eyes. Rebecca screams and fights back all the way through. But the creature is simply too strong.

Afterwards, it leaves the room.

This time, it locks the door.

DAY 4

Early next morning, before the sun is up, the door is suddenly unlocked.

Rebecca is already up, sitting by the window, looking into the blurry darkness outside, when she hears the key turn. She turns to look at the door, which is fuzzy to her, expecting it to open—but it doesn't. Instead, she hears faint footsteps from the hallway as the creature walks downstairs again.

Rebecca gets up from the chair, then flinches at the pain in her feet. The new wounds hurt worse than the old ones, making it even harder for her to stand up now. In an effort to dull the pain, she wrapped her feet in plenty of gauze, turning them into clunky lumps. She also bandaged the hand she cut on the fence.

She goes to open the door and finds the hallway empty and almost completely dark. The stench of the creature is still in the air, but so is something much more inviting: the smell of food.

Rebecca is starving, but the last thing she can think about is food. She hardly slept last night; she just sat by the window, watched the moon rise and set again, and waited for the sound of sirens which never came.

She doesn't get it. What's taking them so long? She's been here for three days now. They must have begun looking for her by now, so why aren't they coming?

Rebecca doesn't feel like waiting anymore. She's going to do something about it.

The stairs are too big of an obstacle for her throbbing feet, so she has to sit on her buttocks and climb down one step at a time, like a toddler would do it. It takes a little longer, but it gets the job done.

Once she reaches the bottom, she limps out into the kitchen, supporting herself against the wall. She immediately sees the creature; it's sitting at the table, eating from a plate, its back to her. A second plate is laid out across from it. She can't tell what's for breakfast using her eyes, but the unmistakable smell of eggs and bacon makes her mouth water.

Rebecca has no intention of joining the creature. She stays in the doorway and stares at the blurry outline of its bald head, her heart throbbing in her throat—both from fear, but also something else.

"Sit down, Alice," the creature says with its rusty voice, not turning to look at her.

"I'm not Alice," Rebecca says, feeling anger arise. "And I'm not going to eat your nasty food. I don't want to be here. I want to go home."

The creature doesn't reply. It just keeps eating calmly.

"You'll go to jail for this, you know," Rebecca says. Tears are starting to form in her eyes, and her voice trembles. "Once the police find me, you'll go to jail for the rest of your life."

The creature still doesn't look at her, but it hesitates a second before it continues eating. "Sit down and eat your breakfast, Alice," it says.

"I'm not Alice!" Rebecca shouts. "Now take me home!"

"No."

"Take me home!"

"No!" The creature only raises its voice slightly, but it's enough to startle Rebecca.

"Fuck you!" she retorts, and turns to leave.

The creature reacts with frightening speed. Rebecca hears the chair screech across the floor, four quick footsteps, and then it grabs her from behind.

Rebecca screams as she's lifted up, then put down onto the chair.

"Sit," the creature growls in her ear, pressing her down so hard it hurts. "Now, eat."

It lets go of her, and Rebecca immediately goes to get back up, but the creature slams her down once more, this time hard enough for Rebecca's teeth to clamber.

"Eat your breakfast, Alice," it demands.

This time, Rebecca stays seated as the creature has made its way back to the other side of the table. It sits down across from her, picks up its fork and resumes eating like nothing has happened.

Rebecca fights back tears, breathing in through suppressed sobs. She looks down at the plate in front of her, her appetite completely gone now.

She just sits there, defiantly not touching her meal, while the creature finishes its own. Rebecca doesn't want to look directly at it, so she keeps her gaze low, listening to it chewing.

When it's done, it looks across the table, sees her plate still full, and asks with a mild tone of surprise: "Not hungry, Alice?"

"No," Rebecca says firmly. "I'm not hungry. And I'm not Alice."

The creature is looking right at her, and despite her fuzzy vision, Rebecca can see its demeanor change. "Watch your tone, Alice," it says in a low voice.

Rebecca crosses her arms, trying not to show how scared she feels. "Can I go now?"

The creature looks at her for a moment longer, then it says: "Yes. You can go, Alice."

Rebecca gets up and limps upstairs, her feet sending painful jolts up through her legs with every step. She slams the door to the room, throws herself on the bed and cries into the pillow.

Her feet are hurting worse than ever. She can feel the fresh wounds bleed again. She cries and cries as she thinks about her family and Andy who heard her knocking from the van, she knows he did, and he'll tell the police, and the police will find her, she's sure they will, but maybe it'll be a little while, and she cries because she doesn't want to spend another minute in this house, but she can't get away, not on her own, because there's no way she can climb the fence.

Her thoughts go on like that for a while, until they finally lose speed and without knowing it, Rebecca drifts into sleep.

In her dream, Rebecca sneaks out into the garden, which has suddenly grown much, much bigger—in fact, it looks more like the park. But it's still hemmed in by the fence, and the fence is way too high for her to scale it.

She looks up at the house—except it doesn't look at all like the house, more like a big, black castle, like the one Dracula lives in. She can't see the creature in any of the windows, yet she knows it's in there somewhere and that it might look out any minute to see her trying to escape, which means she needs to hurry, so she turns to the fence, and to her surprise sees Andy standing there right on the other side, holding his bike and waving at her.

"Come on, Becca!" he calls to her. "Come out here!"

"I can't! The fence is too high, and there's barbed-wire at the top."

"You don't go *over* it," Andy says, grinning and shaking his head the way he always does when he finds her silly. "You go *under* it!"

Rebecca looks down and sees a small hole in the lawn right up against the fence. It looks like a cat or maybe a fox has dug its way under the fence.

She throws herself down and begins widening the hole by digging eagerly with her fingers. It's a lot easier than she thought; the ground is very soft and comes away in big chunks.

Soon the hole is large enough for her to crawl through. And so she does, squeezing under the fence and jumping to her feet.

"I did it!" she exclaims with joy, looking around. "I did it, Andy! ... Andy? Hey, where did you go?"

Her brother is nowhere to be seen. Suddenly, the day seems a lot darker, as heavy, black clouds have covered the sky above.

"What are you waiting for, Becca?"

Andy's voice makes her turn around. To her astonishment, she sees Andy grinning at her from the other side of the fence.

"Quit messing about, Becca," he says, his smile faltering a little. "Come on out here."

"What are you talking about?" Rebecca says. "You're the one who—" She stops talking when she realizes she's still in the garden. She must have crawled back by accident somehow.

She gets down, squeezes through the hole, gets back up, and ...

And is still in the garden.

"Seriously, Becca," Andy says from the other side—he's starting to sound scared now. "It's not funny anymore. Just come out here, okay?"

Rebecca crawls under the fence again. And again. Each time she does, she ends up right back in the garden.

"Hurry up, Becca!" Andy shouts suddenly, pointing towards something behind her. "It's coming for you!"

Rebecca doesn't have time to react before a strong, cold hand grabs her shoulder, and she awakens with a gasp. She sits up in bed, breathing heavily, as she remembers where she is.

In the room with the brown wallpaper. In the creature's house.

Outside, the sun is setting. She feels like she was only gone for twenty minutes or so, but once again she slept most of the day. The pain in her feet has lessened. Instead, her stomach aches from hunger.

She rubs her eyes and looks around to test her vision. It's better, but not perfect. She sniffs at the smell of food and sees the plate on the desk.

She gets up, but sits back down again right away, as lightning shoots up from her feet. She can't walk, so she gets down on her hands and knees and crawls to the desk, climbing up onto the chair.

Rebecca eats the whole meal. It's mashed potatoes with bacon bits just like yesterday, and it lands heavy in her belly. There's also a big glass of milk. It's lukewarm, but she downs it all in one go anyway.

Then, she leans back in the chair and sighs deeply. Somewhere in the house a melody is playing; it's probably the radio.

She recalls the dream she had. She can't remember it exactly, but it was something about Andy. She spoke with him. His voice sounded so real in her mind. She bites her lip to keep back the tears.

There was something else in the dream. An idea. It's floating around right at the outskirts of her memory, threatening to dissipate forever. She concentrates hard.

What was it? Something about the fence, I think.

She slips down from the chair and crawls to the window, pulling herself up by the arms. There is no moon or stars out this evening, as the sky is cloudy, so everything is very dark out there. But she can still make out the hedge separating the garden from the surrounding fields. And she knows the fence is right on the other side.

I had an idea. A way to get past the fence. What was it?

Then it comes to her. She dreamed she crawled under the fence instead of over it. She dug a hole—no, a tunnel, actually, just like inmates would do in old-school movies when trying to escape prison—and then squeezed through it.

Rebecca feels invigorated. It's a good idea. It just might work.

But not yet. Not until tonight. When it's sleeping.

Rebecca stares out of the window a little while longer, then she crawls back to bed, heaves herself up and rolls onto her back.

She just lies there, waiting for night to come, listening for the melody playing downstairs. Now she doesn't feel quite as hopeless. Now she has a plan.

DAY 5

She must have slept some more, because when she suddenly sits bolt upright, it's even darker in the room. And the house is completely silent.

It's time.

She swings both feet to the floor, gently putting weight on them. The feet immediately object with painful jabs, and it makes her hesitate. The mere thought of making her way through the house, downstairs and out into the garden is enough to almost make her postpone the plan. Maybe it's better to wait a few days—just until the wounds have healed enough for her to walk again.

"No," she whispers, gripped by a sudden determination. She won't spend one more night in this house. Even if it means she has to crawl out of here.

So, she gets to her feet and limps to the door. She opens it tentatively and looks out into the dark, empty hallway. She walks to the stairs, leaning on the wall as she does so, then scales the stairs using her toddler-method.

She heads for the scullery, walking slowly and stepping carefully, trying to make as little noise as possible. As she crosses the hallway, she picks up a whistling snore from a door standing ajar. She peeks in, holding her breath, and sees a large bed with a thin figure lying under a blanket. At the foot of the bed is a dark lump which suddenly comes to life and lifts its head. It's the dachshund, looking over at her.

Rebecca puts a finger across her lips in a silent shushing. The dog probably doesn't understand the gesture, but it stays put anyway and doesn't make a sound.

Rebecca's heart is pounding away by now. The creature is probably very easily stirred awake, so she needs to be extra careful.

She slips out into the scullery and places her hand on the knob. It won't move. Instead, she turns the lock very slowly. It clicks with a sound like a gunshot. Rebecca freezes and just stands there for ten seconds, listening.

Nothing happens. No sounds from the bedroom.

Once she's satisfied the creature is still sleeping, she opens the front door and is met by a breath of fresh, cool night air. She steps outside and closes the door behind her.

The sky is no longer cloudy, and the moon shines bright enough for her to see.

As she steps out onto the gravel, her bare feet—which are hurting plenty by now—give off renewed shots of pain as the pebbles press up into the bandages. But there's no way back now.

She looks to the gate. It's closed and probably also locked, although she can't see the chain from here; still, she knows it would be a waste of valuable time to go check it.

Instead, she heads for the garage.

The walk across the gravel is the closest thing to torture Rebecca has ever experienced. She attempts to place the weight on her heels, but it only reduces the pain a tiny bit.

When she finally reaches the garage and steps onto the cold concrete floor, her feet are turned into a couple of burning lumps, and tears are running down her cheeks.

She wipes them away and looks around in the dark, blinks and strains to see. There is a lot of junk in here, and a long table filled with tools, but she can't see what she came for. Perhaps it's not here. Perhaps the creature doesn't even own a—

Then she sees it. It's hanging on the wall right next to her along with a few other garden tools. Rebecca reaches out and carefully takes the shovel off the hanger.

She limps back out of the garage and around the back. This time, she can use the shovel as a cane, leaning on it to take some the weight off her feet.

The lawn is wet with dew, and the bandages quickly soak through and turn icy cold. She doesn't mind, though, as it actually soothes the pain from the wounds.

Rebecca already chose the spot from the window. It'll be behind the large bushes down in the farthest corner of the garden.

She walks determined across the lawn, darting a look back for every ten steps. She halfway expects one of the windows to light up and the silhouette of the creature to appear. But the house remains dark. And once she limps around the bushes, she disappears from sight.

There are a few yards between the bushes and the fence—more than enough room for Rebecca to work in. She places herself close to the fence and puts the shovel to the ground. It's difficult to get it to sink in, because the ground is pretty hard. She tries to use her foot to press down the shovel, but it hurts too badly, so she simply leans on the shovel. With a little effort, it gradually goes in.

But the task turns out to be a lot harder than she had imagined. It takes a lot of strength just getting the shovel into the ground, and the hole only grows very slowly deeper. With this speed, she won't be out until sunup.

Yet Rebecca is firmly determined to get away, so she bites down and keeps working. Sweat begins to run down her forehead. A couple of blisters form in her palms. But the hole grows deeper, and the ground becomes softer.

I'll make it, I'll make it, she repeats to herself over and over. *I'm getting away from here. I'll make it.*

Once the hole is about two feet deep, the shovel meets something hard, giving off a sharp CLANG!

Damnit, I must have hit a stone.

She kneels down, brushes away the dirt and reveals something white. Feeling around the surface of the stone, she can tell it's bigger than a softball and very smooth to the touch. Rebecca scoops it up and is about to put it aside, when she gets a closer look at it.

That's funny, she thinks to herself, turning the stone over. *It looks almost like a—*

Rebecca screams as she sees the two large, empty eye sockets and the grinning mouth. She drops the skull and stumbles backwards, wiping her hands frantically on her pants.

She breathes fast, wanting to run away, but forces herself to stay, as she stares at the skull grinning up at the stars.

Questions race around her head.

Is it a human skull? Why is it so small? Is it from a child, maybe? What is a child's skull doing buried here? How did the child die? Was it killed? Did the creature kill it, then bury the body here? Was it—

Rebecca's thoughts are interrupted as she senses a movement out of the corner of her eye. She turns her head and gasps at the sight of the creature standing there. Once again, it has come sneaking up on her completely without a sound.

"Alice," it croaks.

"I ... I wasn't trying to ..." Rebecca fumbles for an excuse, but of course the creature has already gathered why she's here; it's staring at the hole. She ought to run away, she knows that, but there's nowhere to run.

"Alice," the creature says again, still speaking very low, shaking its head like a disappointed parent would. It's still looking at the hole and not at Rebecca. "Oh, Alice," it says, the voice sad and almost whiney now, like a child about to cry.

And then it suddenly hits her. The creature isn't addressing *her*.

"Who ... who was that?" Rebecca says, hardly aware she's speaking.

The creature snaps its head around, and even in the darkness and even despite her still slightly blurry eyesight, Rebecca can see the black eyes lock on her.

"Alice," it says again.

This time, the voice is thick with rage.

The creature drags Rebecca back inside the house and up to her room. For the third time, it drips liquid into her eyes and burns her feet. But this time, it keeps going until Rebecca's feet are completely covered in burn wounds and she is halfway unconscious from pain and fear, having screamed herself hoarse.

Only then does the creature leave the room, leaving Rebecca alone in the silence. She produces a sound, not quite crying; she has no more strength left to cry. She can't move, either. She just stares with her burning eyes into the watery darkness in front of her.

There are no more emotions, no more thoughts. Only emptiness and pain.

And then, in the silent space, a realization appears.

Rebecca has just met Alice.

DAY 10

Several days pass before Rebecca is able to walk again.

She spends those days lying in bed. Sometimes she sleeps, sometimes she's awake. Days and night melt together. Now and then she hears the door open, as the creature brings her food. Every so often she will hear the melody playing downstairs, repeating over and over. Other times, the house is silent.

The pain from her feet is really bad, but the creature only gives her disinfectant and gauze—no burn gel to help the pain. The best way to alleviate it is to sleep.

The entire time Rebecca lies in bed she hopes the next time she wakes up, it will be to the sound of police cars approaching. More than once she dreams that Andy has come. Yet every time she wakes up to find she's still alone.

Her sight returns a little more with each day, but it doesn't go all the way back to normal; everything still appears as though through a thin veil.

As far as she can see, the burn wounds on her feet have healed over, but the slightest touch or movement makes them bleed again.

Even after the pain has lessened considerably and the wounds are healed enough for her to stand up again, Rebecca stays in bed. She has realized escape is impossible. The creature has some supernatural sense, alerting it if she tries to run away. And the next time it will probably hurt her even more badly; perhaps even kill her.

Now her only hope is to wait for rescue. And she plans on staying in bed until that happens. And of course it will happen. It just takes a little longer than she expected. The police apparently have had some trouble tracking her down. But they will. Missing persons always get found.

Don't they?

DAY 11

Suddenly, one afternoon, she hears a scraping at the door.

Rebecca sits up in bed and listens. The scraping continues, very discretely. Is it the creature? If it wants in, why doesn't it just open the door? Is it some sort of game?

Then there's a whimpering from the hallway.

Rebecca gets up and limps to the door. She opens it, and the dog looks up at her with mild bemusement in its dark eyes, as though it wants to say: "How long are you going to stay in there?"

Rebecca leans out and peers down the hallway No sign of the creature. She's not sure how, but she can somehow tell the creature is not in the house. It's almost like the atmosphere is different.

So, Rebecca decides to finally leave the room.

She slips down the hallway and stops by the next door. It's ajar, and she can make out an empty room.

She steps inside and walks across the dusty carpet to the window. From here she can see the courtyard and the garage—the van isn't there.

Rebecca's heart speeds up a little. The creature really isn't home.

She leaves the empty room again, almost stepping on the dog, who's waiting for her just outside. She steps past it and limps over to the stairs, scaling them one painful step at a time, then heads straight for the scullery. She grabs the front door, but finds it locked. And it's one of those old-fashioned ones where you need a key from both sides. She considers trying the dog hatch, but she can tell it's too small.

Instead, she heads for the living room and the terrace door—but that one is also locked.

"Damnit," she whispers and looks around for another way.

She tries the living room windows, but they can only open a few inches due to short safety chains.

She goes to the kitchen, but the windows here also have chains. She searches the entire ground floor—even the creature's bedroom, where the smell is so bad, she has to hold her nose—and finds all windows impossible to open.

The dog follows her along wherever she goes, the tiny bell on its collar chiming softly, until finally, Rebecca goes back into the living room and sinks down on the couch with a sigh. Her feet are throbbing painfully, so she pulls them up to give them a rest.

She looks around. There are no signs of anyone else living here besides the creature. The carpet has several big stains and is worn right down to the wood in more than one place. Every window is dusty and tarnished, making it hard to see through. From the ceiling hangs large cobwebs and the wall paintings are big, faded landscape portraits in heavy wooden frames. There are a few decorative items, like porcelain animals, embroidered pillows and brass candlesticks. There's also a single photograph, standing on a tiny, dust-covered table next to the couch.

Rebecca reaches over and takes the frame. Her eyesight is still blurry, but by holding it close, she can just make out the face in the picture. It's a girl with platinum blond hair—just like Rebecca always wanted, but Rebecca's hair is raven-black. The girl is wearing a yellow shirt and white pants, sitting on a chair, smiling nervously at the camera, almost like she has a secret with whoever took the picture.

Something sniffs her knee. Rebecca looks down to see the dog.

"You want up?" she asks.

The dog is obviously no stranger to being on the couch, because it willingly lets her lift it up and immediately curls up next to her.

"I never found out your name," Rebecca says, searching with her fingers in the dog's fur for the old collar. "Boris," she reads. The dog's ears move slightly. She smiles. "Hi, Boris. I'm Rebecca."

Boris looks up at her, friendly, but not particularly interested. Its pupils look cloudy, and Rebecca is pretty sure that means it's almost blind; just like her.

"Do you know who this is?" she asks Boris and shows him the photo. Boris just sighs and puts his head back down. "Nah, me neither," she mutters and studies the blond girl and her shy smile. The picture could be very old. Maybe the girl is grown up by now. Maybe she's very old, or even dead. Maybe—

Suddenly, it hits home.

Rebecca can't explain why, but she knows for a fact that the girl in the picture is Alice, and she feels goose bumps come crawling all the way up her back. She quickly puts the photo back—all of a sudden, she doesn't want to touch it; it feels wrong, somehow. Like it creates an unwelcome connection between her and the dead girl.

Then she hears a faint rumble, like a car driving on gravel.

Rebecca jumps to her feet and limps to the kitchen. Through the window over the sink she can see the courtyard and the rear-end of the yellow van as it drives into the garage.

It's back!

Rebecca goes back to the living room, scoops up Boris and hurries out to the staircase. She's not sure why, but she doesn't want the creature to know she's been snooping around the house. So she hurries up to the room and closes the door. She sits down on the bed and listens.

A few minutes pass by.

Then the stairs give off their unmistakable creaky sounds as the creature comes upstairs.

The door is opened slowly. The tall, gangly figure towers in the opening. It's too tall to look into the room unless it bends its neck slightly. The arms and legs are also long, unnaturally so, and the way it moves them sometimes makes it look like they each have an extra joint. Like a spider.

The creature steps into the room, but doesn't go more than a few steps. It just stands there, staring at her.

Rebecca doesn't want to look right at it, so she keeps her gaze at its feet. "What do you want?" she asks, her heart pounding in her throat, making her voice jumpy.

The creature doesn't answer, just stands there, breathing slowly.

Boris grows restless in her arms and gives off a small bark. Rebecca realizes the creature isn't looking at her, but at the dog. She doesn't want to let Boris go, but she's also afraid to keep him if the creature wants him, so she bends over and puts him on the floor. She expects the dog to run to its owner. But to her surprise, Boris sits down between her feet.

She glances towards the creature. "I think ... I think he wants to stay with me."

The creature just stands there for another long moment. Then, it turns around, leaves and closes the door behind it. She hears it walk downstairs again.

Rebecca breathes out in relief. She bends over and pats Boris. "Thank you," she whispers. "I'm glad you chose me. But we can't become too friendly, you know. I'm not staying here for much longer."

Boris just sighs, as though he doesn't really care, then makes himself comfortable between Rebecca's banded-up feet.

"I don't care if you believe me," Rebecca says. "They'll come for me. Soon. You'll see."

She's not sure if she's telling the dog or herself.

DAY 18

The days go by.

Rebecca waits.

No one comes for her.

Gradually, she learns the routines of the creature. It eats the same three meals every day: scrambled eggs, ham sandwich and mashed potatoes with bacon bits. Every night, before it goes to bed, it sits down by the piano and plays the same melody over and over—that's what Rebecca initially took for the radio. She knows the song, but she can't quite place it at first.

The worst part of the routine is the burning of her feet and the liquid it puts in her eyes. It does it every third day now. In the evening, before bedtime, it comes to her room, the lit cigar between its grey lips.

Rebecca fights it every step of the way, even though it makes no real difference. She can't help it, though; she can't just let it harm her without offering resistance.

The weird thing about it is, the creature doesn't seem angry at her at all. It doesn't make a sound during the procedure, and it doesn't seem to derive any kind of pleasure from it. It's almost like it simply needs to be done. Probably, Rebecca figures, to keep her from doing any more attempts of escaping. By keeping her halfway blind and unable to walk properly, Rebecca has a very bad chance of running away.

The creature also changes its attitude towards her; it begins demanding things.

First, it stops bringing her food. If she wants to eat, she has no other choice than joining it in the kitchen. Rebecca tries to avoid it by waiting until the creature is done, then sneaking down to the kitchen to find something to eat. But every time she does so, the creature appears, staring at her menacingly, causing Rebecca to slink away again.

The third time it happens, she tells it, with as much defiance as she can muster: "I want something to eat."

The creature shakes its head and answers: "Not time for eating now, Alice."

Rebecca knows what will happen if she proceeds. She stares at the fridge for a few seconds, feeling her stomach rumble with hunger.

Then she turns on her heel and leaves the kitchen, scoffing: "Fine. I wasn't really hungry anyway."

But she was. And the next time a meal is served, Rebecca goes to the kitchen.

She tries to take the plate and leave, but of course, the creature won't let her: it gets up and grabs her with incredible speed, forcing her back down.

Rebecca tries a few more times to find a way to eat alone, but the creature is relentless. She has even tried eating while the creature went out one day. She took two eggs from the fridge and fried them on the stove instead of scrambling them, as the creature would always serve them. Then she ate the eggs with great relish, happy with finally having outsmarted the creature.

But as soon as it came home and found the two eggs missing from the fridge, the creature came up and burned her badly.

So finally, Rebecca resolves to join it for those three meals a day, not look at it, not speak to it, just chow down the food, then go back up to her room. She can do that, even though she doesn't like it. But it's a matter of survival.

The creature makes other demands, some of which are much harder for Rebecca to come to terms with.

For instance, she wakes up one morning to find her clothes and her shoes, which she always puts right next to her bed, missing. The creature must have been in here while she slept and taken it.

She has been wearing the same outfit ever since she got here, and by now it is turning pretty smelly, since Rebecca hasn't showered even once, so her first thought is that the creature took it to wash it.

But that turns out to not be the case.

Rebecca never sees her clothes again. Instead, she finds a bunch of clothes on the desk. It's six identical outfits of yellow shirts and white linen pants; the exact same clothes as the girl in the photo down in the living room.

Rebecca really doesn't like the thought that some dead girl once wore the clothes, but she dislikes the thought of walking around in her underwear even less, so she has no real choice.

DAY 20

A few days later, Rebecca learns that the clothes were only a small sacrifice, as she wakes up to find a plastic bag on the floor next to the bed. She looks inside and finds a hair bleach kit.

At first, Rebecca almost laughs at the idea that the creature apparently wants her to dye her hair. But then, the more she thinks about it, the fun of it evaporates.

The girl in the photograph—Alice—has blond hair. And Rebecca is already wearing her clothes.

"It can't be serious," she tells Boris. "I'm not going to dye my hair—no freaking way."

She throws the bag in the downstairs trash can.

The next morning, it's there again, next to her bed.

Rebecca hides it away in the back of her closet.

The next morning, it's back again, and the creature is there, too, staring at her.

Rebecca sits up with a jerk. Boris wakes up with a confused whimper.

"Get out of here," Rebecca tells the creature in a hoarse whisper.

It just stares at her, holding out the plastic bag.

Rebecca shakes her head. "I'm not going to do it. I won't dye my hair. You can't make me!"

But of course, the creature can.

It reaches out and grabs Rebecca by the arm, pulling her out of bed. Rebecca screams and fights to get free. It drags her out into the bathroom, puts the bag in the sink, then leaves and locks the door.

Rebecca is left alone, kicking the door. She rubs her arm and forces back angry tears.

"Fuck you!" she shouts. "I'm not doing it!"

She waits for an answer, but can only hear the sound of the stairs, as the creature walks calmly downstairs.

Rebecca sits down on the toilet and breathes deeply. She can't do it. She can't change her appearance like that—wearing the strange clothes is one thing, but dying her hair—she'd rather starve to death.

And that seems to be exactly what will happen.

The creature comes back a few times to check on her; just a brief look, before it closes the door and locks it again.

Rebecca drinks water from the sink and tries to make time go by without thinking about her hair or the hunger, which becomes more and more intense.

She stays in the bathroom all night, sleeping in the tub.

The following day, the creature again checks in on her a few times.

When noon comes around, Rebecca is so hungry, she can't take it anymore.

"It's just hair," she tells herself in the mirror. The Rebecca staring back at her looks thin and pale and has dark circles around her eyes. "It's just hair, it doesn't mean anything. Besides, I always wanted to be a blonde."

She tries to smile, but it turns into tears, as she opens the bag with trembling fingers.

She follows the instructions of the packet, finishing off by washing her hair in the tub.

Just as she reaches for the towel, she sees the door in the mirror. It's open. The creature is standing there, smoking its cigar, looking in at her.

"What are you looking at?" Rebecca snarls. "Isn't this what you wanted?"

The creature takes a long drag on the cigar and blows out the smoke. "Good, Alice," it whispers. Then, it simply turns and walks away, leaving the door halfway open.

"I'm not Alice!" Rebecca shouts. "My name is Rebecca!"

She takes one last look in the mirror. She did a pretty awful job; the roots are still dark, and some places are whiter than others. But she doesn't really care anymore. She just wants something to eat.

When she comes downstairs, the creature has prepared an extra-large ham sandwich for her.

For once, Rebecca is allowed to eat alone.

DAY 21

The following evening, after dinner, as Rebecca has gone up to her room with Boris, the creature comes and opens the door without knocking.

"Downstairs, Alice," it tells her from the doorway, then turns and leaves without waiting for a reply.

Rebecca's pulse immediately rises. This is something new, and she has a bad feeling about it.

She considers staying here, or even trying to hide. But she knows that won't work. Also, she can feel the creature's patience becoming thinner and thinner the more she resists; anymore disobedience, and she'll likely get punished severely. Her feet are aching from the last burn. So, she decides the wiser course is to simply follow the creature downstairs and find out what it wants.

She picks up Boris and brings him for moral support.

All the way down to the living room, her fear and dread for what's to come rises steadily, until her knees feel shaky.

She clutches Boris to her chest and peers into the dimly lit living room. She spots the creature by the piano, the cigar it in its mouth and its back to her.

Slowly, it turns its head and lifts one boney hand to wave her closer.

Rebecca approaches the piano but stops a few paces away.

"What ... what do you want?" she asks, her voice thin.

The creature doesn't answer her. It takes out the cigar and places it in an overfilled ashtray on top of the piano. Then it begins playing, and Rebecca immediately recognizes the melody she has heard many times. What she at first took for the radio must have been the creature playing.

She watches in silent wonder, almost forgetting her fears, at the gangly figure producing those soft, melancholy tunes. And she realizes she knows the song. It's the lullaby Mom used to sing when Rebecca was little. She hasn't heard it for years, but she can still remember the lyrics, and her eyes fill with tears, as she whispers along to the melody.

Once the verse is over, the creature plays the melody over again. Then, the third time around, it says: "Sing, Alice."

And Rebecca finally realizes why the creature brought her here. It doesn't want simply to play to her; it wants to play *with* her, to hear her sing.

"No," Rebecca croaks, almost sobbing now.

"Sing, Alice," the creature repeats, staring over once more.

Rebecca doesn't want to sing, but she knows what will likely happen if the creature needs to tell her a third time, so she begins singing softly along with the melody:

"Hush-a-bye baby
On the treetop,
When the wind blows
The cradle will rock.
When the bough breaks,
The cradle will fall,
And down will fall baby
Cradle and all."

The creature starts over, and Rebecca sings the verse again; it's the only one she knows. The creature doesn't seem to mind, and it plays the melody over five or six more times, accompanied by Rebecca's low singing.

Finally, it stops, takes the cigar and heaves a deep drag, blowing out the air slowly and watching it drift to the ceiling.

"Can ... can I go now?" Rebecca whispers, her cheeks wet from tears, Boris sleeping in her arms.

The creature doesn't answer, but it turns its head slowly and gives a tiny nod. Rebecca hurries back upstairs.

As she lies in bed a few minutes later, trying to sleep, she feels a weird mixture of feelings. She misses her family more than ever, but she's also afraid. In a strange way, singing with the creature was worse than getting her feet burned. Rebecca can't figure out why, but she feels terrible inside.

"I hope that was the only time it wants me to sing," she whispers to Boris, who's snoring at the foot of her bed.

But it wasn't.

Every evening from then on, the creature comes to get her after dinner, uttering those same two words from the doorway: "Downstairs, Alice."

And every evening, Rebecca goes downstairs to sing the lullaby while the creature plays the piano, feeling awful afterwards.

DAY 23

The creature also demands other, smaller things from Rebecca. Some of them rather peculiar.

Like, one morning, at breakfast, it suddenly tells her: "Other hand, Alice."

Rebecca, who's shoveling down eggs, looks across the table at the open newspaper, which the creature is holding.

"What?" she asks.

"Other hand," the creature repeats.

She just stares at the newspaper for a few seconds, before it begins to dawn on her what it means.

She puts the fork in her left hand. "Like this? But I'm not left-handed."

She continues eating with her right.

"Other hand, Alice," the creature says, its voice rising. And this time, it lowers the newspaper enough for its tiny black eyes to stare at her.

Rebecca immediately looks down on her plate and shifts the fork. Eating with her left hand seems like a very little sacrifice, so she doesn't make a fuss about it.

In the days to come, she forgets about it almost every meal, but the creature reminds her patiently from across the table: "Other hand, Alice," and Rebecca slowly gets used to eating left-handed.

Rebecca knows the reason for these things, of course. She knows the creature wants her to be Alice, to be like the dead girl it once knew.

She tells herself it's no big deal, that she can do it in order to survive, that it's simply a matter of keeping her head down until she can get away from here.

But from a deeper part of her, a sense of growing dread gets a little bit bigger each time she voluntarily adjusts her own behavior. It goes against who Rebecca is in her heart, and it scares her.

The weirdest thing is, other than those areas, the creature seems oddly non-interested in how Rebecca spends her time—as long, of course, she doesn't act disrespectful or try to escape.

And so long as Rebecca does what it wants, they fall into an almost peaceful coexistence.

Besides for the burnings and the blindings every third night.

DAY 28

More days go by; still no one comes for her.

Rebecca begins to venture out of her room more and more. She prefers to do so whenever she can sense the creature is outside, working in the garden or fixing something in the garage. Whenever it drives off in the van, it always locks the doors beforehand, trapping Rebecca in the house.

Her fear diminishes as she realizes the creature isn't going to kill her or do anything worse than burn her feet and blind her eyes—which is bad enough, of course, but she also somehow gets used to the pain; or at least, she learns to get through it.

It provides her with a sense of comfort knowing what to expect from the creature. She can predict approximately when it'll leave and when it'll be back again, when it's safe for her to walk around the house, when the meals will be served, when it goes to bed, and so on.

Whenever it's at home, Rebecca stays mostly in her room; not so much because she's afraid it'll harm her if it sees her, she just doesn't like being around it when she doesn't have to. She can never really tell where in the house it is, as it moves very quietly.

Boris sleeps in Rebecca's room every night, curled up by her feet. Whenever she wakes up from a nightmare, she's thankful the dog is there.

Every evening, after they have played and sang together, and Rebecca has gone to bed, the creature comes up to her room to say good night.

The scene is always the same: Rebecca lies in bed. She hears the stairs creak. The door opens. From the doorway, the creature whispers: "Sleep tight, Alice," right before closing the door.

Rebecca never answers; she's grown wary of correcting the name, which the creature seems determined to call her. Until one night, when Rebecca is in a bad mood.

"I'm not Alice," she says loudly. "Alice is dead."

The creature freezes in the doorway. Though the lighting is dim and Rebecca's eyesight is blurry, she can tell the tall figure is shaking its head.

"No," it whispers. "No, no, *no!*" The voice turns into a thunderous roar, causing Rebecca to sit up and Boris to begin whining.

For one fearful moment, she's sure the creature will come at her. It actually looks like it struggles to keep itself back, trembling in the doorway, clutching the frame with both hands.

Then, it simply shakes its head once more, and repeats calmly, "No," then closes the door.

For the first time, that night, the creature doesn't go to bed at the usual time. Instead, it stays up, playing the piano over and over again for almost two hours, that same lullaby.

And as Rebecca lies in bed, listening, she can't help but whisper along, while thinking about her mom and her dad and Andy and Cindy, and she cries deeper than ever before.

And while she does so, it's as though something shifts inside of her—or rather, falls into place. It's a realization which makes her scared, but even more sad.

Rebecca realizes that no one will come for her right now. That it could be many days, perhaps even months, before she gets found.

Which means, that for now, this house is her new home.

DAY 76

Rebecca is sitting on the chair in the room with the brown wallpaper and staring out of the window at nothing in particular, hardly noticing the open fields or the orange evening sky above.

She has no idea how long she's been here; she long since gave up counting the days. But when she came here, the fields had tiny, green sprouts, and now the wheat is knee-high. The weather is warmer, too, and the days longer.

She's spent many hours right here, on the chair in front of the window. Down in the living room she can hear the grandfather clock. Rebecca counts twelve chimes. She hates that clock. No matter where she is in the house, she can hear it. Every hour it reminds her that time is moving. And it reminds her of the church bells she could hear from her room. The sound makes her homesick.

"Duuip!"

A cry from a bird in the distance. The sound makes Rebecca straighten a little.

It's them. They're back.

She leans forward and listens. Another cry, closer this time. She can't see the birds yet. She opens the window and listens. Another couple of cries, before the birds finally come into view.

"Duuip! Duuip!"

Although Rebecca doesn't have her bird book or access to the Internet, she still remembers the names of most of the local species, and these are without a doubt lapwings.

The birds circle above the house, disappear out of sight for a moment, then reappear and land on the lawn. They mince around on their skinny legs, looking for food in the grass. From this far away, Rebecca can't make out any details, but she still smiles to herself. She leans her cheek against the cold window glass and watches the birds.

Then, suddenly, they take flight, soaring close by the window, and Rebecca listens as their cries disappear into the distance. She wishes she was a lapwing herself and could go with them.

The stairs creak. The familiar sound of footsteps.

Rebecca gets up and waddles to the bed where she sits back down. The door opens. The creature looks in at her.

Rebecca doesn't like looking, but she doesn't like not looking, either, so she fastens her gaze on the greyish hand resting on the doorknob. She can't make out the long, skinny fingers very well, but she knows the touch of them intimately; they're rough and chapped and very cold. The smell from the creature fills the room.

"It's time, Alice," it whispers. "Lie down."

"My name is not Alice," Rebecca says, still staring at the hand. "It's Rebecca."

She has said it hundreds of times, perhaps even thousands. The creature doesn't care; it just keeps calling her Alice, as though it doesn't even hear her.

The hand lets go of the knob and goes to the collarbone, where it scratches the skin through the shirt. Rebecca stares at the hand because she doesn't want to look at the face, which always gives her the shivers. It's too narrow and the forehead is too high, topped off with white tusks of dying hair. The nose is a thin, sharp edge, running from the grey upper lip to the brow protruding like a cliff, hiding the eyes in a permanent shadow.

And they are the worst.

The eyes.

Small, black, circular and gleamy. No life behind them. Glass-like.

She only looks the creature in the eye when she absolutely can't help it.

The hand stops scratching and goes to the front pocket. The long fingers pull out a cigar and places it between the cracked lips. Rebecca watches as the creature finds the lighter and lights up the cigar. The smoke fills the room almost instantly.

The creature repeats the command: "Lie down, Alice."

Rebecca hesitates for another few seconds, then lies down on her back, her legs slightly apart and her arms at her sides. The creature comes over and sits down at the foot of the bed, making the springs creak.

Rebecca clutches the bed linen with both hands, breathes through her nose and looks up into the ceiling. She tries to imagine she can hear the lapwings somewhere in the distance. That she has X-ray vision and is able to see them fly around above the roof.

The creature sits for half a minute, pulsing on the cigar. The wait is always the worst.

Then she feels its rough hand grab her ankle and lift up her bare foot. Rebecca squeezes her lips together tightly, but she doesn't close her eyes—for some reason, the pain is worse with eyes closed.

The low seething sound comes first, boding the pain which follows half a second later. Rebecca gives off a whimper, as burning needles force their way up through the sole of her foot and spreads out into the toes. There's a long second of rising pain, reaching almost an unbearable level, then it subsides. The creature lies her leg back down on the bed and takes the other one.

"Now the other, Alice."

The same exact words, the same exact tone.

The creature takes a long drag off of the cigar, firing it up again, before repeating the procedure with the other foot. The needles sink in, the pain increases until the point where she almost screams out—and then it goes away again, turning into a dull throbbing.

Rebecca goes limp all over, feeling the sweat on her forehead and her heart pounding dully in her chest.

The creature lets go of her ankle and goes on to the eyes. They are a lot easier to deal with than the feet; the pain is nowhere near as bad.

Rebecca holds her breath so as to not breathe in the stench from the creature as it leans over her. She turns her eyes sideways, staring into the wall and not at the figure looming over her. The creature breathes calmly as it administers the cool drops to Rebecca's eyes. She blinks as the liquid runs down her cheeks like sluggish tears. A slight sting, and she blinks it off.

The creature gets to its feet. "It's done. You did well, Alice."

It doesn't wait for an answer, it just heads for the door.

"My name is not Alice," Rebecca automatically replies, wiping the excess liquid from her cheeks. "It's ..."

She pauses, and for a terrible moment, the name is gone. Her mouth is open, but no sound comes out.

"It's ..." she says again, trying to force it to appear. "It's ..." And then it comes. "Rebecca!" she blurts out, feeling a deep sense of relief. "Rebecca Wisler! My name is Rebecca Wisler."

She lifts her head and looks to see if the creature is still here. It is. Standing in the doorway. And through the blurry haze, she sees its face in the light of the cigar, and she is almost certain she sees a smile on its lips as it whispers: "Sleep tight, Alice." Then it closes the door and leaves Rebecca to the silence.

She feels like crying. She decided a while back that she wouldn't cry anymore, that she wouldn't give in to it, that she would act brave; but she's not brave, not at all. She misses her family so much and she's scared. Scared of the creature, scared that she'll never be found, scared that she'll eventually forget her name.

She gets up, wipes the tears from her still stinging eyes and wobbles to the table with small gasps of pain with every step. She can feel the burn wounds bleeding, but she doesn't care; she's so used to the pain by now, she hardly registers it.

The table is stuffed with pieces of paper, drawings of birds, mostly lapwings but also other kinds. She found the pencil and the paper in a drawer downstairs, and the creature apparently didn't mind her bringing it to her room.

She grabs the pencil and a blank piece of paper and writes in big, bold letters:

REBECCA WISLER

She stares at the name, then writes it again. And again. Smaller and smaller as she runs out of blank space. Writing her name alleviates some of the fear.

Afterwards, she looks at the paper and realizes it's no good having it around. The creature will not stand for it. It will confiscate it as soon as it finds it—and it *will* find it, no matter where she hides it. It searches the room now and then, and if it finds something it doesn't like, it'll punish her with an extra-long and drawn-out round of feet-burning.

Like the time she had written a letter for help which she planned on taping to the back of the van, in the hope that the creature wouldn't notice it the next time it went for a drive.

Or when she stole a knife from the kitchen, planning to cut the creature as it came up to say good night. She wasn't sure she could really go through with it, but she was so pissed off that day, she was willing to try.

She never got the chance, though, because right on that same day—just like on the day she had written the letter and hidden it under the carpet—the creature came to search the room and found her secret.

Because it knows. Somehow, it always knows if Rebecca has done something she shouldn't have.

Writing her real name all over a piece of paper will almost certainly spark its fury.

But I need to write it down **somewhere**, Rebecca thinks to herself, looking around the room. *Or I might forget it.*

She limps to the window, bends down and examines the windowsill. The lower part protrudes a few inches from the wall. There is just enough space for her to write on.

She glances at the door, then kneels down and writes her full name on the underside of the windowsill. She writes it again and again, tracing the letters and pushing the pencil harder each time, until there's a slight crevice in the board and the tip of the pencil is worn flat.

She looks at the name, feeling better now.

Back in the beginning, Rebecca had hoped the cigars would kill off the creature. Mom often told her how smoking is bad for you and can cause a lot of diseases. Lung cancer, for instance.

When Rebecca sometimes lies awake at night, thinking about her family, fighting the tears, she desperately hopes for the creature to fall ill and die. If that happens, she will leave the house, unlock the gate and run down the gravel road as fast as she can, not looking back and not stopping until she reaches another house or meets a passing car.

Unfortunately, the creature doesn't seem ill in any way. And Rebecca has long since rejected the hope that she will outlive it.

"My name is not Alice," she whispers as she goes to the desk and picks up the paper. "My name is Rebecca, and I'll never forget it."

She tears up the paper into tiny pieces.

That night, somewhere around midnight, Rebecca wakes up and notices the light. It's coming from the closet; a thin, white strip streaming out from the crack in the door.

The closet across from the bed is built into the wall. The door is made of dark wood with a cut-out ornament which makes Rebecca think of leaves and butterflies.

At first, Rebecca is confused as to what causes the light, and she even suspects this might be a dream. But no, she feels awake.

She pushes the blanket aside, waking up Boris, who looks at her from the foot-end of the bed with sleepy eyes. Rebecca gets out and slips over to the closet. She places her hand in the stream of light, as though to check it's real. She lets her fingers play with the tiny, fine flecks of dust in the air. Then, she carefully opens the closet door.

On the shelves, her clothes—white pants and yellow shirts—are neatly folded up, just like Mom taught her. Rebecca washes her clothes in the sink and hangs them out to dry on the line in the garden, so they don't start to stink.

The light is coming from the top of the closet. There's a crack in the boards, and this is where the light comes in.

Rebecca reaches up. She can't quite reach the opening, but she can feel the cool breeze coming in.

And she realizes the crack is a hole in the roof, and that the light is moonlight.

Why haven't I seen this before? Why doesn't the sun shine in through here too?

The answer is obvious, of course. In the day, everything is bright, and the stream of light wouldn't be visible. But now, when the room is completely dark, the strip of moonlight is free to show itself off.

Rebecca closes the closet and goes to the window. She leans against the glass and can just make out the moon high above. It's only one-third full, but its white light shines down over the house and the garden.

For some reason, Rebecca thinks of Andy. She imagines him sitting in his room, looking out the window and up at the moon, just like she is now.

Could he be thinking about her? Is he wondering where she might be? Or did he forget about her? Do they all assume she's dead? Maybe Mom and Dad even decided to have another child. If it's a girl, it can have Rebecca's room.

The thought makes her so sad she begins to sob quietly. She sits there for a long time, crying by the window, bathed in the moonlight, thinking about her family, wondering if she will ever see them again.

DAY 89

One morning, as Rebecca wakes up and gets out of bed, Boris doesn't jump to the floor as he usually does, eager for Rebecca to let him out for his morning pee, then feed him breakfast. Instead, he just stays snuggled up at the bottom of the bed.

"Hey, sleepy head," Rebecca yawns, nudging him gently. "It's morning. Time to wake up now."

The dog doesn't react at all. Rebecca knows he's pretty old and doesn't always hear too well, but him sleeping this heavily is quite unusual.

"Boris? Wakey-wakey."

She strokes the back of his neck, surprised to feel how cold he is. She nudges him harder. Still no reaction.

"Oh, no," Rebecca whispers, as she realizes with a sinking feeling what's wrong. "Boris!"

She grabs him and shakes him, but he's all limp, his eyes are closed and his mouth open. She lets go of him again with a gasp, and he just slumps back down onto the bed.

"Oh, no, no, no," Rebecca whimpers, putting both hands to her mouth. The shock is overwhelming; Boris had shown no signs of illness, so how can he just have died overnight? The thought of losing her last friend is too much to bear, and Rebecca buries her face in her hands and starts crying loudly.

A moment later, she senses the smell and looks up. Through tears she sees the creature standing in the open door.

"He's ... he's dead," she sobs. "Boris is dead."

The creature comes into the room and stops by the foot of the bed. Rebecca just looks at Boris and sniffles. The creature picks up the dog, gently, then carries it out of the room. She hears it go downstairs, and a minute later, the sound of the front door.

For a minute or so, Rebecca hopes that the creature will fix Boris. Maybe he wasn't really dead after all. Maybe the creature has some sort of supernatural power which can bring him back. She almost begins to hope.

Then something draws her attention towards the window. She gets up and goes to it. Down in the garden, she sees the creature walking with Boris under one arm and the shovel under the other. It goes behind the hedge at the place where Alice is buried.

Rebecca starts crying again and throws herself onto the bed.

She stays in the room for the rest of the day and the days to come.

It feels like she lost more than just a good friend. It feels like she's lost everyone and is left completely alone in the world. She misses Boris badly, particularly in the morning when she wakes up and finds the foot of the bed empty. The only sound in the house that could make her happy was the low ringing of the bell in Boris's collar, telling her the dog was somewhere nearby, and that she wasn't alone with the creature. But now there is only the silence and that damned grandfather clock and the creaks from the floorboards as the creature moves around.

Rebecca can't bring herself to leave the room; she's too depressed. The creature brings her food while she sleeps. Rebecca has hardly any appetite and struggles to eat.

The only consolation is that the creature stops burning her feet and dripping her eyes for a few days. Yet Rebecca doesn't really care. She would have almost welcomed the pain. Anything would be better than the emptiness left by Boris.

She's never felt this lonely in her life.

DAY 91

One evening, as Rebecca leaves her room and goes to pee, she suddenly hears a sound from downstairs.

It's the ringing of Boris's bell.

She feels her heart open like a flower, and for a moment she imagines Boris has returned, that he wasn't really dead after all, that the creature didn't really bury him, but instead took him to the vet who has now fixed him. But of course, it's a silly thought.

Then what's making the ringing?

Rebecca goes downstairs and peeks into the living room. Her eyes are a little better because the creature hasn't given her the liquid for almost a week, and she immediately sees the puppy sitting on the floor, playing with a sock. It's a dachshund, the exact same color as Boris, and it's wearing Boris's collar, even though it's too big for the tiny neck.

The sight of the puppy is so unreal, Rebecca feels like she's looking at Boris reincarnated. She steps into the room.

The puppy looks up and sees her. It yelps happily and runs to greet her on its stumpy legs. It jumps up and down in front her, whining impatiently as the bell rings.

Rebecca kneels down and picks it up. The puppy licks her chin and bites her hair. Rebecca can't help but snigger.

"Who are you?" she asks, holding out the puppy to study it. It just looks back at her with a silly expression, mouth open and the pink tongue hanging out.

Rebecca checks the name tag on the collar. It still says BORIS.

"Oh, so your name is Boris too," she smiles, rubbing her nose against the puppy's snout, then laughing as it tries to lick her nostrils. "Are you going to live here now?"

The puppy yelps again, squirming joyfully in her hands, and Rebecca feels her heart beating warmly in her chest.

She has been so taken in by the puppy that she hasn't noticed the creature until now. It's sitting in the armchair over at the corner, halfway hidden in shadow, only its skinny legs visible, and of course the orange glow from the cigar. It's been sitting completely quiet, watching her.

Rebecca feels a cold shiver run down her back. She doesn't like how the creature saw her reaction to the puppy, saw her laughing happily. It's almost like she's been exposed. She quickly puts down the puppy, then rushes out of the room and back upstairs.

Later, as she lies in bed, trying to sleep, she can't stop thinking about the puppy downstairs. Once or twice she hears it yelp. She wishes now that she had brought it up with her.

She awakens during the night because she dreams Boris is licking her cheek. The sensation is so real, she can even smell his fur, and she smiles dreamily.

As she becomes more awake, she blinks and rubs her eyes, and the warm feeling from the dream turns into sadness when she remembers once more that Boris is dead and gone.

But then she hears someone breathing right next to the pillow, and she turns her head. The puppy is looking at her with small, sleepy eyes, before licking her cheek one last time, then lying down with a sigh.

Rebecca stares at the door. It's closed. Which means the puppy can't have ventured in here on its own. Besides, how would it have climbed the stairs? Old Boris could only just manage the steps, and he was three times as big. That can only mean ...

Rebecca doesn't care at all for the thought that the creature has been in here while she slept—she hates when it does that. But she is happy that New Boris is here. She places her hand on its back, feeling its rapid breathing and tiny heartbeat.

She falls asleep and sleeps well the rest of the night.

DAY 97

Rebecca instantly becomes best friends with New Boris. He sleeps in her bed every night—not by her feet, like Old Boris would, but right up against her pillow.

In the daytime, they play in the room or out in the garden when the sun is shining. Rebecca feeds him twice a day like she did with Old Boris, taking the food from the bag in the scullery. She's not entirely sure how much food the puppy needs, so she gives him plenty. After all, he needs to grow.

Rebecca doesn't feel quite as sad about Old Boris being dead anymore. She has a new friend now. And yet something about the thought of Old Boris keeps nagging her whenever she remembers him. She's not quite sure what it is, though.

One day, Rebecca realizes the puppy is actually a she. She has brought it out into the garden to pee—she's seen it pee many times, but watching it now, it suddenly occurs to her that it doesn't pee quite like Old Boris did. Whereas Old Boris would raise one hindleg up high, New Boris simply bends both hindlegs.

Rebecca picks up the puppy and turns it over to make sure. It checks out. New Boris is definitely a she.

That same evening, after mulling it over, Rebecca decides to make it right.

She brings the puppy down to the kitchen, where the creature is sitting by the table, reading the newspaper and smoking. Even though its back is turned, it apparently senses Rebecca standing there, because it stops reading and turns around on the chair. It doesn't say anything, just looks in her direction, as though waiting for her to speak.

"You need to buy a new name tag," Rebecca says. "It can't be called Boris. It's a girl."

The puppy yaps in agreement.

The creature, however, shakes its head slowly and says simply: "Boris."

"No, she can't be named Boris," Rebecca says patiently. "Boris is a boy's name."

"Boris," the creature repeats, still shaking its head.

"She's a girl," Rebecca persists, stepping a little closer. "Look. She doesn't have a—"

The creature slams both hands onto the table with in a sudden ferocity and bellows: "*BORIS!*"

Rebecca staggers backwards, almost dropping the puppy, who jerks and begins whimpering in her arms. Rebecca turns and flees upstairs.

As she closes the door to the room and clutches the puppy to her chest, she can't really tell if it's her own or the dog's heart that's beating faster.

That evening, for the first time since Old Boris died, the creature begins burning her feet and giving her the eye-liquid again.

Later on, as she lies in bed with the puppy snoring softly next to the pillow, Rebecca can't fall asleep. She just stares up into the blurry ceiling, as thoughts keep going around her head, and her feet throb painfully under the fresh bandages.

Rebecca turns her head sideways and strokes the puppy's back as she broods. Now she understands what was bugging her about the thought of Old Boris.

As she lies in bed now, in the dark room, it all comes into place in her mind, and she finally realizes no one will come for her. It's been way too long now.

In fact, she has known it for a while, she just didn't want to face it. But losing Old Boris somehow brought it to the surface.

The truth is, if she wants to get away from this place, she needs to do it herself. Or else she will spend the rest of her life here, without ever seeing her family or even another human being again. And one day, if she turns fatefully ill or the creature grows tired of her and decides to kill her, she will end up in a hole in the ground out behind the hedge next to the bones of Alice, and the creature will go on to find a replacement, just like it did with Boris.

The thought makes her both angry and very sad. The creature tries to forget that Old Boris is dead, that he was even really here. But he was. Rebecca remembers him, and she always will.

"Your name isn't Boris," she whispers to the puppy. "From now on, your name is ... Doris."

Rebecca smiles and breathes deeply through her nose. Something has changed within her. Something has been brought back to life. Something which had almost gone away forever.

She's scared at the thought of fleeing—terrified, actually—but somehow, weirdly, she also feels relief. Even if it should fail and the creature catches her and punishes her, the punishment can't be worse than staying here, waiting to die.

"I'm going to try," she tells the sleeping puppy. "I really am. And I'm bringing you with me, Doris."

Rebecca closes her eyes then and falls asleep with surprising ease.

And for the first time in a long time, she dreams about Andy and the rest of her family waiting for her back home.

DAY 98

Rebecca spends an hour the next day, when the creature is out, going around the house, looking in every room, thinking.

It's the first time she goes through the house like this, and she finds something quite unexpected in the creature's bedroom. In the closet, which she presumed only contained the creature's clothes, she finds a shelf full of different shoes, including Rebecca's own. They're all around the same size, and all seem to be girl's shoes. Some of them are very old. She counts at least six pairs.

She considers for a moment taking her own shoes, but that would of course be a blatant mistake; the creature would find out and punish her for it. Besides, she's quite used to walking around in her socks by now, even when she's outside.

She leaves the shoes and goes on investigating while she ponders the plan. There are a lot of questions she needs to answer.

Should she do it in the day or in the night? Should she try while the creature is sleeping or wait for it to leave in the van? If it's out, it will lock the doors, meaning Rebecca needs to smash a window to get out of the house. But even if she does, the biggest obstacle will still be the fence. She can't climb it because of the barbed-wire, that's too dangerous. Which means she needs to go either *under* it or *through* it.

There is, of course, the beech. It's a big, old tree by the side of the house, and it has long branches reaching out over the fence. If she could somehow climb up there, she might be able to climb over the fence and jump down on the other side.

The problem is, though, that the lowest branches of the beech sit very high, too high for her to reach them, even if she brought a chair to stand on. She would need a ladder. She knows there is one in the garage—she saw it one day, when she was out playing with the puppy and it ran into the garage—but it's firmly chained to the wall; as though the creature predicted the ladder might be used to scale the fence. So, the beech is not really an option, either.

Later, in the afternoon, Rebecca goes outside and checks the garage. The creature has returned home and is taking a nap in its bedroom.

She finds a pair of pliers which might be big enough to cut the fence—if Rebecca has the strength, that is. She picks up a piece of wire from the floor and tests the pliers. She manages to cut the wire, but it takes a lot of effort, and the fence is even thicker. Besides, she needs to cut it in at least ten places in order to make an opening big enough to squeeze through; probably more like twenty. How long will that take her? Will she tire out before she's done?

There is also still the option she already tried once: digging her way under the fence. The biggest problem with that option is how long it'll take. The first time she tried it, the creature had time to sense what she was doing and showed up. Which means, if she chooses to dig her way out, she needs to do it while the creature isn't home.

But then the next question pops up: what does she do if she makes it past the fence? Where does she run to? There are open fields in every direction and she has no idea which way town is. Of course, she can follow the gravel road until she reaches the highway, but if she flees while the creature is out, she runs the risk of it returning and seeing her on the road.

It might be better to just choose a direction and make a run for it. At some point, she's bound to meet a house or a town.

Then how much of a head start will she need? If the creature sets after her, which she feels pretty certain it will, she better make sure she's far enough away that it can't catch up with her. Even more so if the creature follows her in the van.

Unless she sabotages it, of course. She's seen in the movies how people will cut a wire or something in the engine of a car, and then it won't start. Maybe she can do the same before she makes a run for it?

There are so many things to consider, Rebecca's head is spinning, but she wants to make sure she doesn't overlook anything, so she prepares herself mentally for staying another couple of days, just until she has got it all figured out.

Then, suddenly, a completely unexpected chance shows itself.

DAY 99

Rebecca hears it already from very far away, as she's out playing with Doris in the garden. She immediately recognizes the sound of tires on the gravel, and at first, she thinks it's the creature who has left in the van. But she hasn't heard the engine start up or the rattling of the chain at the gate.

So, she picks up the puppy and goes around to the courtyard. The yellow van is still in the garage.

Some distance up the gravel road, she can make out a red car coming this way. The gravel is very dry and creates a tall, narrow cloud of dust rising towards the blue sky.

Rebecca feels her heart rate rising. She turns and looks at the house. The creature is in there somewhere. Has it heard the car yet? Why hasn't it come out? Perhaps it's napping—it sometimes does that around this time of day.

Rebecca looks toward the approaching car again. It's driving along at a leisurely speed, with no hurry.

Who is it? Someone who knows the creature and wants to pay it a visit?

Rebecca never even considered the possibility of the creature having relatives or friends, and it seems highly unlikely.

She stands there in the courtyard, uncertain what to do, watching the car come closer. Still no sign of the creature as the car reaches the gate. It stops but doesn't turn off its engine.

Rebecca can't see through the windshield due to the reflection of sunlight. The driver's door is opened and an older gentleman steps out. As soon as Rebecca sees his face, she understands he's not a friend of the creature.

"Hello?" he calls out, waving at Rebecca. "Hello, there! Could you please help me, darling?"

Rebecca is completely unprepared for the man's thick accent. It's British, as far as she can tell, like the way old, fancy people from Europe talk in movies. The man sounds very nice, and he's smiling at her and waving her closer.

Rebecca glances back at the house again. The front door is still closed. The creature would have heard the car by now. Perhaps it really is napping.

She bites her lip. *Should I go for it?*

The old guy is still waving and calling for her.

Rebecca can't open the gate, and neither can the man, since it requires a key, which the creature has. And if she tells the man to call the police or go for help, and the creature shows up to see her talking with him, she will no doubt be punished. In fact, just standing here looking at the guy might be considered a disobedience by the creature. Perhaps she ought to simply go inside the house.

On the other hand, this might be the chance she's been waiting for. Rebecca decides to take it.

She runs to the gate.

"Hello, sweetheart," the old man says, holding out a brochure of some kind. "What a lovely little dog you've got there. Listen, I'm looking for this motel, you see, but I've been going 'round for hours on end now, and I just can't seem to—"

"You've got to help me," Rebecca interrupts. "You need to call someone."

The man's smile falters. "I ... I'm sorry, sweetheart, I'm not quite sure I follow?"

Rebecca grabs the cold metal bars of the gate. "Help me!" she says earnestly. "Help me get out of here!" She darts a look back towards the house.

The old man follows her gaze, frowning. "What … what's wrong, darling? Are you all right?"

"No! I'm not all right! I'm being held hostage. Call the police!"

The man raises his eyebrows. "The police? But, really—"

"Yes! The police! Call them now!"

The man hesitates for a moment longer, looking from the house to Rebecca, then seems to decide to believe her and goes to his pockets. "Shoot, where's my bloody cell phone?"

He goes back to his car.

Rebecca's heart is pounding away in her throat, Doris is shaking in her arms.

And then she hears it. The front door.

She turns her head like in slow motion to see the creature come out of the house. It looks right at her, but weirdly, it's walking in a different direction; it's headed for the garage.

The old man has found his phone and is coming back towards the gate, fumbling with a pair of reading glasses.

Rebecca reaches her arm out through the gate, pointing frantically. "Hurry up! Call them! It's coming! The creature is coming! Call them, just call them!"

"Now, hold on a minute," the old man says, and then he says something more, which Rebecca doesn't pick up, because she's looking back to see the creature coming back out from the garage, holding the shovel and coming this way.

"Call the police!" Rebecca screams. "Call them now! Please!" She lunges for the phone, but the old man steps backward with a look of utter confusion.

He looks to the creature and says: "Good afternoon, sir. Could you please explain to me why this young lady seems to be terrified? What exactly is going on here?"

"*Call the police! Call them!*" Rebecca screams, as the creature grabs her and drags her aside. It produces the key and unlocks the chain.

Rebecca is still screaming, the old guy is still talking to the creature, but now he's also backing away towards his car, the cell phone still in his hand.

"*Run!*" Rebecca screams to him. "*Get out of here!*"

Finally, the seriousness of the situation dawns on the old man, and he turns and makes for his car. The creature has just pulled the gate aside and is still far enough away that the old guy can actually make it—but his shoe slips on the gravel, and he grabs the door so as to not fall down.

It gives the creature the five seconds it needs to get to him and raise the shovel.

Rebecca doesn't actually hear the blade of the shovel connecting with the old guy's skull, because her own scream drowns it out.

She doesn't see it, either, because thankfully, the creature is blocking the view.

But she does see the man fall to the gravel and she sees the creature swing the shovel three times more and she sees the man's bloody face.

Then, she only sees the blue sky and finds herself lying flat on her back, Doris barking somewhere nearby.

I guess I fainted, she thinks curiously, looking at the white clouds drifting by.

She tries to lift her head and is surprised to find she actually can. She sees the creature come walking across the courtyard, dragging along the old man by one leg.

Rebecca feels very faint and weak, but she uses her last strength to turn her head towards the gate. The old guy's car is still right outside, his cell phone lies in the gravel, only a few yards away from Rebecca.

But the creature has closed and chained-up the gate once more, so the car and phone might as well be on Mars.

Then, Rebecca rests her head on the gravel and looks back up at the clouds.

That was my chance, she thinks. *Now the creature will kill me.*

She drifts off.

PART THREE
AMBROOS VAN DE GOOR

DAY 103

The creature doesn't kill her.

It burns her feet until they're both like one giant, oozing wound. It drips the liquid in her eyes and blinds her. It doesn't feed her for three days. And it keeps her locked in the room the entire time.

But it doesn't kill her.

Rebecca lies in bed for a week as her feet slowly heal and her eyes recover somewhat.

The pain is so bad the first couple of days that she barely sleeps. She drifts in and out of feverlike dreams, where she witnesses over and over again the creature beating the old man to death with the shovel. She hears crunching on gravel, her own scream and the sharp thud of a metal blade connecting with a skull.

But she also sometimes dreams about Andy and the rest of her family; they call to her from behind a thick window. She can't hear their voices, but she can see them waving and banging the glass.

Rebecca reads Andy's lips. He keeps repeating the same three words:

"Come home, Becca!"

On the fourth day, the creature brings her a bucket to use as a toilet and starts bringing her meals again. It doesn't look at her or talk to her, though.

As Rebecca slowly recovers in bed, she gradually becomes able to think straight again. And she realizes the thought of trying to escape is even worse, now that she knows what the creature is willing to do to keep her here. She harbors no illusions that it will kill her without hesitation if she tries to run and it catches her.

And why wouldn't it? After all, Rebecca is pretty replaceable. The creature could easily find a new Alice. Maybe it even has done so before.

The way the creature simply replaced Boris makes Rebecca wonder if she is the first one to get caught by the creature? It would explain the many girl's shoes she found.

How many Alices have gone before her? How many exactly are buried around the garden?

So what happened to them? Did they simply grow too old? Or perhaps they refused to toe the line. Perhaps they refused to forget their real name or their family. And finally, one day, they tried to run away. And the creature caught them. And now, their bones lie buried in the ground out back, their flesh eaten away by maggots.

The thought brings out a deep dread in Rebecca.

Though she feels terrified at the thought of trying to flee, she has also already made up her mind to do it. At least it will offer her a chance to see Andy and Mom and Dad and Cindy again, even if the chance is slim. If she does nothing, however, she won't see them for sure.

She also realizes, as she spends the week in bed, how she will do it. It comes to her in a half-dream in the middle of a night full of pain, as she suddenly opened her eyes and stared right at the solution.

Actually, the idea has already occurred to her several days back, maybe all the way back to the night she first saw the moonlight shining in from the closet; she just hadn't realized what it meant until now.

It's obvious, really, when she thinks of it.

It's like a sign from heaven.

Her way out.

And besides, what other way is left? Now that the creature won't even let her out of the room, all of her other options are gone.

She will escape through the closet. The hole at the top leads right onto the roof. And from there, she can make it to the tree. And via the tree, she can climb over the fence and jump down on the other side.

That's the plan, anyway.

If it's doable, she has no idea, and she doesn't really concern herself with the question. She's going to try—that's all that matters. In a couple of days. As soon as her feet are healed enough for to walk again.

There is only one last thing she needs to figure out: how will she bring Doris?

She hasn't seen her since the old man came. The creature won't allow her into the room anymore. Rebecca hears her several times a day, whining from the bottom of the stairs.

Rebecca won't run without Doris. She won't leave her here with the creature.

So, she begins to think out a plan. That's how Andy would do it. Andy is brainy and very meticulous when it comes to problem-solving. He loves riddles and always finds a solution to difficult challenges, using only his mind. Rebecca tries to think like Andy would.

It's going to be difficult getting Doris up here since she can't leave the room, and the only time the creature unlocks the door is when it brings food and empties her toilet-bucket.

Rebecca spends an entire afternoon sitting by the window, gazing down into the garden as she broods.

Once or twice she sees Doris, as she comes out through the dog hatch in the terrace door, strolls about the garden, pees, then goes back inside.

Slowly, an idea starts to form.

DAY 104

The next day, Rebecca sets her plan into motion.

She begins to leave a small portion of each meal. A bit of scrambled egg, small pieces of sandwich and three bits of bacon. She hides it in a sock which she places under the mattress.

She spends a few hours by the window every day. As soon as she sees Doris in the garden, she whistles three times, then drops a little food from the open window.

To begin with, Doris has trouble catching on, and she doesn't notice the food right away. Then, the fourth time Rebecca does it, the dog looks up and sees the food falling. After that, she quickly figures out what the three whistles mean.

DAY 107

Rebecca continues the training the next day and the day after that. By the third day, she can get Doris to come running out from inside the house by whistling three times.

Rebecca also spends the days on another part of her plan: making a rope.

She collects all sorts of things: the string from the blinds, the wire from the desk lamp and a thick thread from the carpet in the corner where it's already unraveled. She binds everything together to form a single, long piece, until she's confident it can reach all the way down to the ground. It's very thin and definitely not strong enough to carry Rebecca's weight—but it's not supposed to carry *her*.

Finally, there's only one last piece to the plan: the bucket. The one Rebecca uses as a toilet.

The creature empties it every night as it brings dinner. Five minutes later, it comes back and drops the bucket on the floor. It's been rinsed out and smells of sanitizer.

Rebecca worries the smell might scare off Doris. She can only hope the smell of the bait is more prominent.

Rebecca hides the makeshift rope under the mattress as the creature comes on the third day to bring her evening meal. It puts the plate on the desk, takes the bucket and closes the door again behind it without even looking at her.

Rebecca immediately goes to eat, plucking away three bits of bacon and devouring the rest of the meal.

When the creature returns with the cleaned-out bucket, Rebecca has already stuffed the bacon away and is sitting on her bed, looking innocent.

Normally, the creature would have found out. It would have looked at her closely and figured out she was hiding something. But because it's still punishing her and hasn't spent any time with her lately, its ability to sense that something is up seems to have weakened.

Yet this time, it suddenly hesitates in the doorway. Rebecca doesn't look over at it, but she senses how its eyes rest on her.

"Alice," it whispers.

Rebecca doesn't move. Sweat is prickling her back. Did the creature figure it out after all? Did it hear her whistling for Doris through the window? Or has it been in here when she slept and found the rope? Does it know she's planning to flee?

"Alice," it whispers again.

Rebecca turns her head halfway towards the door and, for the first time ever, she answers to the false name by saying: "Yes?"

She's surprised at how sincere her voice sounds.

The creature doesn't say anything else. It just stands there, staring at her. Then, it closes the door and goes downstairs.

Rebecca begins breathing again. *What did that mean? Was it a warning?*

The creature didn't sound either angry or threatening—in fact, there was almost warmth in the voice. Maybe it didn't figure out her plan after all. Maybe it just wants to make peace.

Rebecca can't tell for sure. But she knows she needs to make the plan happen now, tonight.

DAY 108

Never before has time gone by so slowly.

Andy twists and turns. He keeps checking his phone. Every time he does so, only a few minutes have passed since he last looked. If time would just hurry up so he could get going.

Finally, he can't wait any longer. It's only 0:23 AM, and he meant to wait until 1:00 AM, but he's pretty certain both Mom and Dad are sleeping by now.

So, he gets up, gets dressed and arranges the bed like he has done hundreds of times before.

But this time is special. This time might be the last.

He checks his phone. The address is a fair way outside of town—way too long for him to have ever found it on his nightly outings, anyway—almost twelve miles. It will take him most of the night just to reach it. His legs are in pretty good shape, but he'll probably still get very sore muscles tomorrow.

Andy doesn't care if he'll walk sideways for the rest of his life. Rebecca is at the end of the twelve miles, and that's the only thing that matters.

He takes out his bag from under the bed. It's loaded with crackers, a Mars bar, a water bottle, *The Wendigo* and a boxcutter.

He's not exactly sure why he brings the book, but he somehow feels braver knowing it's with him. He picks up the boxcutter and slides out the blade. It shines up at him. Andy swallows dryly. He really hopes he won't need it, but he might end up in a position where he has to defend himself or Rebecca, and it was the best weapon he could find in Dad's toolbox.

He zips up the bag and swings it over his shoulder. Then, he crawls out of the window, uses the drainpipe to slide to the ground, runs around the house and remembers to duck as he passes his parents' bedroom window, even though the curtains are drawn.

He sneaks into the garage but leaves the lights off. He knows the surroundings well enough to locate his bike in the dark. He pulls it out to the driveway and is just about to head off, when he notices something is wrong. He looks down to see the back tire completely flat.

"Oh, crap," he whispers. "Not now!"

He gets back off the bike again and looks at it for a moment. He doesn't know how to fix a flat tire—Dad always does it for him. Which means he needs to postpone the whole thing till tomorrow.

The thought of waiting another day makes him very ill at ease. He goes back into the garage and takes out his phone, using its flashlight to look around.

Mom's bike is dismantled because Dad is in the progress of fixing the gears. Dad's bike is too big for Andy. And Cindy doesn't own a bike.

Andy moans and feels like kicking something out of frustration. He feels so close, but now he has to wait.

Then he sees Cindy's scooter.

Andy hesitates for a moment. He did actually try it once, last summer, where Cindy let him have a go on it without Mom and Dad knowing about it. He even knows how to start it—and he knows where to find the key, too.

Andy decides to do it.

He sneaks into the house. In the entrance hall the key for the scooter hangs from the rack among other keys. Andy steps over and carefully takes it, when suddenly, there's a sound from the bathroom.

Andy freezes. Steps are coming this way. There's nowhere to hide.

The door opens, and Cindy appears. She jumps a little when she sees him. "Oh, you scared me, Andy. What are you doing up at this hour?"

Andy tries to reply, but only a dry croak comes out.

Cindy looks down and notices Andy is fully dressed, shoes and all.

She sighs. "Goddamnit, Andy. Are you still sneaking out at night? Mom will kill you if she finds out."

"I ... I have to, Cindy."

"No, you don't, actually. You need to move on. Rebecca won't come back, okay?"

The words connect with Andy's stomach like heavy blows. He forces down a deep breath, reminding himself that Cindy means well. And she doesn't know what *he* knows.

He keeps the key for the scooter hidden behind his back and hopes she won't notice it missing from the rack.

"Come on upstairs with me, Andy," she says pleadingly, stepping closer. "You can sleep in my room if you like."

For a moment, Andy is so surprised at the offer, he almost feels tempted to go with Cindy. He hasn't slept in her room since he was very little. Before Rebecca was born. Back then, he and Cindy still played together.

"Cindy," he says, not even considering what he's about to ask her. "Why aren't you sad that Rebecca's gone?"

The answer is obvious from Cindy's face right away, as she struggles to not let it crumble.

Instead, she shakes her head. "How thick are you, Andy? Of course I'm sad. I cry myself to sleep every night. I just … I just don't wear my emotions on my sleeve."

"I … I didn't know," Andy says, feeling stupid.

Cindy sighs again. "How would you? We're all wrapped up in our own shit right now, aren't we?"

"I guess so," Andy says, looking at Cindy in a completely new light.

The haircut, the makeup, the new clothes. It all happened after Rebecca disappeared. And maybe it wasn't at all about Cindy's looks after all.

"I'm sorry, Cindy," he says, realizing his sister might have been suffering just as much as he has over the loss of Rebecca.

"It's fine," Cindy says, managing a smile. "Come on upstairs with me, won't you?"

Cindy makes as though to go, putting a hand on Andy's shoulder, but Andy stays firm.

"I need to go, Cindy," he whispers.

Cindy is about to answer, when she looks at him and sees the tears in his eyes.

"This will be the last time," he says. "I promise."

Cindy eyes him, a look of deep sadness coming over her face. "All right," she mutters, nodding.

"You won't tell Mom, will you?"

"I guess I should, but ..." Cindy shrugs. "If this is your way of dealing with things, then who am I to tell you otherwise? Just promise me to be careful. Put the lights on your bike, okay?" She squeezes his shoulder, then heads upstairs.

Andy breathes out. His entire body is trembling. The key is sweaty in his clutched hand.

***

Rebecca can't sleep.

She lies awake, staring at the ceiling. She knows this will be the last time she lies here. The last time she sees this room. One way or another.

The hours drag on. She doesn't have a watch, but she listens to the grandfather clock downstairs, counting the chimes. Finally, she decides it's time.

She sits up, already dressed. She finds the rope and the sock full of food, moving as quietly as possible. She ties the rope to the handle of the bucket and empties the sock into the bucket. There's almost an entire meal. She hopes it'll be enough to tempt Doris.

But first she needs to take care of something else.

Rebecca slips over to the closet and opens it. The moon is full and its light is streaming in through the crack in the roof. Rebecca steps up onto the lower shelf and reaches up with one hand. It takes some meddling, but she manages to pry one of the roof tiles loose. It's very heavy. She carefully lowers it and places it neatly on the floor, before stepping back up and loosening the next one.

When three tiles are gone, the hole is big enough for her to fit through. A rectangular piece of black, starry sky is visible, and the cool night air seeps in, inviting her.

Rebecca steps out of the closet and closes the door again. Her heart is thumping away; the creature might open the door to the room at any point and ruin everything. But so far, it hasn't. And Rebecca moves on.

She opens the window and picks up the bucket. Then, she whistles three times. It sounds very loud in the silence. She waits a minute or so, but Doris doesn't show up. Rebecca knows the puppy is sleeping in the living room right below her, and the creature's bedroom is way over at the far end of the house. But which of them sleeps deeper?

Rebecca whistles again, a little louder.

Still, no Doris.

She whistles a third time, as loudly as she dares.

And then she hears the dog hatch open. Doris comes trundling out, shakes her fur and looks up at Rebecca with sleepy eyes.

"Hey, Doris," she whispers and waves.

The tail starts wagging.

"Don't make any noise now," Rebecca instructs her. "The creature mustn't hear us."

Doris sits down and waits patiently for her treat.

"I've got something special for you this time," Rebecca whispers and lets the bucket slip out of the window, lowering it carefully with the rope.

Doris looks curiously at the bucket as it comes closer. Rebecca lands it gently next to the dog. Then she makes a few sideways jerks with the rope, causing the bucket to tip over on the side.

Doris steps a little back. She whimpers and sniffs the bucket suspiciously. She can obviously smell the food, but isn't quite sure if it's safe to dig in.

"Just go for it," Rebecca whispers. "It's okay, just take the food, Doris."

She glances back. The door is still closed.

After a little more sniffing around, Doris decides to chance it and tentatively reaches into the bucket. Rebecca can hear her eating.

"Just a little farther," Rebecca breathes, staring at the dog and the bucket.

Doris takes another step forward. She's halfway inside the bucket now. Still not enough. If Rebecca tries to lift the bucket now, and Doris slips out, she's afraid the puppy will be too scared to go near the bucket again. She only gets one shot.

"Just a liiitle more ..."

Finally, Doris steps all the way into the bucket, only her tail is showing now.

Rebecca jerks the rope upwards. The bucket tilts back upright and lifts off the ground. Doris gives off a little yelp of surprise. Rebecca hauls the bucket up quickly. Doris jumps to get out, and the bucket sways dangerously. For a terrible moment, Rebecca is sure the puppy will fall out and hurt herself badly on the stone terrace below.

But Doris falls back into the bucket and a moment later, Rebecca grabs the handle and pulls it into the room.

"You did so good," she whispers and lifts up Doris. "Good girl, good girl."

The puppy licks Rebecca's face and whines happily at the reunion. It's been several days since they last were together.

"Sssh," Rebecca shushes. "We need to be very quiet now."

She unbuttons the front of her shirt and places Doris inside it. The puppy is warm against her stomach, and it settles in immediately, giving a satisfied yawn.

"That's right, you rest. I'll do the work."

Rebecca goes to the closet. So far, so good. Now comes the tricky part. She breathes deeply, opens the closet and climbs up the shelves. She sticks her head up through the hole and surveys the roof for a moment. It's steeper that she thought, and it's also wet from dew.

I can make it. I just need to be careful.

Rebecca steps up onto the top shelf and raises herself up onto the roof. She's really high up. Luckily, she has never been scared of heights. Still, a fall from up here might results in several broken bones.

She tests the roof with her foot, the socks slipping easily. She takes them off and tries with her bare feet. The burn wounds hurt a little, but the soles of her feet have a little more grip without the socks.

Slowly, she begins the climb. The tree is on the other side of the house, which means she needs to scale the rooftop. A few times she almost slips, but then she figures out a method where she grabs the edge of the tiles. They are pretty sharp and rough on her fingers, but she ignores the pain.

Doris is sleeping calmly against her stomach.

Rebecca reaches the top of the roof and moves along the ridge until she's right next to the beech. Now, she only needs to get down to the branches.

The biggest problem with her plan, she realizes now, is that the tree is right outside the creature's bedroom, and she will be climbing right over it. Which means she needs to be extra silent.

Rebecca begins the descent. It's a lot harder than going up. After only a few feet, she loses her grip and slips. She almost screams out as she slides down the slippery roof, her buttock giving off small bumps with every tile, moving faster and faster, the branches rushing towards her, and then she meets them, groping wildly for something to catch on to. One or two of the thinner branches break off, and she is very close to sliding right through, when, at the last moment, she grabs a branch thick enough to halt her.

Rebecca sits still, clutching the branch, her heart racing. Doris moves under the shirt.

"It's okay," she whispers. "We're okay. Go back to sleep."

Rebecca listens for noises from inside the house. The bumps from her wild ride might have been enough to wake up the creature.

Then get a move on!

Rebecca climbs onto the tree. It's more difficult than she imagined, the branches aren't very thick and are also slippery, but she manages to make her way to the trunk of the tree.

She stands still for a moment and looks down. She can see the window to the creature's bedroom. It's dark in there, but the window is open, letting the night air in.

Rebecca looks out over the branch that reaches across the fence. From here, it looks a lot thinner and less supportive than it did from the ground. And there are several feet down. She feels so close to freedom, but she still needs to cross one final, dangerous stage.

And suddenly, unexpectedly, Rebecca is gripped by the most overwhelming fear she has ever felt in her life. For a moment, she wants to drop everything. To climb back up onto the roof and slip back inside her room. Lower Doris back down onto the lawn and go to bed.

Would it really be so bad living here? Is it really worth risking her life to get away? If she just does as the creature asks of her, she has really nothing to fear. She could live here for many years to come.

But she knows she can't do that. She knows there's only one way for her, and that's out over that fence, no matter how scared she is.

She breathes deeply, forces her hands to let go of the trunk and begins walking. Rebecca is pretty good at balancing. The first half of the way, she has other branches to hold onto for support. But then they run out, and she needs to walk on her own. The branch isn't much wider than her feet, and it bobs gently under her weight. The burn wounds at the soles of her feet begin stinging badly, but she ignores the pain, steps slowly, one foot at a time.

She's almost above the fence now.

Two more steps. She is very close.

Two more. One.

And then she's over.

Rebecca kneels down and grabs the branch with both hands. Out here, it's not much thicker than a broomstick. She shivers all over. Now she just needs to make the jump. There's almost ten feet to the ground. She's never made a jump this high before. She could swing herself down and hang from her arms, that way making the jump shorter, but she's afraid the shirt might open and Doris could fall out if she stretches out like that. So she needs to just jump.

Come on, you can do it. It's the last thing you need to do, and then you're free!

Rebecca closes her eyes. Then she jumps.

She wooshes through the air, faster and faster. The fall seems to go on forever.

Then she hits the wheat and the soft ground below and rolls to her back to soften the blow on the feet. Her ankles hurt a bit, but it soon wears off. She didn't break anything. Doris wakes up and moves around.

Rebecca gets to her feet and looks around. The wheat is knee-high, but she can see very far.

I ... I did it ... I'm free! I—

A movement above her. Rebecca looks up and sees something white swoop through the air. A large, snowy owl lands in the beech and looks down at her with big, round and yellow eyes.

Rebecca stares back at it, dumbfounded.

The owl blinks at her. Then turns its head to look at the house.

Rebecca follows its gaze. And freezes when she sees the creature.

It's standing right on the other side of the fence, glaring at her.

"Alice."

The word comes creeping through the night air. The voice is low. Ominous. Furious.

Rebecca shakes her head and begins backing away through the wheat. She can't take her eyes off the creature. She's certain it will take off and scale the fence in one giant leap at any moment. But it just keeps standing there.

"Alice," it says again, a little louder.

"No!" Rebecca says, and the sound of her voice is like a spell-breaker. Suddenly, she can turn around and run.

She looks back and sees the creature move along the fence. It's headed for the courtyard and the gate. Which means it's can't scale the fence after all. That should give Rebecca courage, but something about the way the creature moves scares her more than anything. It doesn't run, it just walks with long, casual strides.

Like it knows it doesn't need to hurry.

Like it's got all night.

Like Rebecca's flight is doomed to fail.

The owl takes flight and glides noiselessly over her head before disappearing into the darkness.

Rebecca runs for her life.

***

Andy gives it full throttle as he races along the dark highway.

To begin with, he rode carefully, but now he's got the hang of it, and he feels comfortable about going at full speed. The road is mostly straight, and the light from the scooter helps him see the dew-wet asphalt ahead. He's been riding for close to half an hour now.

Now and then he stops to check his phone and make sure he's on the right track.

Until he got out of town, he was afraid of getting stopped by a police car. He only met a few late drivers, though, and none of them paid any attention to him. He's wearing Cindy's helmet, so hopefully no one can tell he's only thirteen.

Out here in the country, the chance of getting stopped is obviously a lot smaller, and he hasn't met a single car yet. Only the stars above keep him company.

Something dark appears ahead.

It's a forest, Andy realizes as he gets closer. It fits with what the map told him: the house he's looking for will be on the other side of the forest. Which means he's close now.

The road cuts right through the trees. The darkness grows thicker around him as he enters the forest, and there are leaves on the asphalt, making it slippery, so he lets off the gas a little. Crashing with the scooter would be almost as bad as getting caught by the police. Just the thought of having to call home, admit the whole thing and ask them to come get him ... Andy shivers. That mustn't happen. But as long as he's careful—

Suddenly, he sees it.

It appears out of nowhere, like a jack-in-box, completely unexpected.

He stops the scooter and puts his feet to the ground. He pulls off the helmet and stares open-mouthed at the yellow van parked at the roadside.

Although it's been almost four months since he saw it, there's no doubt in his mind he's looking at the exact same van.

He squints, adjusts his glasses and tries to look through the windshield. As far as he can tell, no one is behind the wheel. He looks around in the darkness, peering in between the trees.

No figures in sight. He feels alone, but ... how can he be sure?

Andy shuts off the scooter's engine and puts it on the kickstand. Then he quickly takes off the bag, opens it and reaches in for the boxcutter.

He steps a little closer to the van, holding his breath as he listens.

The night is absolutely quiet.

Not a breeze stirs.

Not a leaf rustles.

Only Andy's heart is buzzing in his ears.

He walks closer to the van, clutching the boxcutter, ready to push out the blade, in case he's walking into a trap.

He walks around the van. All the doors are closed. Andy tries to open the back door. It's locked.

"Rebecca?" he whispers. "You in there?"

No reply.

Andy's intuition tells him the car is empty. He goes around to the front and places his hand on the hood; it's a trick he learned from a detective's novel. It's still warm. The van can only have been left here a few minutes ago.

Andy suddenly gets a strong feeling that someone is looking at him, and he spins around.

No one to see. Except—

He looks up and sees the owl eyeing him from the nearest tree.

That does it. The owl must be a sign. There's still almost one mile to the house, but now Andy knows Rebecca is nearby.

"Where is she?" he asks the owl. "Tell me!"

The owl blinks. Then it takes flight and swoops over his head without a noise, headed into the forest and quickly disappears in the darkness.

Andy stares after it and sees the trail snaking between the trees. It's too narrow for a car, so whoever came in the van has probably parked it here and continued into the forest on foot.

Andy swallows dryly. He's suddenly very much aware that he's standing in the middle of nowhere all alone in the dead of night. No one even knows he's here, and now he's about to go pursue a dangerous monster with only a boxcutter to defend himself.

If I'm afraid, how must Rebecca feel?

The thought makes him breath hard through his nose.

"I'm coming, Becca," he tells the night.

***

Rebecca isn't really aware that she's headed for the forest until it's right in front of her. She just runs across the field as quickly as she can. It's hard, because the wheat keeps trying to trip her, and her pants are completely soaked through from dew.

The full moon lights up the land, allowing her to see a little ahead despite her blurry vision. A few times she stumbles, but quickly gets back up.

She keeps looking back, expecting to see the creature come running for her, but so far that hasn't happened, and by now the house and beech tree have turned into nothing but a tiny, dark blotch.

Yet she knows it's coming.

She knows it won't just let her leave.

She sees the forest and stops to catch her heaving breath. Doris moves under the shirt, whimpering.

"I know," Rebecca pants. "But you can't get out yet, Doris."

She considers for a moment if it's wise to go into the forest. On the one hand she'll be less easy to see once she's no longer out in the open. On the other, she has a feeling the forest is where the creature moves most naturally. After all, it was in the park forest it was waiting for her when it took her. Perhaps it's better for her to run around the forest. Maybe she ought to—

The wind whispers at her. It's only the slightest breeze.

"Alice."

The name is just barely audible.

Rebecca spins around and looks in every direction. She's still alone in the field. But suddenly, she doesn't *feel* alone.

She runs into the forest, clutching the puppy against her stomach as she zigzags between the trees. It's extra hard to see in here, because most of the moonlight is drowned out by the treetops, their leaves and branches creating flickering shadows all around. The forest floor is uneven and overgrown in ferns, causing her to almost stumble.

She reaches a clearing and stops, looks around, panting, straining her eyes.

The shadows from the trees play with her imagination, making it seem like one of them could step forward at any minute, revealing itself as the creature.

No, it can't be here already, Rebecca tries to tell herself. *I had a good head start and I ran as fast as I could all the way over. Unless, of course ... unless it* **drove** *here ...*

The thought sends icy chills down her sweaty back. What if the creature knew she was headed for the forest? What if it just casually walked to the van and drove over here? Perhaps it's already here. Perhaps it's even waiting for her ...

The feeling of being watched creeps up on her from every side. She wants to run, she feels exposed in the middle of the clearing, but she doesn't know which direction to take.

"Hello?" she whispers, spinning slowly. "Is anybody here?"

No answer comes. At least not from a human voice. But the breeze stirs again, floats through the clearing, causing the ferns to rattle, and carries the creature's squeaking little-girl-voice to her.

"*Alice ...*"

The breath is pulled from Rebecca's mouth. She wants to scream, but can't. Her entire body is trembling, her knees threaten to buckle. She turns and turns, desperately trying to get eyes on the creature.

"Where are you?" she croaks.

"*Alice,*" the wind whispers.

"*Where are you*!?" Rebecca screams.

The sound throws an echo and a flock of sleeping crows take flight from the treetops. Their shrill shrieks fill the air, and their flickering shadows flow across the clearing, before the birds are gone and silence once again descends over the forest.

Rebecca holds her breath and listens. The breeze is gone now. Everything is quiet. Rebecca feels a faint hope. She can't hear the voice anymore. Maybe the creature got distracted by the crows. Maybe it's—

"Alice."

This time, the voice comes from right behind her.

Rebecca spins around with a scream, just as the creature steps out from the shadows. As the moonlight hits it, Rebecca sees to her utter horror that it's fully naked. The pale, greyish skin covers the thin limbs and gives it a sickly look. It moves in a strange, almost dreamlike fashion on the long, spiderlike legs, and the black eyes lock Rebecca in place.

She wants to turn, to run, to get away, but she can't move a muscle, can only stand there like a statue and stare at the creature sweeping towards her, and she knows that this is it, knows without a shadow of a doubt that the creature will kill her now.

Rebecca notices very faintly a distant sound growing louder. At first, she takes it for her own pulse buzzing behind her eardrums. But once the sound grows louder, it reminds her more of an angry wasp coming this way. And then the sound rises even further, turning into an angry roar.

The creature hears it too, because it snaps its boney neck and looks to the side, just as a sharp, white flash lights up everything for a brief second.

Rebecca turns her head in a slow, dreamy movement. She catches a glimpse of the scooter as it comes crashing into the clearing, bumping wildly over the forest floor. She also sees the creature caught in the headlight like a surprised animal. It raises its arms and lets out a hoarse scream, but the sound is cut short as the scooter collides with it and sends it sprawling backwards. The scooter does a somersault and the driver flies off before it lands and both the headlight and the engine die.

Rebecca blinks and stares at the driver, who has landed right in front of her. With a moan of pain, the person comes to their feet and pulls the helmet off.

Andy looks at her.

He's taller, thinner, and his hair is longer. But it is Andy. He smiles, and the smile is exactly the same.

"Hi, Becca," he says, a little out of breath.

Then his smile goes away as he turns to look at the creature. Rebecca follows his gaze and sees the thin figure on the ground starting to stir.

"Come on," Andy says, grabbing her by the arm. "We've got to go."

The feeling of his hand on her arm wakes Rebecca from her trance. She follows him to the scooter, which he lifts up with a groan. He turns the key, and the engine whirs and comes to life.

"Hop on!" Andy says, getting on the scooter himself.

Rebecca jumps up behind him. She puts her arms around his waist and squeezes him so tightly that Doris is almost flattened between them.

Andy revs up the engine and turns the scooter around. In the movement, the glare from the headlight sweeps across the clearing, and Rebecca gets another glimpse of the creature, who's already halfway back to its feet. It clutches its side as it stares at them in a wordless sneer.

Then, it's gone, and the scooter is bumping through the forest, and Rebecca tries her best not to fall off.

***

It feels like forever before they finally reach the road.

Andy is pumped up on the adrenaline still coursing through him. He barely felt any pain when he collided with the creature, even though he went flying head over heels. He'll probably find a host of bruises all over his body later, though, but for now he only feels exultant.

Rebecca is squeezing him tightly, and he still can't believe it's really her—that he really found her!

She doesn't really look like herself, though. She has lost some weight, and there are dark patches under her eyes. Also, her hair has been dyed blond for some strange reason.

But nonetheless, it *is* her.

The forest floor is very uneven, yet Andy gives it almost full throttle, biting down hard to prevent his teeth from chattering. Without the helmet it's actually easier for him to see.

Suddenly, the ground changes into asphalt, and Andy hits the brake, stopping the scooter in the middle of the road. They've come out at the exact same place he went in: a few yards from the yellow van.

"That's how I found you," Andy says over his shoulder. "When I saw the van, I knew you were in the forest somewhere."

"We have to get away from here, Andy," Rebecca says in his ear. "It's going to follow us."

"I know," Andy says, getting off the scooter and putting it on the stand. "But we need a head start."

He goes to the van, kneels down and studies the tire. He finds the valve and tries twisting it. With a little effort, he manages to loosen it, and the valve gives off a hissing as it lets out the air.

Andy makes sure the tire is completely flat before he runs back to the scooter. He notices Rebecca eyeing him with something close to awe, and he feels a wild sense of pride. He jumps up and revs the engine.

"Right, hold on."

They speed along the road headed for town. Andy can feel how Rebecca keeps turning to look back.

"I think it might have gotten hurt when I hit it," Andy says. "Maybe it doesn't have the strength to take up pursuit."

"I wouldn't count on it," Rebecca says grimly, adding: "It's not human."

"I know," Andy says.

Rebecca is silent for a few seconds, then she asks: "How do you know?"

"From a book," Andy says. "It's a long story, but I think it's a wendigo."

"A what-now?"

"A wendigo. It's a monster from old stories, like vampires and stuff like that. It's—" Andy feels something move against his back. "What's that?" he asks, looking back.

"It's just Doris. It's a puppy I brought with me from the creature's house."

"Oh, okay."

They drive for some time without speaking. Andy feels Rebecca looking back a few more times, then she stops. As they get out of the forest and the shadows, the moon and stars light up the open landscape around them.

"I didn't think anyone would come for me," she suddenly says in his ear. Andy can tell she's almost crying. "That's why I ran. I thought you had all given up on me."

"I didn't give up on you," Andy says firmly. "Never."

"Then why didn't the police come for me?"

"They said there was nothing more they could do. And Mom and Dad, well … they believed it, I guess.

But I didn't. I knew we could still find you and get you home."

"Is that why you came alone? On Cindy's scooter?"

"Yeah. Mom and Dad don't even know I'm gone." He breaks into laughter. "Imagine their faces when we show up!"

Rebecca is quiet a little while. "How did you figure out where I was?"

Andy begins explaining, and once he starts, the whole story comes out. Everything from the book to the woodpeckers to New Mom to *Anatomy of the Human Eye*. He even tells about Lisa.

Rebecca listens while he talks. Andy can't recall she's ever listened for so long without interrupting him.

When he's finished, she simply says: "So, ghosts are real then."

"I guess so. At least this one is." Andy can feel Rebecca's arms tremble. "Are you cold?"

"Yes, very."

"It's only ten more minutes to town. Hang on a little longer, Becca. Can you do that?"

Andy expects her to scoff and says something like: "What do you think?" or "Of course I can, I'm not a baby." That's what the old Rebecca would have said.

Instead, she answers meekly: "Okay."

Andy feels a stab in his heart. What was it the wendigo did when it caught someone? It broke down the person's mind and spirit, sucked the life force out of them, until they weren't even a human anymore.

Andy really hopes the wendigo didn't suck too much life force out of Rebecca. He really hopes she's still Rebecca.

The sky has started to lighten, and the moon and stars have lost some of their shine, when they finally see the town up ahead. The night is turning into morning, and very soon the traffic will set in.

They have just passed the town limit, when the scooter gives a jolt.

Andy looks to the dashboard. A red light next to the fuel-indicator is blinking.

"Oh, crap."

"What is it?"

"It's out of gas."

The scooter jerks again and loses speed. Andy pulls onto the sidewalk just as the engine dies and they come to a halt.

"We have to walk the rest of the way," Andy says, putting the scooter on the stand, before helping Rebecca down. It's only now he notices she's barefooted. "Where are your shoes?"

"I had to leave them," she simply says, cupping the bundle on her stomach.

"You want me to carry you?"

"No, that's okay."

They begin walking down the sidewalk. It feels unreal to Andy, strolling alongside Rebecca again. She limps a little.

"So, what was its name?" she asks, glancing at Andy.

"The wendigo?"

"Yes, you said you knew right away when Regan found the name."

"Here, let me show you ..." Andy finds his phone and types in the name.

Rebecca reads the name, then frowns. "What a strange name."

"I know. But try to sound it out."

Rebecca does so. "Ambroos van de Goor ..." At first, she doesn't seem to get it. Then she squints her eyes and repeats it. "Van de Goor ... it sounds a lot like 'wendigo.'"

"Exactly!" Andy says, smiling. "I guess it made up its own name, trying to pass off as a human being. It must have had a social security number and everything, since it could take a book from the library."

"Maybe it was a human being once," Rebecca says, her tone distant, as Andy can tell she's thinking back on something.

"Why do you say that?"

"There was a picture of a girl at its house."

"A girl? What girl?"

Rebecca shakes her head. "I don't know. Someone the crea ... the wendigo loved. I'm pretty sure she's dead now."

Rebecca falls silent, and her eyes seem to stare at nothing as they walk on.

Andy glances at her once more. "Did it ... did it hurt you, Becca?"

Rebecca keeps looking straight ahead. "It burned the soles of my feet with a cigar and dripped something in my eyes which made them sting."

"That monster," Andy whispers, feeling shivers run down his spine, and anger well up in his chest. He looks at Rebecca again. "I can tell your eyes are kind of pink—can you see all right?"

"Not really. Everything is blurry."

"I'm sure it'll pass."

"It did so in the beginning, but not anymore."

Andy clenches his fist. He feels so bad for Rebecca, but he also feels furious at the police, at Mom and Dad, at himself, at everyone for not finding Rebecca sooner.

Now she might have permanent eye damage due to what the wendigo did to her.

"What about your hair?" he asks.

"It made me dye it."

"Did it do anything else to hurt you?"

Rebecca is silent for a long time.

Andy begins to think she won't answer.

Then, she says very quietly: "It kept calling me Alice."

"Alice?"

"Yes. I told it over and over my name was Rebecca, but it just kept calling me Alice."

"Why would it do that?" Andy asks, frowning.

Rebecca keeps looking forward as she says blankly: "It wanted me to forget my real name."

Andy notices her face tremble slightly as they walk on. He can see thoughts going through her head, and he can tell how badly it has affected Rebecca's mind being trapped by the wendigo for that long.

"But you didn't forget your name, did you?" he asks tentatively.

Rebecca hesitates just a second, then shakes her head. "No. I wrote it down."

"Good. That was clever."

"It also ... it also killed an old man," Rebecca goes on. "I saw it."

Andy swallows. "Who was he?"

"I don't know, some guy who came by looking for directions. It beat him to death with a shovel."

"Holy crap," Andy mutters, then thinks of something to change the subject: "How did it catch you? I mean, how did it get you into the van in the first place? 'Cause you *were* in the van, right? When I heard you knocking from the inside?"

Rebecca nods. "I was, and I saw you through the crack between the doors."

"How did it happen? Did it just scoop you up outside the library?"

"No, I went to the park."

"The park? Why?"

"I wanted to give you a scare. You know, because I was mad at you."

Andy shakes his head. "Well, that's just typical you, Becca. You should have stayed and waited for me like I told you."

He sounds a lot more accusatory than he meant to, and he immediately regrets saying it.

"I know," Rebecca says, breaking into sudden tears. "I know I should have waited, and I'm sorry, Andy, I'm so sorry!"

She stops, turns and puts her arms around him.

Andy is so surprised to see Rebecca cry, at first, he just stands there, dumbfounded, as she holds him in an awkward, sideways embrace.

Then, he puts his arms around her. "It's okay, Becca."

"It's not okay, it's my fault, I should have stayed!"

"No, it's *my* fault," Andy says, tears coming to his eyes now. It breaks his heart to hear Rebecca blame herself, but at the same time, it makes his own guilt easier to bear, and it enables him to say what has been on his lips ever since he saw Rebecca again: "I'm so sorry I left you, Becca. If I had never gone into the library that day, none of this would have happened. Can you ever forgive me?"

Rebecca tries to say something, but it drowns in sobs, and Andy just holds her as she cries uncontrollably into his chest. He hears someone whisper soothingly, and realizes after a while it's himself.

"It's okay. It's okay now. You're back. You're safe now. It's okay."

Finally, Rebecca's crying dies out, and she wipes her eyes. "I'm so glad you came for me, Andy."

Andy smiles, discretely blinking away a single tear. "I'm just sorry I couldn't have been there earlier. You've been really brave."

Rebecca looks down. "My feet are really hurting. I think I'd like you to carry me now."

"Sure, hop on the Andy Express."

That's what he used to call it when Rebecca was very little and wanted a piggy-back ride.

He kneels down, allowing Rebecca to climb onto his back. They haven't done this for years, but luckily, Rebecca isn't very heavy.

Andy begins walking, and they move through the still sleeping town, the streetlights casting their yellow glare from above.

"What do you think will happen to it?" Rebecca asks. "The creature, I mean."

"It'll be arrested for sure. As soon as I give its name to the police, they'll track it down and put it in jail. Or maybe they'll even kill it once they find out it's not human."

"Good," Rebecca just says.

"Look, we're almost at the library," Andy says, nodding ahead. "Ain't that weird? It was right down there we spoke and saw each other last, right before you disappeared."

Rebecca doesn't answer right away. Instead, she says: "Do you hear something?" A note of tension in her voice.

Andy stops and listens. He *does* hear something. It's a rumbling *ga-dunk, ga-dunk, ga-dunk*, growing both louder and faster, and it's coming from behind.

Andy turns and feels his stomach drop.

The yellow van is approaching fast, tilted to one side and flapping away on the flat tire, but still going very fast.

"Oh, shit!" Andy exclaims. "It's coming!"

"*We've got to run, Andy!*" Rebecca screams into his ear—quite unnecessarily, as Andy has already spun back around and is running as fast as he can, Rebecca bopping up and down on his back.

The street ahead is empty; there are no side streets, no driveways or other places to turn, and no people to call for help, either. Andy can't do anything but run straight ahead.

Rebecca shouts something, but Andy doesn't register the words. He can hear the yellow van gaining on them fast. He darts a look back and sees it now driving with two of the wheels up on the sidewalk. Behind the dark windshield he glimpses the pale face staring out at them, and he realizes with a jolt of cold fear that the wendigo is going to run them both over.

There is still nowhere to get off the street, only fences and hedges, but they have almost reached the library now, and if he can just make it another twenty feet or so, he can cross the street and run into safety behind the bike rack on the parking lot. But the sound of the van is so close now, Andy has no choice but to make a dash for it, so he turns out onto the street. The turn proves a little too sharp, however, and the already spent muscles in his legs give way, causing him to stumble and fall to his knees with a painful thud.

"*Watch out, Andy!*" Rebecca screams.

Andy looks up at the last moment, just as the sharp headlights swallow up everything in his visual field. It's too late to lunge forward, too late to go back, too late to get out of the way.

Andy does the only thing he can; he throws Rebecca off.

Then the van hits him.

***

Rebecca lands halfway onto the sidewalk, scraping her palm and hurting her knees, but hardly noticing either.

She immediately turns her head to look back at Andy. And she sees it all happen. Just like the time the creature killed the old man, everything turns to slow-motion.

The van isn't going quite as fast as it did, but it's still moving at a considerable speed when it collides with Andy and sends him flying across the asphalt.

He rolls over several times before coming to rest on his back, his legs and arms splayed out to the sides, his head tilted sideways so Rebecca can see his face. His glasses are hanging from one ear, his eyes are closed and his mouth is open. A dark stream of blood runs from the corner of his mouth. She stares at his chest. It's not moving.

He's dead, a thought tells her from somewhere very far off. *Andy is dead.*

She can't take her eyes off Andy's face; everything else disappears around her. She just stares at him, willing him to open his eyes, to begin breathing again, to make him lift his head or move a hand. But Andy just lies completely still, not breathing, not opening his eyes and not moving anything.

Something stirs under Rebecca's shirt, and she vaguely remembers the puppy.

Somewhere nearby she hears the sound of a car door opening, slow steps coming across the sidewalk. The tall, gangly, naked figure of the creature comes into view. It stops next to Andy. Stands there for a moment, staring at him, in the middle of the empty street.

Leave him be, Rebecca thinks, trying to turn it into words, but failing.

The creature bends over, scoops Andy up and carries him back to the van.

Rebecca's thoughts are broken. She feels distant and dizzy, black dots are dancing in front of her eyes and she blinks to try and keep herself awake, but it's a losing battle.

Call for help, she thinks, but still can't find her voice. She couldn't call out any more than she could take flight. She can't even get up or turn her head. Out of the corner of her eye, she sees how the creature opens the back doors of the van and puts Andy's body inside.

When the creature comes to take her, she can't do anything to fight it. She feels the cold hands grab her and lift her up, and then the blackness comes rolling in, rushing over her like a wave of tar, drowning out the last of her conscious mind.

Rebecca faints.

***

Andy wakes up very gradually from a very deep sleep.

At least, so it feels.

But something is different. He feels so much lighter, like his body has turned into warm air. And when he opens his eyes, something is different with his vision as well.

He stares at a dim sky with faint stars overhead, but everything appears like he's looking through a window wet from rain.

He sits up, realizing where he is, but remembering nothing about how he got here. He's outside the library, in the middle of the street, and it's either late evening or very early morning, judging from the dark skies overhead.

Even though he recognizes the surroundings, they look simultaneously very strange, somehow more fresh and vibrant, almost like he never really saw them before. Everything is shimmering slightly, the road, the houses, the library, even the air around him.

"*I must be dreaming*," Andy thinks—or maybe he actually speaks it out loud, because the words seem to reverberate around him for a few seconds, before drifting away.

He gets to his feet, amazed at how easily he can move—it's like he simply forms the intention to move, and then it happens without any effort on his part. He feels weightless, like he is mostly part of the air around him, like he isn't really there.

"*I'm not really here*," he think-speaks, listening to the words, trying to understand them.

He looks at his hands, turning them over slowly, studying them as they flicker and blur in front of his eyes, the edges constantly trying to bleed out into the air, as though his body is reacting to an unfelt breeze, almost taking off.

"What a strange dream this is."

The words float around him for a while, then dissipate.

Then, new words appear: "*It's not a dream.*"

Andy turns around—at least he thinks he does, but it feels more like the world around him revolves, spinning like a giant disc—until he faces the library, from where the new words seemed to come. The darkish building is swimming before his eyes, and a bright figure comes floating towards him, touching the ground but not really walking. It's a girl, wearing blue, her long, dark auburn hair floating around her head and constantly moving as though she were underwater.

Andy tries to focus, tries to look at the girl more closely, but discerning her features is like pinning down a piece of soap you dropped in the sink.

"*Who are you?*" he asks the figure with his mind.

"*I'm Lisa,*" the girl replies, hovering in front of him. "*You remember me, Andy.*"

That's not true, Andy doesn't remember anything. He didn't even remember his own name until the girl mentioned it just now.

But then he does remember, very vaguely.

He remembers having talked to a girl named Lisa sometime very long ago in a distant place far from here.

"*I do remember you*," he says in his head and out loud. "*You're the dead girl at the library.*" Suddenly, more memories return, and they turn into speech. "*You died right here outside the library.*"

"*So did you*," the girl tells him, her voice betraying no emotion. It's funny how the words sound, like birdsong in the air. "*We're both dead.*"

Andy bursts into laughter. Somehow, that seems like the appropriate response to someone telling you you're dead. Of course he isn't dead. Dead people don't speak, don't hear, don't experience anything.

"*I'm not dead*," he tells the girl. "*I'm just dreaming. You're in my dream.*"

"*Look closer, Andy.*"

Andy stops smiling and looks closer. He notices something behind the girl, something in the sky above the library. The background is changing, turning into something else. It's a bright purple sky with foreign planets drifting around; then it shifts again into something else. This time it's a desert, and then it's an old castle, then an open flowery field, an active volcano spewing lava, a battlefield strewn with dead soldiers, a schoolyard full of children.

The sky keeps changing, the scenes bleeding into each other, all of them trying to appear at the same time, and Andy notices he can call forth new ones, open up the ones he wants to look at. And he recognizes some of them.

There is the Shire.

There is Hogwarts.

There is the space station of Solaris.

He feels something different with each reality appearing in front of him, just like he did when he read the books.

"*Worlds behind worlds*," he speaks, not really sure where the words come from or what they mean.

The girl in front of him doesn't say anything; she simply hovers there.

Andy forces himself to look away from the shifting universes above and fixes instead on the girl's face, trying hard to see her for real.

He remembers her now, at least partly. She's Lisa Labowski, the dead girl who spoke to him through the books. And he desperately wants to see her face. But her features keep drifting in and out, bleeding and flickering. He can only make out the auburn hair, the pale skin and the darkness around the eyes.

For some strange reason, Andy feels a pang of fear. He doesn't understand; why would the girl scare him? She is his friend, he knows that.

"*I wanted you to come in here so badly, Andy,*" she says. "*I wanted to be with you forever.*"

Lisa moves then, or maybe it's the surroundings spinning again; either way she floats around him, disappearing from sight, speaking again from behind him.

"*I've been alone for so long. I just wanted someone to talk to.*"

Andy is stricken by a deep sadness. He wants to help Lisa, wants to make her happy again. He doesn't want her to be all alone.

"*I'm here now,*" he tells her, turning around, but not seeing the girl. "*You're not alone anymore. I'll stay here with you.*"

"*Help her, Andy,*" a voice inside his mind tells him. "*She needs you.*"

Andy turns and turns, trying to find Lisa, but he can't. The fear comes creeping back. "*I want to help you,*" he says out loud. "*I want to help you, Lisa! Where are you?*"

No answer from the girl.

Andy is alone in the street.

The universes above the library are still changing, displaying one marvelous scenery after the other, offering so many different moods and feelings, Andy's eyes are drawn to them.

"*I'll stay here with you,*" he whispers. "*We'll live inside the books together.*"

He walks towards the library, moving his legs but not really using them. The glass doors of the library open, a warm orange glow welcoming him, dispelling the darkness around him and the fear in his heart.

"*Help her, Andy!*" the voice tells him again.

"*I will,*" Andy whispers and is about to step through the open doors and into the glow.

Then suddenly, the dead girl is right in front of him, and for a split second, he sees her face clearly, and he can tell she really is very dead.

Andy recoils, the fear overwhelming him for a moment, and he wants to flee, wants to throw himself into the library and the many worlds awaiting him, but Lisa Labowski blocks the way, and she's suddenly grown very tall.

"***Help her, Andy!***" she bellows, her voice shaking the world. "***She needs you!***"

"*I can't!*" Andy cries out, covering his ears and trying to look away. "*I can't help her! I'm scared!*"

He doesn't want to look, but he can't help it, and he sees the dead girl in front of him. She's no longer towering over him, but has shrunk to her regular size again, the size of a thirteen-year-old girl.

"*We're all scared, Andy*," Lisa tells him, her voice calm and dreamlike once more. "*But the things we're scared of are never real. Not really. They're just stories.*"

The girl looks up, and Andy follows her gaze. The sky above them has stopped shifting and has come to rest showing a single scenery. It's a dark forest, four men clad in old-fashioned hunter's uniforms walking between the tall trees.

"*The wendigo*," Andy says. "*The wendigo is real. It took Rebecca.*"

"*Then you take her back*," Lisa tells him, her voice rising again as she moves closer, very close, close enough for Andy to feel a breath of cold air on his face.

He shuts his eyes, waiting for Lisa to shout at him.

But instead, he hears her voice very gently inside his mind: "*It's okay to be scared, Andy. You simply go on anyway.*"

And when Andy opens his eyes again, Lisa is floating backwards towards the library, the doors opening once more, the tempting orange glow surrounding her like a halo.

"*Don't go,*" Andy says, almost crying now. "*Don't go, Lisa.*"

"*Go, Andy,*" Lisa tells him. "*Help her.*"

Then she sinks into the orange light and it swallows her up as the glass doors slide shut.

Andy looks up at the sky still portraying the scene from *The Wendigo*. The men have now set up camp, and darkness is falling upon the forest. Andy remembers the story; he knows what comes next: very soon, the wendigo will come creeping and take one of them.

"*Not this time,*" Andy says, and he turns away from the library and the breathtaking scenery.

***

Rebecca wakes up with only a vague notion of being inside a car. She can hear the rumble of the engine and the *ga-dunks* from the flat tire below. She can also smell motor oil and the stink of the creature.

She has no idea how long she has been out, but her head feels heavy. There is almost complete darkness around her, but Rebecca is used to not seeing well, so she instinctively feels around with her hands. She finds someone lying next to her and she lets out a gasp as her memory comes rushing back.

"Andy!"

She bends over, finds his face and puts her ear close to his mouth, praying to hear him breathing. But he doesn't. There is no air flowing in or out of Andy's slightly open mouth.

"Oh, Andy," Rebecca moans, starting to cry. "Oh, Andy, wake up! Please, wake up!"

She hugs him and shakes him, begs him again and again to wake up.

And then, suddenly, he does. A single, faint breath.

Rebecca stares at him, sensing only a dim, blurry outline of his face.

"Not this time," Andy whispers almost inaudibly. Then he takes another breath. He doesn't open his eyes, though, and he's still not conscious, but Rebecca doesn't care; her heart is almost bursting with joy at the thought of Andy being alive!

She hugs him again, gentler this time, so as to not hurt him. She just lies there next to him for several minutes, listening to him breathe, feeling his chest rise and fall, thanking God and heaven that Andy didn't die when the creature ran him over, that she isn't left alone with the creature.

Then she hears something sniffing next to her ear, and she reaches out and feels Doris. She pulls the puppy into her arms and hugs her, too.

She is so exhausted from being afraid that she begins to nod off, the soft rocking of the car almost lulling her to sleep, when it suddenly stops.

Rebecca hears the rattling of the metal chain and knows exactly where they are. The van rolls on into the courtyard, and the creature shuts off the engine, then gets out to close the gate again.

Rebecca stares at the crack where a faint daylight is coming in, feeling a dreadful sense of déjà vu from the day the creature caught her the first time.

This time around, it also opens the back doors to the car, but it makes no attempt to hide. Its boney, still-naked frame is visible in the opening against the now dimly lit horizon. Before Rebecca has time to react, the creature reaches in and grabs Andy's ankle.

"*No!*" she cries, as the creature pulls Andy towards it.

Rebecca throws herself on top of Andy, but the creature shoves her aside like it would an annoying fly over its dinner, and she bangs against the inside of the car, knocking the wind out of her.

Somewhere, Doris begins to bark angrily.

"Stop!" Rebecca croaks, fighting to get her breath back. "Let go of him!"

The creature doesn't listen. It lifts Andy up like he weighs no more than a doll, then slings him over its shoulder like a bag of potatoes. Andy gives off a moan.

Rebecca scrambles to her feet and throws herself at the open doors, but the creature steps aside, and Rebecca falls onto the gravel.

"Come back!" she screams, her lungs working again. "*Don't you hurt him!*"

She sees the creature walk towards the garden, still carrying Andy, and she jumps up and runs after, ignoring the pain from her feet.

She catches up with the creature and grabs Andy's leg, but only manages to pull off his shoe. She grabs hold of Andy's pantleg, but the creature is way too strong and simply drags Rebecca along as it strides across the wet lawn. Instead, Rebecca begins punching the creature in the back.

"*Stop it! Put him down!*"

The creature ignores her. It carries Andy to the place behind the hedge, then drops him on the ground. Andy moans again and rolls onto his back. He mutters something and looks like he's trying to open his eyes.

Rebecca throws herself down next to him, hardly noticing the creature stepping back.

"Andy?" she says, her voice trembling. "Are you okay? Can you hear me?"

"Becca?" he murmurs, sounding very weak. He opens his eyes halfway but can't seem to get them to focus. "Where ... are ... we?"

"We're back at the—"

Rebecca stops talking as she notices the creature coming back into view from the side. She turns her head and gasps.

It only stepped away to pick up the shovel, which was lying a few feet away. Even in the dim morning light, Rebecca can see the blade shining as the creature raises the shovel high above its head.

"*Nooo!*" Rebecca screams, and without thinking, she throws herself over Andy, readying herself for an intense pain in the back as the shovel will probably shatter her spine—but the pain never comes, because the shovel never comes.

Rebecca glances up and sees the creature hesitate, the shovel still halfway raised.

"Move aside," it whispers hoarsely.

"N ... no," Rebecca says, shaking her head defiantly. "You can't hurt him."

"Move aside."

"No!"

The creature bends over, grabs her by the neck and pulls her aside. But Rebecca scrambles back as soon as it lets go and raises the shovel again, once more covering Andy with her body.

"Becca," Andy mutters dully below her, apparently not really aware of what's going on.

"Don't worry," Rebecca tells him, her voice trembling. "I'll make sure it doesn't—"

She's interrupted as the creature grabs her again and flings her away. This time, she rolls around a couple of times, then jumps back up and half crawls, half lunges herself over Andy once more, a split-second before the creature can let the shovel fall.

It gives off an irritated grunt, then throws down the shovel.

Rebecca feels a brief, intense rush of victory.

It gave up!

But then the creature grabs her hard by the arm and drags her back towards the house. And Rebecca realizes what it intends: it'll lock her in the house, then go back outside to kill Andy with no more interruptions. Then it'll use the shovel to bury him next to the bones of Alice and the still-fresh grave of the old, British guy.

Rebecca begins fighting to get free, heaving and kicking, but the creature is simply too strong. It's like being dragged behind a car. She strikes it, kicks it, even tries to bite its hand, but it just pushes her head back using the free hand. All the while, it pulls her around the house, across the courtyard, into the house and up the stairs.

Rebecca is very close to panic now. If the creature locks her in the room, it's over; there will be nothing more she can do.

She begins begging. "Stop! Please, stop! I'll do anything! I'll never run away ever again; I promise! Just please don't hurt him!"

No reaction from the creature; it just drags her down the hallway.

"I'll ... I'll stay here!" Rebecca says. "I'll stay here for the rest of my life! I swear!"

Still, no reaction. They reach the room, and the creature opens the door.

Rebecca searches frantically for the right words. And then, just as the creature shoves her inside the room and is about to close the door, they come to her.

"I'll be Alice!"

It's like a magic formula.

The creature freezes, the door halfway closed. It turns its head slowly to look at her.

Rebecca breathes quickly, blinking in an effort to see more clearly. Through a veil of tears she can almost make out the expression on the creature's face. It stares at her, waiting.

"I'll be Alice," she repeats. "Forever. If you just don't hurt him."

The creature looks at her for several seconds. The only sound is Rebecca's own, ragged breathing.

"Alice?" it finally whispers, a question in the word.

"Yes," Rebecca whispers back, nodding. "Yes, I'm Alice from now on."

Then something incredible happens. The creature simply turns and walks away, leaving the door open. Rebecca slips back out of the room, seeing the creature walk downstairs. She follows it. It goes outside and back to the garden.

The morning is lighter now, the sun is peeking over the horizon, coloring the sky orange and purple.

Rebecca follows the creature back to the place where they left Andy. Her brother has fainted again, lying on his side. Rebecca is ready to jump in and protect him again, if the creature still wants to hurt him. But somehow, she knows it won't.

It simply bends down, picks up Andy and walks back to the house. Rebecca follows at its heels, as it carries Andy upstairs and into the room next to Rebecca's. It puts him down on the bed and turns to leave.

As it passes by her, it briefly reaches out and strokes her cheek, the touch surprisingly tender. Rebecca is completely unprepared for the gesture and it's all she can do not to recoil.

"Alice," the creature whispers, and the warmth in the voice is the most terrifying thing Rebecca has ever heard.

Then it walks out of the room and leaves Andy and Rebecca alone.

DAY 113

Rebecca opens the door very carefully and slips inside the room.

Her eyesight still hasn't recovered from the last treatment, and her feet are still sore from the fresh burn wounds.

To her surprise, the creature didn't punish her particularly bad this time, despite her attempt to run away. Probably because she made a promise to be obedient from now on. To be Alice.

Andy's room is bathed in a golden evening light streaming in through the drawn curtains. Her eyes as usual go to the bed in the corner, and to her surprise, she sees Andy sitting up this time, wearing his glasses.

"It's just me," she says, closing the door softly behind her. "I have your dinner." She brings him the plate.

Andy takes it, but just puts it on his lap. "I'm not hungry," he mutters.

"You need to begin eating."

"I can't. My head hurts too bad."

"What about the pills? Are they still not helping?"

"Not really, no."

Rebecca sits down next to Andy on the bed. It's weird; part of her knows she has plenty of reason to be scared and worried, and yet she feels a lot safer now that Andy is here. He hasn't been able to do anything but lie in bed, sleep, throw up and complain about the headache and his busted-up leg, but just having him here is a great comfort.

She knows, of course, that even if Andy had been in fine shape and not hurt at all, he still wouldn't have been able to help her escape. She has come to terms with that. She is Alice now—in a way, at least—and her last chance of getting away is gone, which means she will likely spend the rest of her life here. Still, the thought is much more bearable with Andy around. At least she won't be alone anymore.

"How are your feet coming along?" Andy asks.

"Better. They still hurt, but I can walk again."

She made sure to bite down hard and not scream during the latest burning, because she knew Andy was in the room next to her and could hear if she cried out. She didn't want to worry him.

It's amazing how quickly things have gone back to normal. The creature has taken up its usual routines and acts like nothing really happened.

The only exception, really, is that Andy is here now. The creature doesn't speak to him and never enters his room. It's obvious it doesn't care about him, but it doesn't stop Rebecca in caring for him, either.

So, she brings him food and helps him to the bathroom. She also asked the creature for painkillers to help with Andy's headache—she did it with no real hope of getting it, she just couldn't take Andy's painful writhing anymore—but to her utter astonishment, the creature actually brought her some.

There is one other thing that's different now: the way the creature acts around Rebecca. It looks at her differently. At first, she couldn't figure out what it meant, but now she gets it.

There is affection in its voice now. Warmth.

It touches her now and then, always briefly, always when she doesn't expect it. Rebecca still has to control herself so as to not draw back—she fears it'll enrage the creature if it sees her flinching away from its touch.

But even though the creature seems to have warm feelings towards her now that she has agreed to become its Alice, she can still feel how closely it watches her. How those black eyes follow her around whenever her back is turned. How it keeps an eye on her every time she takes Doris outside to pee. How it checks her room discretely whenever it comes to say good night.

Rebecca holds no illusions: The love the creature shows her is conditional. It'll only treat her this way as long as she stays obedient. Just below the surface, a constant, unspoken threat lurks.

Rebecca is pretty sure this is her very last chance. If the creature catches her doing anything she shouldn't, there will be no more leeway. It'll kill both her and Andy and go find a new Alice.

"How is your leg?" Rebecca asks.

Andy bends his knee. "It doesn't hurt as bad anymore. I don't think it's broken after all. It probably just got busted pretty bad when the van hit me."

There are still black and blue bruises running up Andy's calf and thigh, but they are lessening day by day.

If the leg isn't broken, that's great news, and it means Andy will be able to walk again. Unfortunately, his head was less lucky. Rebecca can still recall seeing it bounce off of the asphalt as Andy fell. Already the following morning, he had a huge, red swelling behind his left ear and he started throwing up all the time.

Rebecca had a concussion once. She was very young. It was the first time her family went skiing. An older boy on a snowboard knocked her to the ground, and she hit her head pretty badly. She's pretty sure Andy now has a concussion and she remembers how painful it is.

A low scraping from the door. Rebecca goes to open it, and Doris slips inside, runs across the floor and jumps up into bed.

The dog has also changed since they tried to run away. Now, it'll only be with Andy and Rebecca, and it growls whenever it sees the creature.

Andy picks a piece of bacon out and offers it to the dog. Doris swallows it eagerly.

"We've got to make a plan," Andy says, looking at Doris.

Rebecca sighs. "We've been over this, Andy. You can't even walk yet."

Andy doesn't seem to hear her. "Does it go to work?"

"Work?"

"Yeah, I mean, does it ever leave for work?"

"I ... don't think so."

"But it leaves sometimes, right? It has to. It needs to buy stuff, groceries and stuff."

Rebecca considers it for a moment. "I think it goes to town once a week, maybe, but you know it locks the door before it leaves. And it's hard to tell how long it'll be gone; sometimes, it's only half an hour."

Andy gives Doris another piece of bacon. "So it knows about the hole in the roof now, right? It knows how you got out?"

"Yes. It sealed the roof."

"That means we need to find another way out."

Andy is still looking at the dog, frowning slightly as he concentrates.

It's the first time Rebecca has seen him act like his old self. In one way, it makes her happy—but in another, it's also heartbreaking, because he looks so determined, so confident. He clearly hasn't accepted the reality of their situation yet.

"The windows up here are too high, and there is nothing to climb down," he goes on. "So either we need to pick the lock to the door, or we have to smash a window downstairs."

"Andy, listen. I really don't think—"

"It'll probably take too long to pick the lock," Andy interrupts. "So I think the better choice is busting a window. Is there anything inside the house heavy enough to smash a window?"

He finally looks at her.

Rebecca looks back at him. Even despite her blurry vision, she can tell how adamant he looks.

"Andy," she says softly. "It's not going to work, no matter how we do it."

Andy's frown grows deeper. "Why not?"

"It won't allow us to flee again. It just won't."

"Of course it won't allow it, but it's not up to it. We decide, Rebecca. We'll find a way to—"

"No, Andy. That's not what I mean. I told you this already. It watches me now. Everything I do. It's always nearby, listening. Like it's just waiting to see if I try anything again."

"Right," Andy says, closing his eyes and rubbing his forehead as the pain obviously comes back. "Then we just need to ... need to be more clever ... we have to outsmart it."

"But if we fail ..." Rebecca takes his hand and lowers her voice. "If it catches us again, Andy ... it will kill us. This time, it won't be merciful."

"Merciful," Andy repeats, almost sneering. "You think it's been merciful keeping you here like a prisoner? Was it merciful of it to burn your feet and damage your eyes?"

"No, but—"

"So what do you think, we should just stay here for the rest of our lives?"

"Maybe ... maybe someone will come by and find us."

"Like who? Some random stranger who the creature will just kill and bury? That's not going to work."

"Then maybe the police."

"The police," Andy scoffs. "They've probably already given up. They couldn't find you, remember? And even if they are still looking for me, how would they find me? They have absolutely nothing to go on. When you disappeared, at least they had a witness—me!" Andy stabs himself in the chest with a thumb. "The problem is, they didn't listen to me! And now, they have nothing—*nothing*, Becca!"

Rebecca doesn't know what to say. Andy is too upset to listen to reason, and she doesn't want to argue with him, so she gets up and is about to leave the room, when Andy grabs her wrist and pulls her back down.

"We need to run away," he says, talking low, his face close enough for her to smell puke on his breath. "As soon as possible. We can't give up. And we can't count on help from the outside. You did it once, and you can do it again. I'll figure out the plan, but I'm going to need your help. You know this place and you know the wendigo. You need to come up with an idea for a way to escape—however small it seems. When you got something, come to me, and I'll do the rest. All right? All right, Becca?"

Rebecca breathes deeply a few times. Andy looks so desperate; she can't bring herself to say what she thinks. That it's no use. That they'll never find a way.

That trying to flee is suicide. And that she's not going to risk their lives.

So, instead, she forces a smile, then lies to him: "All right, Andy. I'll come up with an idea. Just give me time."

DAY 114

"Hello?"

Regan blinks and comes to. For a moment, she has no idea where she is, and she looks around to find herself behind the desk at the library. On the other side is a girl around seventeen, looking at her with mild bemusement.

"I'm sorry," Regan mutters and smiles at the girl. "I guess I just drifted off for a moment. What did you say?"

The girl holds out a book. "I found this book ..."

"Sure, you want to borrow it? Just run it through the terminal over there. Do you need me to show you how—"

"I don't want to borrow it," the girl says. "It was just lying around on the floor, so I didn't really know what to do with it."

"Oh, okay. Thank you," Regan says, taking the book.

The girl goes back to browsing the shelves.

Regan stares at the girl for a while without really seeing her; she's already lost in thoughts again.

She can't stop thinking about Andy. He's been on her mind ever since they officially reported him missing yesterday—no, even before that. Ever since the first day Andy didn't show up at the library. Of course, it's happened before that he skipped a day or two, but Regan still had a weird feeling this time. A feeling that something bad had happened.

And when Andy didn't come the day after that, her feeling grew stronger.

And by the third day, when they began talking about him in the news, she already knew her feeling was right.

She almost went to the police; had actually gone to her car twice to drive down to the station, but both times she changed her mind. Because what could she tell them? That she had had a hunch Andy would disappear? How would that help them find him?

She had no idea where Andy was now or what had happened to him. And the police seemed to have no idea either. Their spokesperson on television kept uttering phrases like "ongoing investigation" and "still looking into leads" and "keeping all possibilities open"—and that was exactly what they kept saying when Andy's sister went missing in the spring.

It's so terrible. First Rebecca and now Andy.

Rumors were already circulating town. She heard a couple of old ladies talk together just yesterday, right here at the library. They were certain that Andy had run away from home because he was still devastated over losing his sister.

Regan knows better. While it's true Andy was still sad about the loss of Rebecca, he wasn't devastated. In fact, he had seemed very eager the last time she spoke with him. Almost like he ... like he *what*?

"It's got something to do with Rebecca."

Regan has played their last conversation over and over in her mind. Something about it keeps bugging her. Something her brain tries to tell her. It keeps pulling her back to that one thing Andy said.

"It's got something to do with Rebecca."

The glass doors open as an older gentleman enters the library, the sound pulling Regan out of her thoughts once more, and she decides to get on with what she was actually doing: putting back returned books.

Perhaps she needs to stop brooding about it. There's nothing she can do anyway. The thought that Andy is missing makes her deeply sad, and what good is that to anybody? She can't go on like this, spending the days lost in gloomy thoughts, barely able to function.

She takes a deep breath and goes to the book cart, when she notices the book still in her hand—the one the girl handed her. She completely forgot about it.

"It was just lying around on the floor."

Regan stares at the faded, anonymous leather cover. She knows this book. It's *The Wendigo*—the one Andy spoke so highly about. She's seen him sit around the library reading it a ton of times.

The funny thing is ... she also picked it up from off the ground yesterday, when she found it lying in front of the shelves, as though someone had taken it out and just dropped it.

Regan goes to row B, finds the empty slot and is just about to slide in the book, when a strange feeling comes over her. It feels almost like she can sense someone talking to her, but without any sound.

She looks around discretely to make sure no one actually did talk to her, but finds herself alone in this part of the library.

Regan bites her lip, considers for a moment, then she opens the book and leafs through the pages, skimming the text, not really sure what she's looking for.

Why was Andy so obsessed with this book? He must have read it a hundred times. Is it really that exciting?

She stops on a random page and reads a bit. The language is fluent and picturesque, and the storyline seems appealing. But it doesn't tell her anything about what fascinated Andy so much about the book. She closes it again with a sigh, puts it back and turns to go back to the cart.

She's only taken three or four steps, however, when there's a sharp thud behind her.

Regan stops and turns back around.

The book is lying on the floor. Regan stares at it.

How did that happen? I thought I put it in properly.

Apparently, she didn't. She must have spaced out again and didn't push the book all the way in. She goes back and picks it up once more, noticing her heart beating a little too fast. She puts the book back a second time, this time making sure it's all the way in.

Then, she takes a few steps back, keeping an eye on the book, like she halfway expects it to fall to the floor again. Of course, it doesn't.

Regan shakes her head. *I must be really losing it. I need to get a grip.*

She leaves row B and goes back to the cart. Just as she takes the first book, she hears it again. The thud.

Regan's heart leaps into her throat, and she needs to swallow hard to force it back down. She puts the book down and goes back to row B.

The Wendigo is once again lying flat on the floor.

She just stands there, staring at it. She doesn't really want to go near it, is almost afraid to do so.

Must be something about the cover. Maybe the leather is too slippery, or ... or maybe the shelf is sloping outwards slightly. But then why wouldn't the other books fall? It could also be something like static electricity that pushed it out ...

Regan listens to her thoughts' desperate attempt to come up with a rational explanation, while a deeper part of her knows there isn't one. That something else entirely is going on here.

She goes and picks up the book. Brings it back to the desk, places it on the table and stares at it.

What are you trying to tell me?

Andy. It has definitely got something to do with Andy. She can sense it. Sense something buzzing around just outside the reach of her mind. Like when you hear a fly but you can't see it.

"It's got something to do with Rebecca."

Why would Andy say that? What could he have meant? What was he trying to do? To find Rebecca? How could a nonfiction book about the human eye have anything to do with Andy's sister disappearing?

And then it finally hits home.

It wasn't the book Andy was interested in. It was the last person who borrowed it. And Regan helped him find it. She broke the rules because Andy asked her so urgently. Like it was absolutely crucial that he got that name.

But why? What did he need that name for? He didn't say anything, he just stared at the name for a minute, then thanked her and went back to reading *The Wendigo*. Like it wasn't a big deal after all. But now, thinking back, Regan can tell he was only playing cool so as to not draw any more attention to himself.

You clever little rascal ... what did that name tell you?

Did the person know anything about Rebecca's disappearance? That was too far a stretch. If the person really had some information about Rebecca, the police would have been here a long time ago, asking to have a look in the system. Andy is thirteen years old. Could he have unraveled a mysterious disappearance that the police had given up on? Of course not. Things like that only happened in movies. Or in books.

But the timing ...

Andy went missing that same night. Could it just be a coincidence? What if he didn't get kidnapped, and he didn't run away either; what if he went out voluntarily to look for Rebecca? What if he really believed the person behind that name she helped him find had something to do with it? And what if he was right?

It actually made sense. Except it was ludicrous.

But what if it wasn't?

What if this was a chance to find Andy—maybe the only chance there would ever be? Regan's mind is trying to tell her it's all make-believe, a shot in the dark at best, but her gut keeps insisting she's onto something.

Two girls at around Andy's age enter through the glass doors. They're wearing schoolbags, and don't even look at Regan as they pass by the desk, since they're wrapped up in a whispering conversation. Regan catches a few lines.

"Think they'll find him?"

"No. They never found his sister."

Then the girls are gone between the shelves, and Regan is left with a sinking feeling in her stomach.

She looks at the book still in her hand. The book that keeps falling to the floor on its own accord.

And she turns to the computer and begins typing.

DAY 115

Andy is at the library, and he's all alone. He has come to talk with Lisa—there's something vital he needs to tell her, although he's not really sure what exactly it is.

He finds *The Wendigo* and begins talking to the book, but Lisa doesn't answer him.

He leafs through the pages, faster and faster, back and forth, searching desperately for a line from her, but finds nothing. With rising panic he grabs another book from the shelf and looks through it, then, still finding nothing, drops it and takes a new one.

He shouts for Lisa, pleading for her to answer him, and when he looks up, he finds the shelves have grown high as towers, too high for him to even see the tops. And suddenly, the books start coming down over him, hundreds of them, thousands even, hitting him over the head, on his shoulders, and he tries to get away, but he's already up to his waist in books, and they just keep coming, hitting his head again, and it's really painful, his head is throbbing now, throbbing badly, more books hit him, and the pain is causing him nausea, and it feels like he's about to …

Andy barely has time to roll over on his side before breakfast comes bubbling up through his throat and spills down into the tub next to the bed. He pukes for a few seconds while an avalanche of pain rumbles away inside his skull.

He spits one last time, then wipes his mouth on his sleeve, which is already crusty from the many previous throw-ups. He really needs a shower; he reeks of old sweat and vomit, and his skin and his hair are all greasy.

He rolls onto his back, sighing with relief as the headache subsides. It wasn't as bad this time, and it didn't last as long, either. That's a good sign.

He reaches out and finds his glasses, puts them on, then blinks and glances towards the window and can tell it's still daytime from the light seeping in. Rebecca will probably soon come with lunch, or maybe dinner—he's not sure what time of day it is.

He isn't sure how many days have gone by, either. Five, maybe, or six. It feels like a month to Andy.

When he first woke up here in this bed, he was very confused and couldn't remember anything of what had happened. He only vaguely recalled the van chasing them. Then there was a dream where he spoke to Lisa, and then Rebecca was lying on top of him, screaming.

Once he started coming a little more to his senses, Rebecca explained everything to him; how the van had hit him and almost killed him, how the creature had wanted to murder him with the shovel, and how she bargained to save his life.

What a great rescue, an unpleasant voice in his head says. *Not only did you not save Rebecca, you also managed to get yourself caught, **and** you got a nice big concussion to go with the failure. Nice work, Andy.*

The voice sounds like Sheila used to talk, mixed with a taint of the icy cold tone of New Mom. Andy hates the voice and tries not to listen to it. It has haunted him ever since he came here.

He tries instead to tell himself that all hope is not lost yet. That at least he found Rebecca, and now they can figure out a way to escape together.

The problem is, it'll be a while before Andy is fit to run.

And there's also the bigger problem. The problem of Rebecca.

Andy can feel she's reluctant to the idea of trying to flee again. It's like she has spent all her courage on that last attempt, and now she has nothing left to try again.

Andy doesn't care about the deal she made with the wendigo, not one bit. He knows Rebecca only did it to save his life, but he can also sense part of her has accepted the deal.

He can't blame her, of course. She's been very brave, living alone with the wendigo for all this time, constantly fighting to not give in.

Andy isn't sure he could have done it. But Rebecca is very strong and stubborn—at least, she used to be—and if she hadn't been, she would no doubt have succumbed to the wendigo already, losing herself completely and accepting her new life here. Or rather, her non-life. Andy can tell how dull her eyes look, how little of the old Rebecca is left.

It's not too late, though. Rebecca still found the will to flee only days ago. She can still be saved. But it'll be up to him. He needs to be the brave one now. He needs to be the one fighting the wendigo.

Andy is terrified at the thought of the monster. He only dimly remembers seeing its face with those tiny, black eyes; he glimpsed it in the forest right before he rammed it with the scooter, and then again when he briefly gained consciousness out in the garden, with Rebecca lying atop of him and the wendigo towering over them, its grey head silhouetted against the dark sky. He hasn't seen it since. It doesn't come in here. Which is both comforting and disturbing.

Why hasn't it burned his feet or blinded him, like it did with Rebecca? Maybe it simply doesn't care about him. Maybe it knows Andy is still too weak to do anything.

Yet he knows the wendigo wants him dead despite the agreement it made with Rebecca. And maybe it already plans on killing him. It could make it look like an accident, so Rebecca won't realize it was murder. It could easily poison his food. Or Andy could wake up anytime in the middle of the night to see it standing over him …

Andy shivers at the thought.

How would it go about it? How would it kill him if it came in here? Probably with the shovel.

He doesn't want to think about it, but he can't help it. Somehow, he feels he needs to think it through, he needs the fear to motivate him. So he tries to imagine how it would feel to get bludgeoned to death with a shovel.

The pain will be intense—if he even had time to feel it. Maybe the first strike, then it'll probably knock him out. But the wendigo will keep going until it hears his skull crunch …

The nausea comes back, and Andy swallows hard to keep it down.

Concentrate on something else. Figure out a way to get out of here.

The problem is, he has only seen a small part of the house outside of this room. He knows Rebecca's room is next door, and he knows the bathroom is down the hallway. The last time Rebecca helped him to the bathroom, he tried to persuade her to take him downstairs, but she refused because the wendigo was down there.

Andy can't go exploring on his own; he's not strong enough yet. But as soon as he is, he'll be able to check out the house while the wendigo is out, and he's sure he can find a way to escape. He's tired of lying around here, being in pain and feeling useless.

His hand goes to his pocket where he feels the boxcutter. It's a small miracle he didn't lose it when he was run over. The wendigo obviously didn't check his pockets, because if it had, it would have no doubt confiscated the knife like it did his backpack. Now it's Andy's secret weapon. He's not sure how effective a boxcutter is against a mythical creature, but he's going to find out if he has to. If it comes to kill him, he won't give in without at least trying to fight back.

The thought gives him the motivation to get up. He carefully swings his legs out and places both feet on the floor, pushing himself up with his elbow. He tries to lift his butt, and he actually manages to stand. He smiles. Just getting up on his own feels like progress. He feels dizzy, but there is no pain.

He walks back and forth a few times, then sits back down. The room spins for a couple of seconds, but still no headache.

Andy feels very uplifted. It won't be that many days until he's ready to act. But until then, the best he can do is rest. So, he lies back down and closes his eyes.

He has barely drifted off to sleep when he hears quick footsteps come down the hallway, and then the door opens. Andy sits up a little too fast, making his head spin.

Rebecca comes in, closes the door behind her and turns around. Her eyes are big and frightened, and for a terrible moment, Andy is sure the wendigo is coming to kill them both.

"What is—" he begins, but Rebecca cuts him off.

"A car. There's a car coming," she breathes.

Andy's heart leaps, and he stands up, ignoring the dizziness. "You sure?"

Rebecca nods emphatically. "I saw it from my window. It's coming up the gravel road right now."

Andy goes to the window, grabs hold of the windowsill and presses his cheek against the glass in order to look down into the courtyard. He can only see part of the gate and the gravel road beyond. Up ahead, still far away, a car really is headed this way, making its way slowly down towards the house.

Andy squints, looking through the cracked lenses of his glasses. He can tell the car is turquoise. Not a police car, then, which is what he was hoping. But there is something familiar with the car, it occurs to Andy. It's not his parents' and it doesn't belong to any of the neighbors, either. Still, he has seen it before; he's almost sure of it. That color is very recognizable.

Rebecca says something, but Andy doesn't hear her. He just stares at the tiny car coming slowly closer, his heart thumping in his chest, causing a slight headache to sprout behind his forehead, but Andy doesn't even feel it; he just concentrates hard on the car.

Where have I seen it before?

And then it comes to him: Outside the library. Because the car belongs to ...

"Regan," Andy whispers, his breath fogging up the glass.

"What?" Rebecca asks.

"It's Regan coming," Andy says, his brain filling in several blanks in the brief moment it takes him to turn around and look at his sister, who is staring back at him. "She's found us, Becca. She's come to help!"

No trace of joy nor hope appears on Rebecca's face, only fear. "It's going to kill her," she whispers. "As soon as it sees her …"

Andy feels a lump of hot coal appear in the pit of his stomach, as he recalls what Rebecca told him about the old British guy.

"Where is it?" he asks. "Do you know?"

"Downstairs, somewhere. In the living room, probably."

"Did it hear Regan's car yet, you think?"

"I don't know."

Andy looks out the window again, briefly. "We've got to warn her," he says.

"We can't," Rebecca says, shaking her head. "If we talk to her, the creature will punish us. I promised I would be good."

"Listen to me …"

"I promised, Andy! I promised, and if I break that promise, it'll kill us both!"

Andy grabs Rebecca by the arms, hissing into her face: "We can't just stay here and watch it kill Regan!"

Rebecca's lips are quivering.

Andy can tell she's fighting something internally. He eases off his grip slightly.

"You have to do it, Becca. I'm not fast enough. She'll be by the gate in thirty seconds. You need to go down there and warn her."

"No," Rebecca croaks, trying to pull back, shaking her head wildly. "No, I can't, Andy. I can't!"

"Of course you can!" Andy almost shouts, but manages to keep his voice down. He shakes her firmly, once. "You are brave, Becca. All you need to do is run down to the gate and tell Regan to call the police—she'll understand."

"But ... what if the creature comes?"

"Then you run away. Hide somewhere in the garden. As soon as Regan calls the cops, it'll get something else entirely to worry about, and it won't bother finding you."

Rebecca looks like she just might throw up. "What ... what about you, then?"

"Don't worry about me," Andy says, trying to sound assuring. "I'll be fine. I can defend myself if it comes for me. Now go, Becca! There's no more time!"

He shoves her towards the door, and Rebecca staggers along hesitantly. She looks back at him one last time, looking as though she's about to say something.

"You can do it," Andy tells her. "And if you get the chance, run and don't look back."

Rebecca blinks once. Then she turns and leaves the room. A moment later, Andy can hear her run downstairs.

He turns back to the window and sees Regan's tiny, blue car reach the gate and stop. Then the door opens, and Regan steps out.

The sight of her makes Andy catch his breath, and he realizes faintly that this is probably the first time he sees Regan outside of the library. She looks up at the house, shielding her eyes with her hand.

"You found us," he whispers.

Then a smaller figure comes into view. It's Rebecca, running across the courtyard while looking back at the house. And because she's so busy looking back at the house, she doesn't see the garage door opening.

But Andy does.

And he sees the wendigo, too, as it comes striding out on the courtyard, headed for the gate.

In one, boney hand it's clutching the shovel.

***

Rebecca has never been this scared in her life, and the fear drowns out everything else; she doesn't even feel the painful stabs from running on the gravel.

This situation is somehow much worse than when she ran away. Because this time, it's not only her life at stake, but Andy's too.

Andy who never gave up on her.

Andy who kept looking when the police didn't.

Andy who found her.

The thought of the creature killing Andy scares Rebecca more than anything. But it's too late now: she's already made a run for the gate.

The creature can appear any moment. And this time, it won't forgive her. This time, she has promised to be good, to be Alice, and it will realize it can never trust her again.

She's almost at the gate now, and she darts one last look back at the house; still no sign of the creature.

"Rebecca? Is that really you?"

Regan has come out of the car and is now staring at her through the metal bars.

"Yes," Rebecca says, stopping in front of the gate. "It's me. Andy is here too. But you need to get away, Regan. Right now. Drive off. Or the creature will come and kill you."

"The creature?" Regan says, frowning and looking from Rebecca to the house. "Who are you talking about, Rebecca? Where is Andy?"

"Just call the—"

Andy's voice screams from the house: "*Becca! Watch out! It's coming!*"

Rebecca spins around, just as she hears the footsteps coming across the gravel from her right.

Rebecca can't run.

She can't do anything at all.

She just stands there, frozen in place, staring at the creature coming at her with long strides, holding the shovel. Behind her, Regan says something, her voice shrill.

The creature reaches out its hand and shoves Rebecca aside hard enough to almost knock her to the ground. It pulls out the key and unlocks the chain.

Andy is still screaming from the house: "*Run, Regan! Get out of here!*"

Rebecca looks at everything like in a trance, and she sees it all play out.

Regan, who has already caught on to the danger of the situation, is getting back into her car. The creature swings open the gate. Regan slams the door, and Rebecca hears the lock clicking. She sees Regan find her phone and put it to her ear. The creature walks to the car, pulls back the shovel and swings it full force at the side window. The glass explodes with a bang. And then, suddenly, events speed up. Regan screams. The creature reaches in and grabs her by the shirt, pulls her out through the window. Regan falls to the ground, tries to get up, but the creature is faster. It raises the shovel. Regan screams again, covering her face at the last second. The blade connects with her arm, giving off a loud crack. Regan's scream turns into pain. The creature raises the shovel again. Regan's arm is obviously broken, and she can no longer protect her head.

Rebecca knows then, that it's all over.

That she will now get to see Regan die the same way the old guy did. And as soon as it's over, the creature will go upstairs and kill Andy. Then it'll bury them both in the garden. And if it's merciful, it will kill her too. All she can do is hope that she will pass out soon.

Then something completely unexpected happens.

Something tiny and brown comes shooting past her leg. Rebecca blinks dazedly and looks down to see Doris, as the dog sprints for the creature and clamps down hard on its bare ankle.

The creature gives off a grunt, lowers the shovel and shakes the leg to get the dog off. But Doris is not intent on letting go; she growls and bites down harder.

The creature bends down to grab the dog, but Doris sees the hand coming and lets go, only to attack the other ankle. Rebecca can see tiny, bloody marks from the dog's teeth. And she sees Regan reach up and climb into the car, her broken arm all crooked and useless, her glasses gone, but she still fights her way up into the seat.

The creature catches Doris by the neck. The dog whimpers briefly before the creature flings it aside. Then it turns its attention back to the car, which Regan is trying to get into reverse.

She won't make it.

The thought does something to Rebecca. Or maybe it was seeing Doris attack the creature which did it. Whatever the cause, she's suddenly able to move again. And before she knows what she's doing, she jumps forward and kicks the creature on the calf, just as it's about to reach in and grab Regan for the second time. The kick is hard enough to make the creature spin around, and the black pin-drop eyes fix on Rebecca.

For a long moment, they stare at each other, as the creature's face slowly contorts into rage.

Then the car revs up its engine.

The creature snaps its head around just as Regan guns it and the car lunges backwards, gravel spurting from the tires. Both Rebecca and the creature stare after it as it heads back out of the driveway.

"if you get the chance, run and don't look back."

Andy's voice jolts her into motion, and she begins running.

The creature notices her at the last second and grabs for her just as she passes it, its thin fingers missing her hair by less than an inch, and then she's past it.

She runs as fast as she has ever run, pumping her hands up and down, her feet barely touching the gravel road. The car in front of her sways back and forth as Regan backs away from the house as fast as she can without losing control.

"*Regan!*" Rebecca shouts and waves. "*Wait for me!*"

Whether Regan hears her or sees her, Rebecca can't tell, but the car slows down enough for Rebecca to catch up with it. She runs to the passenger side, opens the door and jumps in.

Regan speeds up again, turning in the seat to look back, clutching the broken arm to her chest.

"The road is too narrow," she gasps, sweat running down her cheeks like tears—or maybe it really *is* tears. "I can't turn the car around."

Rebecca looks out the front window and sees the gate grow smaller as they quickly move away from the house. The creature is still standing there, in the middle of the open gate, staring after them. Rebecca feels like it's looking straight at her. Then it turns around and marches back inside the courtyard.

"Andy," Rebecca breathes. "Regan, it's going to kill Andy!"

Regan gives a moan of pain. "We can't go back, Rebecca."

"But it's going to kill him! We need to help him!"

"If we go back, it'll kill all of us!" Regan shouts, her voice breaking. "We need to get away, we need to call for help."

"But ... but ..." Rebecca is on the verge of tears.

"Find my phone," Regan says, wincing from pain and breathing fast. "I dropped it somewhere in the car."

Rebecca looks for the phone on the floor as her eyes fill with tears. She knows Regan is right. And she remembers Andy telling her to not worry about him. And part of her feels immense relief that she has actually made it, that she managed to escape. But the thought of leaving Andy behind like this, with the creature probably already headed up the stairs to kill him, is just too—

Rebecca's train of thoughts get interrupted as something causes her to look up. She stares out the front window, her mouth opening.

"Regan," she hears herself whisper.

"What? Did you find it?"

"No," Rebecca croaks. "It's coming for us."

Regan turns her head to look for a brief second and gives off a tiny scream just as the yellow van comes bolting out the gate like a big, old, hungry predator.

Rebecca's stomach turns to stone.

She thought for a second she had made it. She was naïve enough to think she could escape this easily; that the creature would simply let her go. She thought the only one still in danger was Andy.

She turns her head and looks back. The gravel road goes on for as long as she can see. The highway is still way too far away.

***

Andy sees it all from his window; it feels like being a spectator to the scariest horror movie.

He tried to shout to warn them, but it was too late. If it hadn't been for the dog, the wendigo would have killed Regan.

But now he sees her climbing back up into the car, even though she's obviously hurt badly.

I can't just stand here—I've got to do something.

Andy goes to the door, opens it and heads for the stairs. Looking down the steps, everything grows hazy for a moment, as a wave of dizziness floods him, but he bites down hard, forces his eyes to focus, then descends the stairs.

It's easier than he thought. Soon he's in the scullery. He opens the front door and looks out, afraid of what he will see.

Over by the gate, the wendigo is standing, facing away from the house. It's staring after Regan's car, which is speeding backwards out the driveway. Rebecca is running after it.

They got away!

Andy can hardly believe it, and he is filled with wild excitement.

But he quickly finds out that it's not over, as the wendigo turns and strides to the garage.

It's going to follow them.

Andy feels a pang of panic. He looks out the driveway, and he can still see Regan's car, which has now picked up Rebecca—it hasn't gotten much farther away, though, because it can't go very fast in reverse. The wendigo will quickly catch up with them in its van.

Andy knows what he must do. He steps out the door and crosses the courtyard. He reaches the garage and hears the driver-side door slam shut. Andy grabs the handle to the backdoor and opens it just as the van starts up its engine with a roar. He's about to climb up as it shoots backwards, almost running him over for the second time, but he manages to jump up and land inside the van, the door slamming behind him, but the sound is drowned out as the van backs out onto the crunching gravel. It stops, turns and shoots forward, almost sending Andy sprawling in the dark. He grabs for something to hold onto as the nausea comes rolling up his throat. He forces it back down and makes an effort to see the inside of the van

The only thing visible is a square somewhere above him: a small opening, Andy realizes, separating the cabin from the back. There's a hatch to close it, but right now, the hatch is open, and daylight is streaming in.

Andy crawls towards the light as the van speeds up, the gravel rumbling underneath. They're probably already headed up the road.

Andy manages to get up by supporting himself against the wall, and he looks through the opening. He sees Regan's car still backing away as fast as it can, but the van is gaining on it fast. Rebecca is sitting in the passenger seat.

Andy looks down and sees the arms and hands of the wendigo clutching the wheel.

What do I do? Think! In a minute it will catch up with Regan's car, and it's probably going to ram it off the road. I need to do something!

Andy looks for something, anything he can use. Then he remembers the boxcutter and goes to his pocket. The blade shines in the darkness as he pushes it out.

A new sound reaches him, a hoarse mumbling, and he realizes the wendigo is talking to itself, uttering curses. The van is still gaining speed.

It no longer wants Rebecca, Andy realizes with icy clarity. *It's going to kill them both.*

In less than ten seconds, the van will smash into Regan's car, sending it off the road, maybe even causing it to flip over. The van is double the size, and it's going really fast now, almost flying along the gravel road, stones banging against the undercarriage like gunshots.

Andy reaches the boxcutter through the opening followed by his entire arm.

The wendigo doesn't notice; it's leaning forward now, the bald head visible to Andy. It's mumbling louder to itself as it stares at Regan's car only a few seconds away now.

Andy screams and slashes at the head of Ambroos van de Goor.

***

Rebecca stares at the van coming closer way too fast. The closer it gets, the faster it seems to be going.

Soon she can make out the creature behind the dark windshield. The tall, thin, pale figure is hunched over the steering wheel, and she can almost feel the hate emanating from the black eyes fixed on her.

Next to her, Regan gives off another choked scream; it sounds like a mixture of pain, fear and crying. She's leaning sideways, her eyes darting back and forth between the front and back window, the bad arm presses against her chest, and Rebecca only now notices the piece of white bone protruding through the sleeve at the place where the arm bends.

"We won't make it," Regan says, almost crying now. "It's going to hit us! Buckle up, Rebecca!"

"What about you?"

"There's no time!"

But Rebecca has already leaned over and reached across Regan's shoulder, grabbing the seatbelt and pulling it over. Once Regan is secured, Rebecca buckles up too.

Then she looks out the front window again, and now the view is almost blocked by the van as it's about to collide with them within the next few seconds, and—

Rebecca is just about to close her eyes and prepare for the crash, when she sees a face inside the van, right next to the creature.

It makes no sense.

It's Andy.

***

In the split second before the blade reaches its target, the wendigo snaps its head around and stares right at him. Instead of slashing open the back of its head, the boxcutter cuts along the jawline, opening a thin, dark gash.

The wendigo screams out and lunges sideways, hitting the wheel and causing it to spin violently. The tires jerk to the side way too sharply, and the van goes flying. Andy is thrown up into the ceiling, then to the side, and then he's lying flat on his back.

Everything becomes quiet. The world sways for a moment, before coming to a stop.

***

"Holy hell," Regan whispers and slows down the car as she stares out at the tipped-over van lying halfway in the ditch. "He drove off the road ..."

"It was Andy," Rebecca hears herself saying. She unbuckles, opens the door and jumps out.

"Rebecca! Wait! Come back!"

Rebecca isn't listening. She runs to the van, jumps across the ditch and looks in through the windshield. Behind the wheel is the creature, bunched up in an awkward position. Its face is visible, and Rebecca can tell its eyes are closed, a dark gash running down its jaw and another bleeding on its forehead. But Andy isn't in there.

She runs to the back and grabs the handle. The door resists for a moment, then opens. Andy is lying right inside. He rolls to his side, looking up at her, blinking with obvious effort. His expression is hazy, like someone just waking up.

"What ... what happened?" he croaks.

"You crashed," Rebecca says simply, taking him by the arm. "Come on, Andy. Quickly. I don't think it's dead."

That last part seems to strike a chord with Andy, and he suddenly looks more coherent. He lets her help him out, but gives off a cry as he tries to stand.

"My knee," he winces. "It's hurting really bad ..."

"I'll help you," Rebecca says, placing Andy's arm across her shoulders, supporting him as best she can, as Andy jumps across the ditch on one leg and heads for Regan's car.

"Oh, my head," Andy suddenly moans, stopping and bending over. He wretches and throws up onto the gravel road. It's mostly just spit.

Rebecca hates stopping. They're only halfway between the van and Regan's car. She looks to the latter and sees Regan behind the wheel talking on her phone. Then she looks back and sees the van's driver's door swing open.

"Andy," she says, starting to pull him along. "We need to keep moving—it's coming!"

Andy is still throwing up, but he limps on ahead. They reach the car, and Rebecca opens the back door to help in Andy, who has finally stopped puking.

"Hurry up!" Regan calls, and for a moment Rebecca thinks she's talking to them, then realizes she's still on the phone. She ends the call and gasps aloud. "Rebecca, look out!"

Rebecca is just about to get in, when she turns her head and sees the creature.

It's standing in the middle of the road. Staring right at her.

Regan shouts something.

Rebecca throws herself into the car.

Regan guns it and the car lurches backwards.

Rebecca stares out at the creature, expecting it to run after them—but to her surprise, it doesn't move an inch; it just stands there, staring after the car.

"I think it finally gave up," Regan says, once she realizes the creature isn't taking up pursuit. She slows down only a little. "Thank God. Are you okay, Andy?"

"I think so," Andy mutters, but Rebecca can hear him moan and hold his head in his hands as though it's throbbing. "Thank you for coming to save us, Regan."

"I'm sorry I didn't come earlier, but I didn't figure it out until yesterday, and I ... oh, my arm!"

"You need to get to the hospital," Rebecca says. "You both do."

At that moment, they reach the highway. Regan turns onto the asphalt, stops, and uses her good arm to put the car in drive.

Rebecca looks back up the driveway, and can still see the creature standing there; now it's only a thin, grey line next to the tipped-over van.

Just as they begin to roll down the road, Rebecca sees the blue lights up ahead. "Is that ... the police?"

Andy lifts his head. "The police? Already?"

"Yeah," Regan moans, stopping the car again. "They traced my call the first time, so they had already sent someone out when I called them the second time."

She leans back her head and closes her eyes.

Then, Rebecca turns to look at Andy.

He's very pale and still looks nauseous. Yet he looks up at her and manages a smile, as he whispers: "We did it. This time, we really did it, Becca."

EPILOGUE

"You ready yet?"

Rebecca looks at him from the open front door. Doris is pulling at the leash impatiently, eager to get going. The puppy has grown quite a lot since the first time Andy saw it.

"Hold your horses," he says, fumbling with his laces. "I can't get this knot untied—it's all tangled."

"You're so clumsy," Rebecca sighs and steps over to him. "Let me do it."

She kneels down, shoving his hands aside. With a few brisk movements, she unties the knot and ties his shoe.

Andy looks at her, smiling. When they first got home, he was afraid the wendigo might have sucked too much life force out of Rebecca for her to ever become herself again. And it seemed like it to begin with; Rebecca was very anxious and restless and would often cry. She also rarely spoke and had trouble sleeping at night due to bad dreams.

But it's been nearly two months now, and Rebecca has already changed back to her old, familiar self in most ways: She doesn't cry anymore, and she talks a lot again. And when Andy tripped in the driveway the other day and fell down, she laughed out loud. Andy didn't even get mad at her; he was just so happy to hear Rebecca laugh again.

Now she gets up and says: "There. That wasn't very hard, was it?"

"Thank you," Andy says, smiling at her, his eyes lingering on her face for a moment.

Rebecca squints. "What are you looking at?"

"Your glasses."

"Don't tease me."

"No, they look good on you."

Rebecca crosses her arms, but doesn't say anything.

Andy can't help it, and he goes on: "Remember all the times you called me four-eyes when you got angry with me? Well, now that's come back to bite you in the butt, missy."

Rebecca sighs. "Right, can we get going? Doris is about to pee on the floor."

"I'll just tell Mom we're going." Andy goes to peek into the living room. "Mom? We're leaving now."

Mom is reading a book while eating an apple. She stops chewing and sends him an alarmed look; Andy can see the words building up.

Then Mom thinks better of it, and instead she asks: "You got your phone on you?"

"Sure do."

"Good." She forces a smile. "Have fun."

Andy returns the smile and closes the door to the living room again. Rebecca is not the only one who has changed back to her old self, and it makes Andy happy to see Mom feeling better every day.

Those first weeks were tough, though; she wouldn't let either Andy or Rebecca out of sight, even demanding they all sleep in the same room. But after she went to see a therapist, she slowly began to relax. Now and then she can still fall back to the habits of New Mom and become harsh and overprotective, but Andy feels confident she just needs time.

Dad is also his old self again—in fact, even more so than before. It's almost like his work doesn't mean as much to him any longer. He's cut down on his office hours and spends a lot more time with Andy and Rebecca in the afternoon, which he only rarely did before.

Even Cindy seems different. She eats home every night and she talks a lot more with Mom and Dad than she used to. She has also forgiven Andy for busting up her scooter. Actually, Andy suspects she might even be glad he did, since she used the money from the insurance to start saving for a car. Also, she has stopped dying her hair.

Andy follows Rebecca out into the driveway, where a fresh fall breeze and a golden sunshine greet them. Doris runs around, eagerly sniffing everything.

They walk through town without saying much. It's a quiet Saturday afternoon. All the cars, cyclists and pedestrians move slow, like none of them are in a hurry to get anywhere, but prefer to simply enjoy what will probably be one of the last warm days this year.

A car rolls by, and Andy recognizes the girl in the passenger seat. He waves, and Sheila waves back. Then she's gone.

"Who was that?" Rebecca says, pushing her glasses up her nose.

"Just someone from class," Andy shrugs.

Sheila has begun smiling at Andy whenever their eyes meet. She even talks to him now and then. Andy is pretty sure she's grateful to him that Kristy was finally found.

After the police arrested him, Ambroos van de Goor confessed to kidnapping six girls over the years and killing at least five people. Once the police began digging up his garden, they found plenty of bones—including Sheila's older sister's.

Kristy didn't drown in the stream in the park like the police had originally reasoned. Her clothes and schoolbag had only ended up there, because Ambroos van de Goor had dumped them after he kidnapped her. In reality, she died in his home two years after he took her. She got appendicitis and he didn't take her to the hospital.

Ambroos van de Goor also confessed to being responsible for the death of Lisa Labowski. He kidnapped her six months after he had buried Kristy in his garden. Lisa was kept as a prisoner for four months, but much like Rebecca, she never really stopped trying to escape, and he couldn't leave her home alone, so whenever he had to go to town, he brought her in the back of the van.

One day, Lisa managed to pick the lock and open the back door from the inside. But it happened so unexpectedly that she fell out while the van was still driving. A car coming the opposite way struck Lisa before she could get to her feet and killed her instantly. It happened right outside the library.

Andy can still recall what Lisa had told him.

"kidnapped"

"yellow van"

"blinding sunlight"

Back then, those fragments didn't make much sense to him, but now he can fill in the blanks and vividly imagine Lisa in the back of the van, scared and alone in the dark, fumbling with the lock, and when she suddenly got it and the doors swung open, the sunlight streaming in must have felt very intense. Maybe it even blinded her. Maybe that's why she fell out.

Unfortunately, no one noticed Lisa falling out of the van, so it was never uncovered how she suddenly appeared in the middle of town after having been gone for four months. And no one apparently read too much into the fact that Lisa's hair color had changed from auburn to blond; it only confirmed the suspicion many people had that the girl had run away from home in some sort of teenage rebellion and didn't want to get found.

Andy, of course, figured out the truth: the wendigo had forced Lisa to dye her hair blond just like it did to Rebecca.

After the final fight with the wendigo, Andy spent a week in the hospital. He suffered a bad concussion, a twisted knee and two broken ribs.

As soon as he got home, he went to the library to tell Lisa everything. But once he stood there, holding *The Wendigo*, Lisa was oddly silent. He tried several other books, but she still didn't answer, and she hasn't spoken to him since.

Although he could sense Lisa was no longer in the library, it still took Andy some time to accept she was gone for good. Gradually, he grew to understand she had only lived in the books on borrowed time to begin with, and that she had now gone on to whatever awaits after death.

It still strikes him as odd, though, that Lisa would disappear right after Rebecca came back. The explanation could be that she lingered in the books to help Andy find Rebecca and get her own murderer thrown in jail. That would make sense, Andy figured; after all, ghosts probably have a reason for sticking around. Something that hasn't been resolved. And as soon as it is, they move on.

But there is also another explanation. One that Andy cares a lot less for.

Perhaps the ghost of Lisa Labowski was never really there. Perhaps it all took place in his imagination. All the lines, all the conversations he had with her—it could all be make-believe.

They pass the library, and Andy stops for a moment. It's Saturday, so Regan won't be at work, and the turquoise car isn't parked outside the building.

In the weeks after the fight, Regan wore her arm in cast, and Andy got to sign it with a marker. He wrote: *Thank you, Regan*, and Regan teared up. Their friendship has grown even stronger than before. Every time they meet, Regan hugs him, and she even came over for dinner a couple of times. Mom and Dad couldn't stop thanking her, and Mom bought a huge bouquet of flowers for her.

Andy didn't get any flowers, and he guesses that's only fair. After all, he wasn't actually the one who freed Rebecca, although he played a vital part. Everyone at school has told him how brave he was, but in the media, it's Regan getting all the fame.

Young woman rescues two kidnapped children—risked her own life!

Andy is okay with Regan taking the glory. To him, the most important thing is that Rebecca is home.

"You think they'll ever let him out?" Rebecca asks, pulling Andy from his thoughts.

He looks at her and sees her staring at the library. It's weird standing here with her, on the exact spot where they once split up.

"They say he'll get life in prison," Andy says.

"But that's only about twenty-five years. I Googled it."

"By that time he'll be dead from old age."

Rebecca looks at him critically, and Andy knows exactly what she's thinking. The things they are saying about Ambroos van de Goor in the media are quite disturbing. Something about his DNA being all wrong, and that he seems to be suffering from some hither-to unknown genetical disease, which causes him to age much slower than normal. The medical examiners reported him being at least a hundred years old, and they noted his body temperature never seems to rise above 70 degrees. The weird DNA also explains why the police investigators could never track him down, although they found DNA from him on both Kristy's clothes and Lisa Labowski's body.

But Andy knows better. He knows it's no genetical disease which has messed up Ambroos van de Goor's DNA. The explanation is much simpler: Ambroos van de Goor is not a human being.

It should be obvious simply from looking at him, really. But somehow, other people can't seem to tell right away that the wendigo isn't human; they apparently just see a boney and very tall old man with sharp features, unhealthy, greyish complexion and very dark eyes.

Originally of European descent, he had lived way up in Canada until forty years ago; that's when he came down here and began taking girls.

"Even if they do let him out," Andy says, shaking off the gloomy thoughts, "they'll be watching him closely. He'll never get to kidnap anybody again."

"I hope not," Rebecca says.

"Come on," Andy says, placing a hand on her shoulder.

They go on to the park, where the trees have started to take on yellow colors.

"You think we'll get to see them this time?" Rebecca asks, a growing excitement in her voice, and Andy can tell she has put Ambroos van de Goor out of her mind once more.

"If we're lucky," Andy says, smiling. "Keep your eyes and ears open."

Rebecca lets Doris off the leash, and the dog immediately begins running around in circles, taking in all the exciting smells. Andy and Rebecca stroll alongside each other while they listen and look up into the trees.

Andy glances towards the graveyard and is struck by a strong déjà vu from the day he saw Lisa Labowski's gravestone. He can't help but wonder once more if the ghost was real or not. He was the only one who ever spoke to Lisa, after all. Wouldn't that suggest he made it all up in his mind?

Then suddenly something occurs to him.

The book. *Anatomy of the Human Eye.*

It was Lisa who gave him the title of the book that Ambroos van de Goor took out from the library and never returned. The police found it in his home, and he confessed to having used the book to figure out a poisonous mixture which would blind the girls without taking away their vision completely.

How could Andy possibly have known the name of that book? He couldn't. And that's why the ghost of Lisa Labowski had to have been real.

"There!" Rebecca exclaims, pointing. "You see it?"

Andy follows her finger to a nearby tree and searches the trunk until he sees the hole. And at that exact moment—as though it heard them talking—the woodpecker pops out its head to look down at them.

Rebecca lets out a joyful gasp, and Andy smiles as he closes his eyes for a moment.

***

This story was tough to write, and I nearly gave up more than once. I kept changing viewpoints and formats until I couldn't even tell if it was any good. But something about that brave boy kept pulling me back. After years of tinkering, I finally got the plot right and gave Andy the ending his story deserved.

When I first published *The Girl Who Wasn't There* in Danish, it completely flopped. I assumed the story just wasn't strong enough, which hurt—not only because of the time and effort I'd put in, but because it's one of my personal favorites.

Then I translated it into English, and within months I heard from readers saying it was one of their favorites, too. That told me the problem wasn't the story—it was probably the cover, or the timing. Who knows? What matters is that Andy's story got a second chance, and you got to read it. I hope you enjoyed it.

If you want more of the wendigo, check out my other story, *Human Flesh*, at

nick-clausen.com/flesh

—Nick

Printed in Dunstable, United Kingdom